FINDING THE FIGHT

A STEALTH OPS NOVEL

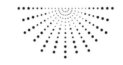

BRITTNEY SAHIN

EMKO MEDIA

Finding the Fight

By: Brittney Sahin

Published by: EmKo Media, LLC

Copyright © 2019 EmKo Media, LLC

This book is an original publication of Brittney Sahin.

Editor: Carol, WordsRU.com

Editor: Anja, HourGlass Editing

Proofreader: Judy Zweifel, Judy's Proofreading

Cover Design: LJ, Mayhem Cover Creations

Photography: Eric Battershell

Paperback ISBN: 9781793204844

❀ Created with Vellum

To a very special lady - Velma McCalla Parker.
This one is for you.

PROLOGUE: RECRUITMENT

New York City

"Asher Hayes."

Asher lowered the bottle from his lips, allowing the rim to hover in front of his face. "The one and only," he responded without turning to track the voice. He finished off his drink and motioned to the bartender for another.

Two hands landed on the sticky bar top next to him—a dark spider web on the guy's left hand and a skull tattooed on the right. "I heard you were here, but I had to come and see for myself."

Asher casually scratched his beard and glanced over his shoulder to match the voice to the name—to lay eyes on a man he hadn't seen in years.

He'd been waiting for an hour in hopes he'd show.

Memories had poured through his mind the moment he'd stepped inside the bar. But now, with Angelo next to him, a waterfall of the past obliterated almost every other thought.

"When did I see you last?" Angelo cupped his jaw and

1

narrowed his dark-green eyes as a grin lifted the corners of his lips. "Was it before or after I banged your sister?"

Asher lowered his head, fighting a smile. Time apart had done nothing to crush the banter from their teenage years.

"Nah, man," Asher said as he caught Angelo's eyes again. "I'm pretty sure it was me screwing yours."

Angelo was quiet for a moment, and his right brow, cut by a fresh scar, twitched ever so slightly. "I see you haven't changed."

Neither had his desire to hit, to pummel flesh, for the sake of nothing other than a good fight. The need burned through his veins and pulsed up into his throat.

It'd been too long since he'd fought for the hell of it.

War was different. Too many rules. Barely any hand-to-hand, even as a Tier One operative.

Asher's fingers united in front of him, and he cracked his knuckles before shifting off the stool to turn around.

Angelo stepped back, and a few other guys now stood crowded behind him, as if itching to charge his way, waiting for a command from Angelo. They didn't know that order would never come.

"Why are you here?" Angelo stroked his jaw. "Looking for a fight?"

His heartbeat kicked higher as he entertained the idea of fighting by the end of the night.

"I heard you're running the fights now." Asher's palm flattened onto the sticky counter at his side.

"You're interested?" Angelo swiped a hand down his inked throat before curving it around the back of his neck. "I don't like easy fights."

After reaching into his pocket, Asher produced a wad of cash and held it between them. "Neither do I, which is why you might need the rest of your guys to go up against me."

He edged closer to him, looking down from his height of six feet four. "Unless you only place bets now and no longer get your hands dirty."

Angelo opened his mouth to speak, but one of the punks behind him yelled out, "You may be some commando now, but military shit is different from the streets."

His words had Asher chuckling and stuffing the bills back into his pocket.

"Kids these days," Angelo said with a touch of humor in his voice.

"Maybe he got kicked out of the military." A second guy stabbed the air, probably the youngest of the gang. A gang Angelo had been running since the days of Vanilla Ice and Michael Jackson.

His stomach muscles banded tight at the guy's words, at the possible truth of what might happen to his career in two days. "I'm just looking for a fight."

Angelo studied him for a brief moment, and every sound in the room fell away. "I got a place all set up. There's a fight already in progress. You and me—like old times."

Asher nodded when he found his words stuck in his throat and his sister's voice whispering in his head to back off.

Too late. He needed this night. He'd needed it for some time now.

Angelo angled his head, motioning him toward the exit. "Follow me, then."

His booted feet moved slowly through the bar, maneuvering around mostly empty tables before going outside.

On the sidewalk, Angelo stole a glimpse at Asher from over his shoulder. Their eyes connected as they neared one of the few working streetlights. Asher tipped his head as if to say *Yeah, I'm real*. Then Angelo looked straight ahead again, walking with his crew. Probably the latest recruits.

He kept his distance behind them, not eager to catch up on the last dozen-plus years. He was honestly surprised Angelo wasn't behind bars or six feet under.

He'd been back to New York since joining the military, but never for long, and never to this part of town. Never to his old haunts.

But this trip was different.

His mom and sister didn't know he was home, and he'd keep it that way.

There was only one mission on his mind tonight: fighting.

His steps slowed as he thought about what had happened two weeks ago on deployment. A violent flurry of anger slammed through his chest, scalding his body beneath the jacket. His hands curled into fists as he seized a breath of the bitterly cold December air.

He shifted his gaze to the left, where a man was pounding his car horn. The guy parked in front of him at the green light finally rolled through the intersection.

Asher shook his head.

New York City was the same as he remembered.

This side of town was still dead. Unnoticed. A blur of nothingness to anyone who drove through.

No twinkling lights or Christmas music playing in storefronts. No big tree. No ice-skating rinks. This was where Christmas carols came to die.

Bars on the windows, graffiti, barbed wire fences, and the stench of two-week-old meat. And death.

He lifted his chin, searching for the moon in the clear sky as he walked, but it was probably tucked away in the Upper East Side, where his mom and sister lived.

Angelo abruptly stopped.

Asher glanced to his right to find a run-down factory. He followed the guys through a side door, surprised to see the inside nothing like the exterior.

The walls had been stripped down to brick and painted over in a bright blue with matching blue benches and chairs circling a cage at the center of the expansive space.

"A beauty, ain't she?" Angelo opened his palms and spun around.

Asher eyed the crowd already gathered around the octagon.

There'd never been cages in his day. No protection from outsiders jumping in to join the fight. It could quickly turn into a free-for-all. Chaos and mayhem.

Of course, that was before soccer moms had started watching UFC and turned it into a household name.

He removed his jacket and flung it near a bench where two classy-looking women were sitting alongside a guy in a suit. They weren't from this side of the city. Clearly, they enjoyed the off-the-books fighting. Blood and money. Nothing new.

"You ready?" Angelo peeled off his shirt, revealing a hell of a lot more ink than he'd had in their youth. Nearly every inch of his skin had been used as a canvas.

Asher tossed his long-sleeved shirt, and Angelo's gaze darted to the tatt on Asher's forearm—the same tatt Angelo had. They'd once been like brothers, and now . . .

Two different directions in life had taken them on vastly different journeys.

Only, here Asher was again. Drawn back to the dark side. To the fight.

He'd kept his shit together in the SEALs. He'd had to, for the sake of his country and his team.

But here he could do whatever the hell he wanted.

He shook out his arms as he gathered a breath and then removed his boots.

"You're going to be the underdog; just an FYI." Angelo smoothed his hand over his jet-black hair, looking more like his Italian father than ever before.

Angelo's dad was upstate . . . in the penitentiary.

"I'm ready," Asher bit out, knowing his old friend was dying to fight him, to unleash on him for abandoning the crew, for putting on a uniform instead of staying on the streets. "Let's do this."

Maybe Angelo was right to hate him for leaving. But it'd been the Navy or prison.

He coughed into a closed fist as he shoved the past from his mind to focus on the present, on the fight.

A girl, probably just out of high school, stood at the center of the octagon with a sign that read *Round One*; she started walking the perimeter of the cage.

Hopefully, he'd go all five rounds tonight and draw this thing out. The night had to last before shit got real. Before he found out if his days on Charlie Team were over.

He entered the cage in jeans and bare feet a few minutes later. At least some things hadn't changed; at least he didn't need to wear ass-hugging short shorts.

He'd learned to fight weighted down with combat gear. Denim wouldn't hold him back.

"Welcome home." Angelo raised his fists into the air then came in hard for a direct attack.

Jab.

Knee kick.

Elbow.

None of which landed.

It was Asher's fists that connected. He executed three

hard uppercuts to Angelo's core, hitting different tattoos with precision.

The crowd hollered. Screamed. Then booed as Asher began pummeling Angelo even more.

Round one blurred by.

He circled his opponent, the race of his heart intensifying with each satisfying swing.

A thrill darted up his spine, and a rush of adrenaline bolted through him.

I'm home. He delivered the final blow in the second round, knocking Angelo out.

"Shit." He knelt by Angelo's side and lightly swatted his cheeks. He hadn't meant to annihilate the guy so early, and in Angelo's territory, no less.

The crowd surged closer to the octagon, and other fighters hungry to throw down with him leaped onto the sides of the cage. Asher ignored them and assisted Angelo to his feet.

"Guess you're still the better fighter." Angelo raised his palms in surrender. "Motherfucker," he said with a laugh, limping toward the cage wall. "You'd better get out of here before you get jumped, though." He pushed open the cage door.

"Sorry it's been so long." What else was there to say? "I, uh—" Asher cut himself off at the sight of a blonde in the crowd.

It couldn't be Jessica, could it?

His heart picked up as he tried to catch her eyes to verify if it was, in fact, her. When he spotted the tall blond man alongside her, he let out a hard sigh. "Yeah, I should go." He left the cage and grabbed his belongings. He needed to get out of there. Now.

"Take the money. You earned it." Angelo held out a wad

of cash double the size of the one Asher had offered back at the bar.

"Nah, I'm good."

Angelo smiled and tossed the roll of money to one of the guys behind him.

Asher surveyed the next set of fighters entering the cage. The itch to get back in there surprised him. Maybe something was wrong with him. Could the Navy be right?

"Well, guess I'll see you in another ten or so years." Angelo folded his arms. "Unless you're thinking of staying. It's been a long damn time since you've come to our part of town."

"I can't stay." His throat thickened as more memories from his past, from the streets, blew through his mind.

Angelo wrapped a hand over his shoulder. "You really came all this way to knock me out?"

Asher stepped out of his reach and shrugged on his jacket, noticing Angelo was blinking a little as the blood near an open cut spattered his lashes.

"I guess I did." But maybe he was also there to remind himself why he left. To understand why he needed the military. "I, uh, better—"

"Go." Angelo nodded. "Do you want me to say *hello* to your pops when I visit next?"

He hung his head. It'd been even longer since he'd seen his old man. "Nah, but you can tell your dad I said *hi*." He started for the exit. Time to leave the past behind. For good.

Outside, the dark night grabbed hold of him and absorbed some of his thoughts. He glanced around, expecting to find Luke Scott waiting for him.

"Hey," he said when he saw Luke come out a different exit, Jessica striding behind him.

Luke stepped forward and extended his hand. "How's it going?"

Asher shook his hand but kept his eyes glued to Jessica standing quietly off to Luke's side.

The guy had retired three years ago, so this couldn't be a work visit. But then, why was a spook with him?

Asher dropped his arm to his side. His breath visibly sailed from his lips in the cool air. "This isn't the best place for a woman."

Jessica's lip caught between her teeth, and even beneath her coat, he knew her chest was slowly rising from the deep breath she was trying to hide.

"We need to talk," Luke was quick to say.

"I, uh, figured." Asher's focus journeyed to the parked Escalade at the curb. "Your ride?"

"Yeah." Luke gestured toward the vehicle and led the way.

"I'm guessing this isn't a social call," Asher said once in the back seat and Luke started to drive.

"Not exactly." Luke shifted his rearview mirror to catch a quick look at Asher.

Asher remembered Luke being hard around the edges, but there was a grim darkness shadowing his eyes now.

Someone must have died. Someone close to him.

He hadn't heard mention of any recent SEAL deaths, though.

"Marcus Vasquez," Luke offered, reading Asher's thoughts. "He died three weeks ago on an op."

Asher squeezed his eyes closed as his heart worked harder in his chest at the idea Marcus was gone. He hadn't known him well, but he'd been a Teamguy. A loss was a loss.

"I didn't hear about that." He'd been cut off from the world on a mission for over a month, though. "But I thought

Marcus was retired." He opened his eyes, leaned forward, and pressed a hand to the top of Jessica's seat.

"To the world he was." Luke stopped at a red light and shifted to the side to catch his eyes. "He worked with me."

Damn. "Sorry, man." Asher settled back in his seat. "You run that security company now?"

"Yeah, I do, but there's more to it," Luke replied.

"I still don't get how you found me."

"Finding people is what I'm good at." Jessica spoke for the first time, and her voice had the hair on his arms standing at attention. "Why were you fighting?" she asked without turning to face him.

"That's not relevant," Luke interjected.

"I think it is," she said.

"Drop it," Luke commanded.

He pressed his palms to his thighs and stared at his now swollen knuckles; the memory of his hands pounding flesh snapped back to mind.

"We're almost at our office. I'll explain everything there. I promise." Although the promise was aimed at Asher, Luke glanced at Jessica before focusing on the streets that became busier as they neared Manhattan.

He wasn't sure if he wanted to hear an explanation, though. Hell, he didn't even know if he wanted to be in the car right now.

He was due back to Virginia in two days to find out his fate with the SEALs. Now that the fight was over all he wanted to do was get stupid drunk.

But curiosity got the best of him, so he stayed tight-lipped until they were in the parking garage of a skyscraper.

He eased out of the car slowly, as if he'd been the one getting battered in the cage tonight.

When he faced Jessica in the garage, she kept her eyes low as she tightened the belt of her coat.

When Luke came around to their side of the car, Asher waved a finger between them. "Are you two together?"

"Hell, no. This is my sister. Jessica."

A rock dropped in his stomach, and he staggered back a step. *Shit.*

"I know, I know." Luke showed his palms. "It'll make sense soon."

Did he really not know Asher had a history with his sister?

Luke pointed to the elevators, and Asher maintained his distance behind them as they walked, ignoring her long legs beneath skinny jeans and tall brown boots.

In the elevator, Luke punched in a passcode, and they began to ascend a moment later. "You good?" Luke angled his head, observing Asher.

"I don't know what I am to be honest." He fought the urge to study Jessica, now that they were in better lighting.

Brother. The word rotated through his mind like a record skipping.

There were rules, and one of them was you didn't bang a Teamguy's sister. Jessica had omitted that part before she'd ridden him like there was no tomorrow.

He rolled his eyes skyward and eased out a steady breath to stop his dick from leaping up at attention at the memory of her tits smashed to his chest.

Luke tipped his head toward the parting doors, but Asher motioned for Jessica to exit. "Ladies first." He told himself he was being a gentleman, and it had nothing to do with his desire to check out her ass, which he wanted to sink his teeth into like a peach.

The khaki wool coat didn't hide the sway of her hips with

each step. Her buns of damn steel—undoubtedly hard-earned —had become a permanent fixture in his memory from the moment he'd laid eyes on her back in Aleppo.

"You sure you're okay?" Luke arched a brow.

Asher blinked, realizing he was still standing in the elevator, simply watching Jessica walk farther and farther away. "Yeah." He finally stepped into the lobby.

"We can talk in Jessica's office," Luke said.

Asher forced his shit-kickers, as his sister liked to call them, to move.

"So." Jessica was standing behind her desk, coat off and arms folded, when he entered. The white cashmere of her sweater accentuated her curves and had his forearms tightening at the sight of her.

Long, light-blonde hair. Ice-blue eyes. High cheekbones. A straight nose. And kiss-me full lips.

He couldn't take his eyes off her mouth, a mouth that had somehow taken every inch of his—

"Asher?" Luke's voice effectively killed his thoughts.

"Yeah?" He went over to the chair in front of her desk and dropped down, gripping the arms to try and pull himself together.

Going back home. The fight. And now her. A parade of the past . . . Maybe it was too much in one night, even for him.

"So, why am I here?" He glanced at the hard set of her jaw. Did she hate him? Hell, she was the one who'd left his bed without so much as a goodbye.

Luke stood off to Jessica's side in a rigid position. "I wanted to recruit you three years ago to our team, but you'd just hooked up with DEVGRU, so I didn't think you'd want in."

Our? His gaze flicked to Jessica before meeting Luke's eyes.

"My sister and I run an on-the-books company with former Teamguys—Scott & Scott Securities. But we also lead a black-ops group for the president which very few people know about. It comprises of two teams—Bravo and Echo. Jessica, myself, and nine other guys." A grimace touched his lips. "Er, eight guys."

Marcus. He straightened in his seat but kept his hold on the chair arms.

"We're a man down. Marcus was our best tracker." A touch of anger reverberated through his tone.

"Did you catch the bastards who took him out?" Asher was back on his feet, his legs itching to rise. He couldn't sit while having a conversation about losing a Teamguy.

"No." Jessica's arms fell to her sides. "Not yet."

"We're still active duty, but we handle ops DEVGRU can't." He pointed toward the floor. "This place is the front."

"And you're asking me to join?" He crossed his arms, the dull throb of his heart like an echo in his ears. Low. Steady. A constant booming. "You should know I might be off the Teams soon."

"I know." Luke shook his head. "You made the right call. I would've done the same as you. Hell, it's one of the reasons I want you."

"Because I don't follow rules?" *Because my superiors think I'm unpredictable? Uncontrollable?* He almost laughed, even though it hurt like hell on the inside when he thought about it.

The Teams were everything to him, and he hadn't been sure what would happen if he got suspended or the boot. Maybe he'd end up back on the streets or in the ring, like tonight.

Black Squadron—Charlie Team—had been his life, but Luke was offering him a second chance.

How many second chances had he already had? Maybe more than he deserved.

"You got the job done," Luke said firmly. "And more importantly, you refused to leave a man behind even when your CO ordered you *not* to go back into the compound."

Luke had left out the part where Asher had slugged his commanding officer across the jaw, but he wasn't exactly itching to relive that moment.

He circled the desk and stood only a foot or so away from Asher. "I need someone on the team who is willing to take risks others may not."

He scratched at his beard. "I don't know." He turned away, needing a moment to gather his thoughts.

"I also need someone to remind me that what's best isn't always protocol." Luke's voice became low, gravelly. "Maybe I shouldn't have followed orders. Maybe I should never have let Marcus go alone on the op that killed him."

His words had Asher slowly turning around, leaving him with only one choice—one answer. This was no time for indecision. It was now or never. "Okay."

He saw the flash of relief in Luke's eyes, like a shit-ton of bricks had been lifted from his shoulders.

Asher's back muscles pinched tight. "But . . . I can't live in this city."

Luke's brows stitched together, but he said, "We have locations all over the States. You don't need to spend much time here."

"Is your past going to be a problem?" Jessica's palms landed on the desk. "Those people you were with tonight will—"

"No." *As long as I don't live here, I'm good.*

"Thank you." Luke faced him with an extended hand. "It might be a rough transition with Marcus being gone, but this will be good for the team." Luke released a hard sigh, and Asher could feel the weight of his loss slam into him.

He released Luke's palm and wrapped a hand around the back of his neck. He wasn't too great at dealing with feelings either.

Luke cleared his throat. "Jessica has a few nondisclosure papers for you to sign from the president, and then we'll handle the rest of the details tomorrow."

"You can't tell anyone, not even the guys from Charlie Team, about this," Jessica added.

"I gotta make some calls." Luke nodded. "I'll be in my office. One door down. Come find me when you're done." And he left without another word.

Asher moved around the desk to confront Jessica now that they were alone. His hands slipped into his pockets to keep himself from reaching out to her. To touch her. To ensure she was real.

"What are you doing?" She tipped her chin to find his eyes and folded her arms as if to build a wall between them.

Still as arctic-cold as he remembered. Except between the sheets, of course.

"Why doesn't he know we worked together in Aleppo?" He thought back to the op. He'd known her last name was Scott, but he hadn't known Luke had a sister, and even if he had, what were the odds they'd be related?

"I didn't see a reason to tell him." She dropped her eyes, hiding her gaze beneath long lashes.

"I don't see why you'd feel the need to keep it from him." He tensed. "Unless, of course, you were worried he'd find out what happened between us."

The way a newbie fires a 9mm, not used to the recoil—

that was Jessica right now. A jerk to her shoulders, to her neck. A quick snap of unease. A lack of comfort at the situation at hand.

"There never was an *us*," she said after a beat. "It was one night."

He casually shrugged. "True. You left before the sun came up."

Her eyes seized his. They were too blue. Too *everything*. "I had a plane to catch. Besides, it was just sex." She stepped back, bumping into her chair.

He assessed her for another moment, trying to get a read on her. "Are you against me joining the team?"

"Yes." She dropped her arms. "But not because of the thing between us."

He angled his head. "I thought there wasn't an *us*."

She looked toward the door, a pinch of irritation flaring on her face. "You make me nervous. You hate authority. You don't ever—"

"You didn't seem to have an issue with me when you were muffling your screams with a pillow so you didn't wake the barracks."

"I don't normally hook up with SEALs." She flicked her wrist. "Or anyone in uniform, for that matter."

He couldn't stop the smirk that tugged at his lips. "So, I was an exception?"

"That night was . . ." She lowered herself back into her seat.

It probably wasn't the time or place to be revisiting the past, but they'd need to clear the air if they were going to work together.

"Why were you really fighting tonight?" she asked, pivoting, and he'd give her an A for effort. "Luke may not care, but I do."

He considered changing the topic, but he knew she'd never let it go. "I like it," he answered, a glib tone to his voice. "And I'm sure a spy like you is aware of my history." *My dark, shitty past.* A past that would reach for him like the touch of Satan if he stayed in the city for too long.

She found her feet again. But even though she was five feet eight with boots on, she couldn't compete with his height. A frustrated twist of her lips had him smiling again.

"Trying to get closer to kiss me, huh?"

Her eyes widened. "Asher," she hissed and glanced at the door. Again.

"You know, I wouldn't even be here tonight if you told your brother we've had sex." He squinted one eye. "How many times did I make you come? Three or four?"

"I . . ."

He brushed the pad of his thumb down her cheek. She didn't flinch. "But don't worry, now that I know you're Luke's sister, I won't even picture you naked while we work together." He placed his hand over his heart. "Promise."

A red crept up her throat and touched her cheeks.

He turned away before he showcased his dick attempting to tent out his jeans when he thought about their night together.

It wasn't every day a man met a woman like her: a strikingly beautiful genius. Hell, her brains turned him on as much as her looks.

He'd been a sucker for smart women ever since his first crush on his teacher in the fifth grade. Hot Miss Klein.

"Please don't make this hard for me," she whispered.

He looked back at her. "As long as you, uh, don't make things hard for me." His brows quickly rose and fell.

A smile almost touched her mouth, and it was like fireworks erupted in his chest.

It'd been over three years since they'd had sex, so why did she have his pulse racing like this?

"Can we be civil?"

"You think I'm capable?"

"No." She held out her palm, and he fully faced her and clasped it. "But I can be hopeful."

"Well," he said, raising both brows and smiling, "here's to hope."

She quickly pulled her hand free of his, went back to her desk, and unlocked a drawer. "Are you sure you don't have any questions before you sign away your life?"

He shrugged. "What's to know? I may be out of a job in two days."

"That the only reason why you said *yes*?" She lifted a brow.

"I guess you'll have to find out, Peaches."

CHAPTER ONE

MITRY-MORY, FRANCE
Three years later

"WE'RE CHASING DAYLIGHT, BOYS," ASHER SAID OVER HIS comm. "Three more tangos left, and we're out of here."

"Bravo One, this is Two." Owen's voice popped into his ear. "We've got a problem. I have two tangos in my sights—they've both got s-belts. They're in the room with the laptop."

Asher peered over his shoulder at Bravo Four, Liam, and raised a fist into the air to hold position. "Bravo Two, this is One. Get them away from the computer before they set those damn things off."

"Roger that," Owen replied, and a battery of gunshots sounded in Asher's ear.

"Coming in for an assist, Bravo Two." Asher clutched his 50-caliber sniper rifle and motioned for Liam to move back.

"Bravo One, you have seven minutes to get to the exfil site," Jessica said over the radio.

"Copy that, but we're—" Asher's words were cut off as a blast from down the hall threw him back, rocking his chest cavity as he fell.

"Asher. Asher?" A voice was in his ears, but he couldn't get his eyes to open.

Salt on his tongue. Wet sand on his back.

Hands and feet bound on the beach.

Why am I back in BUD/S? Asher's stomach squeezed as he tried to force his eyes open, to force the ringing in his ears away.

SEALs aren't made, boy—they're born. His training officer had hollered the timeless saying at him on the beach as he had done flutter kicks. *Twenty-five percent of you won't live to see thirty. You gonna be one of them?*

Asher had shaken his head. *No, sir!*

You gonna be a quarterback, boy? Or a Teamguy?

Teamguy, sir! Asher had shouted as he'd continued to kick, his body fatigued as all hell.

Good. Now get up!

"Asher! Get up, man! Get up!"

He blinked back to the present and finally forced his eyes open, the ringing in his ears subsiding, which was a good sign. "You okay?" he asked Liam. He coughed, attempting to clear his lungs.

"I'm good," Liam answered and handed him his rifle once Asher was on his feet.

"Bravo Two, this is One; you copy?"

Silence.

"Do a radio check," Asher sputtered to Liam.

"Nothing on my end." Liam swiped at the tendrils of smoke still curling in the air around them.

"What the hell?" His brown eyes narrowed as he spied Jessica rounding the corner at the far end of the hall.

But at the sound of something coming from the direction of the blast, Asher whipped around to see a tango charging their way, gun in hand.

"Get Jessica out of here!" Asher hollered.

* * *

"To a job well done." Asher raised his bottle in the air and clinked it with Owen's.

"And to only five more days of you being Bravo One," Jessica added and touched her beer to the gathered bottles amongst the team. "I can't wait until Luke is back to take over with me."

"Oh, come on, you loved having me at your side." Asher tipped back his beer and guzzled it.

"Like a root canal," she said with a laugh.

"Really, though, you two survived over two months without killing each other while Luke's been gone," Knox noted and lifted his brows, a smile in his eyes. "I say that's cause for celebration when we get back."

"Yeah, you're right—I guess I managed not to kill him." Jessica took a seat on the only available barstool and swiveled around to face the team. The rest of the guys—Asher, Liam, Knox, Wyatt, and Owen—remained standing in front of her.

"Not that you didn't try earlier today." Asher touched his abdomen, remembering the bullet that had hit him. "You shouldn't have come into the compound." *You could've died, damn it.*

She took a sip of her Guinness. "And you shouldn't have lost your focus and let that guy get the drop on you."

He rolled his eyes. How could he not lose focus when

bullets were flying, an IED had been detonated, and *she* decided to join the party?

"His vest caught the slug. Just a bruise beneath." Liam tapped him on the shoulder.

His abs had turned purple from the impact, but yeah, he'd be fine. Jessica was good—so he was good.

"But, seriously, a job bloody well done," Wyatt, normally on Echo Team, said. He was taking Asher's spot as Bravo Three since Asher had assumed the role of Bravo One while Luke was on paternity leave.

"It was a huge win for us." Owen nodded and then began texting on his phone. Asher assumed he was contacting Samantha, his fiancée, and letting her know he was okay.

Nine bad guys down. And one laptop full of names of arms dealers supplying weapons to terrorists. It'd been a good fucking day. Even if they'd nearly been blown to hell, and Asher had gotten shot.

Jessica wedged her bottle between her thighs and swept her hair into a messy bun, some loose strands drifting around her face.

"Another round, darlin'." Liam thickened his Aussie accent for the bartender. "S'il vous plaît," he added and winked.

Asher tossed his empty bottle, turned away from the team, and retrieved his phone to check his messages. He hadn't heard from his sister in a few weeks, and it was making him nervous. She always returned his calls. He'd had a former Teamguy, Noah Dalton, check on her the other day, just to make sure she was still alive.

She was breathing and doing fine, which meant one thing: she was avoiding him for some reason. But why?

He tapped out another quick message to Sarah and then stowed his phone before rejoining the group.

"I should've stayed here for the weekend." Jessica's eyes went to Asher's stomach, and her lip pulled between her teeth.

Did she feel guilty about distracting him earlier?

He maneuvered between Owen and Jessica to snatch his new drink from the counter, and he brushed against her shoulder in the process.

A twinge of . . . *something* . . . shot down his spine at the mere touch, and it had him swallowing as he edged away from her.

"You need a vacation?" Owen asked, a smile on his lips. Jessica had forced Owen to take some time off, and it'd ended up with him falling in love a few months back.

"No." She looked at Owen off to her right. "I've got to be in Germany next week."

"Everything okay?" Asher asked. "Why are we only now hearing about this trip?"

"It was a last-minute request for me to come." Her pupils constricted and guilt crossed her face. "It's been six months since I've visited the girls—they need me. And I see my other class a lot more often."

"First of all," Asher began, "the girls in your other class live in New York. It's a bit more convenient, so don't feel bad." He lowered his head a touch to connect with her eyes, to ensure he had her attention. "And secondly, you practically spend all of your free time teaching them online."

"He's right. You have no life." Wyatt nodded to add emphasis to his words. "I understand why you teach kids in the Bronx, but what led you to teach coding and tech skills to refugees all the way over in Germany?"

"Yeah, Jess, why?" Owen cocked his head, a smirk stretching his lips. He'd asked her the same question before, trying to bait her into admitting she was compassionate beneath her tough exterior. She always shut him down, though.

Asher knew the truth behind her motives. She was keeping a secret, and it all had to do with the op they'd worked together six years ago—the one no one knew about, especially not Luke.

Asher took a slow and deliberate breath, the kind someone takes in an attempt to prevent his lungs from bursting when a B-52 drops a bomb nearby. The day he'd first laid eyes on Jessica crept back into his mind, and it had him rubbing his temples with his free hand.

You got any brains to go with that brawn? Jessica had asked from inside TOC. They'd been going over the intel to prep for the mission in Syria.

I say something to make you think otherwise? Asher had smacked a palm to his chest and studied the woman whose looks could bring a man to his knees.

Only every fifth word, she'd quipped with that smart mouth of hers he'd wanted to kiss. Apparently, that mouth of hers had had him stumbling through his words like a damn idiot, leading her to question his mental faculties.

I got the distinct vibe you hated me, he'd said the next day as she'd ripped her clothes off between hungry kisses.

I do, she'd hissed and jumped into his arms a moment later, wrapping her bare legs around his hips.

"It's the least I can do for the girls," Jessica said, obstructing Asher's memories, hurling him back to the present. "I'm hoping to give them a better life in Germany. Not to only be thought of as refugees."

"They'll become mini-yous with all that coding you're teaching them," Liam commented.

"There can never be another Jessica," Asher said, and a few of the guys cleared their throats at his words.

"So, uh, are you going to see family while you're in Germany?" Owen asked, coming in for the assist to kill the sudden awkwardness.

"No, my relatives live in Munich," she answered, but she cast Asher a suspicious look as if she were somehow reading his thoughts. "I won't have time."

"No sense going over the Atlantic just to turn around and fly back this way." Owen dropped onto a now-empty stool beside her. "I can cover you until Luke's back if that's what you're worried about."

"She doesn't want to leave me in charge." Asher gulped his beer, but it was too warm for his taste.

Knox looked at Asher and scratched at his jaw. "Did you guys catch the Giants game last weekend?"

"I don't give a damn about American football," Wyatt said with a laugh, missing the intentional change in topic.

Asher moved to stand directly in front of Jessica, and the team parted like the Red Sea. All he could focus on was her blue eyes. "We can handle things with both you and Luke gone."

Her hand tightened around the bottle, and she brought the rim to her lips, allowing it to hover there. The simple act like a taunt to his dick. A tease of seduction.

Every time he'd see her drink a beer—hell, even a bottle of water—it had his balls nearly falling off from becoming the most navy-fucking-blue ever.

His mind had been in the gutter more than normal since they'd been working nonstop together.

The way she'd bend over to pick something up at the office always had his knuckles wedging between his teeth to prevent grunting like a caveman.

And the cherries. What was with her and cherries?

Why did she have to eat them with her lunch? Every. Damn. Day.

His thoughts seemed to go blank in those moments. But after the pause of blankness, he'd find himself on a collision course with the past.

Six years . . . and he still couldn't scrub the memory of their one night in bed from his mind.

"Stay in Paris," he finally spoke up. He dragged his thoughts out of the ditch, for now at least. "Or hell, head to Munich to visit your family before you're needed in Berlin. Enjoy some time off. We'll all be alive and well when you get back."

Of course, this meant he'd have to stay in Manhattan even longer, but he'd do it. For her.

He'd survived the last two months working out of the city and covering for Luke without going to the old fight club. What were a few more days?

Then again, maybe he wasn't ready to leave her side quite so soon. Who knew when another job would come? And he'd damn sure miss her when he left. Not that he'd admit it, but he would. He'd even miss the cherries.

Really, really miss the cherries.

"No," she said with a sigh. "We need to debrief. Besides, I didn't bring enough stuff with me to extend the trip."

"Paris is filled with stores. Go buy some new things," Knox said.

"She can't let go of control." Asher smirked. "It's not in her DNA."

"I can, but—"

"No, you can't," he challenged, wondering if she'd take the bait. The woman did deserve some time to breathe.

"Find yourself a French stud while you're at it. Or a German dude, if you head there early." Liam's words had a chill rushing down Asher's body. "You need to get laid. How long has it been?"

Jessica shook her head and laughed. "My sex life is not your business." Her eyes caught Asher's as she spoke, and he wondered if she was taking a walk down memory lane, remembering their hookup, as well.

"On that note, I think we should head to the gate," Owen said and raised a brow.

"Yeah, I'll be right there." Jessica turned toward the bar.

"Last chance to stay," Knox said, but she waved her hand in the air without looking at him.

Asher glanced at the guys and then gave a slight nod, letting them know he'd catch up with them.

"Why are you still here?" she asked a moment later.

He moved alongside her and positioned his bottle next to hers before his palms met the counter. "Because you're here." He hadn't meant for the words to escape his mouth, but the truth had slipped free too fast.

"You're not going to convince me to stay." She shifted to face him. "So don't bother." Her gaze swept over him, and her blue eyes narrowed as she appraised him as if he were worth well more than market value. "Let's just catch up with the guys." She started to stand, but he held a hand in the air, urging her back down, and she followed his command. That was almost a surprise.

"I need you to tell me why you stormed the compound this morning."

She looked heavenward.

"You weren't supposed to come in. You always stay outside. What the hell happened?" She'd never taken chances like that when she'd worked alongside her brother.

She fully faced him, a sudden fire in her eyes. "Because I lost you guys on comms. I told you this already."

Annoyance tinged her words, burning the edges, and he felt the flames.

"And I said it was bullshit." He cocked his head and folded his arms. "Tell me the truth."

"I heard the gunfire." She lifted her shoulders. "Then there was the explosion."

"You shouldn't have taken the risk." His stomach dropped at the idea of something happening to her. "Luke would've killed me if you'd gotten yourself shot."

Her eyes skated down to his abdomen beneath his crossed arms. The same pull of guilt on her face reappeared. "Instead, I got *you* shot." She gathered in a hard breath and released it. "I won't make another mistake like that again. I'm sorry."

"I'm fine." He reached for her wrist, feeling her pulse race beneath his thumb. "We can't lose you, though. Got it?"

She stared at his hand as if in a daze. "Why are you being so nice to me lately?"

His eyes narrowed as he tried to rally his thoughts. "You want me to be a dick?" His boots edged a step away from her stool.

"Yes." She wet her lips and brushed her hand down the column of her throat.

"Why?" He knew the answer, but he needed to hear the words slip from her mouth.

"You know damn well why." She stood.

"Enlighten me." His folded arms tensed as he examined her, waiting for her to either lie like normal, or finally expose the truth about how she felt.

Without her brother as a barrier between them the last two months they'd grown closer, even though she'd rather run naked in Times Square than admit it.

And although she was probably right to keep things

professional, it was becoming more difficult with every passing day.

"You know, after spending so much time together lately I thought you'd become more of a jackass."

Deflection, of course. The woman was a master at it.

And with the sound of her ringing cell she'd found a second means to escape from any heavy or real conversation.

"It's Luke," she said after retrieving her phone.

Her brother.

His commanding officer.

A major damn cock-block.

He dragged his palms down his face once her back was to him as she answered the phone.

He caught sight of the bartender eying him. She coyly tucked her short, dark strands behind her ears and slowly rolled her tongue over her bottom lip, trying to get his attention.

The universal signs for *I want you* crossed language barriers.

His body had become immune to such advances, though. He'd had to resort to jerking off like a fifteen-year-old. The only woman he wanted he couldn't have, but for some reason, he couldn't bite the bullet and hook up with someone else. To move on.

"Oh God." Jessica's words had him circling her to find her face.

"What's wrong?"

She lowered the phone from her ear. "A DEVGRU team took out a terrorist cell yesterday and . . ."

"What?" He touched her bicep, worry darting through him.

"It was confirmed it was the men who killed Marcus."

29

He staggered back a step in disbelief. "You're sure? We've been down this road before."

Her brows drew inward. "President Rydell personally called Luke and told him the news. They're certain. It's finally over," she whispered.

And he did the first thing that came to mind. He grabbed hold of her and pulled her into his arms, holding her against him for the first time in six years.

CHAPTER TWO

"To Marcus." Luke raised his glass in the air.

The guys had been sharing memories of him for the past hour at the back of a busy restaurant, Rossi's, which had been Marcus's favorite place to eat.

Five square tables had been shoved together to accommodate some of the guys from Scott & Scott Securities, as well as Bravo and Echo Teams. Plus, there were two new additions to the group: Luke's fiancée, Eva. And Owen's fiancée, Samantha.

"To never forgetting," Asher added with a nod and finished his drink, his eyes now clinging to the far side wall. The vintage Italian signs held his attention and reminded him of his family's restaurant; he breathed in the smell of a million baked pies and melted cheese. The taste of home on his tongue.

But that home was gone. He'd left it behind to join the Navy.

His team was his home now. And with justice served for Marcus, he felt like he could breathe again.

"You good?" Liam asked after another ten or so minutes had passed. "I know you didn't know Marcus well, but—"

"I feel like I did." *I took his spot.* And he sure as hell hoped no one else would ever have to be replaced. He didn't know if he could handle any more losses in his life.

"Well." Liam rubbed his palms together and looked over at Jessica from across the table. "Marcus would want us having fun tonight. He'd kick our asses if we didn't."

Knox cocked his head toward the wall of liquor behind the woman tending bar. Liam nodded and circumvented the table to follow him.

"I think they have the right idea," Wyatt said, pressing his palms to the table. "You need to loosen up, anyway. That woman at our three o'clock has been staring at you since we got here."

"Or maybe she's been eying you," Asher said without following Wyatt's gaze.

"So, you don't mind if I move in?" He was already on his feet, sidestepping the chair.

"Have at her," he replied with a laugh, not sure if Wyatt even heard him.

"Some things never change with you guys," Jessica said once Wyatt was gone.

"Why are you making such a sweeping generalization about us?" He leaned back in his seat and glanced toward the end of the table where Luke and his fiancée sat, then he looked over at Owen and Samantha laughing at something Luke had said.

Two Teamguys down.

Eight more to go.

He wasn't sure how many of his buddies would fall in love, though.

"You guys play the field and never commit," she said

with a shrug before taking the cherry from her soda, placing it in her mouth, and pulling off the stem.

And . . . I hate you. "You're just as bad." He took a sip of his Guinness to try and cool off, to keep from wandering to that blank space in his mind that would quickly shift to memories of their one time together.

He scratched at his chin, his thoughts wandering anyway.

Oh, Asher. You're so, so, so— Her words had turned to a full-on howl-at-the-moon kind of moan before she'd sunk her teeth into the pillow as she orgasmed.

He coughed into a closed fist and regrouped. "Don't pretend you don't hook up with guys and then leave them in the morning, never to call again." *You did it to me.*

Restaurant mood-lighting or not, he could see the rise of red edge up her neck and into her cheeks.

Her attempt to clear her throat was less than subtle. He'd somehow gotten to her, hadn't he?

"I don't have time for relationships." Her lips depressed into a hard line. "Or casual sex," she said in a lower voice a moment later. "But, that's not any of your concern."

"Then why'd you tell me?" He cocked a brow, a smirk touching his lips.

She drummed her nails on the table and her eyes pinned to his. "Where will you be heading Monday when Luke comes back to the office?"

If only he had a bell to ring every time she changed the subject. Of course, he'd probably lose his hearing from the ringing.

"Until we get another job, you mean?" His hands fell to his lap. "I don't know."

"Are you ever going to pick a place to call home?"

"I—" He lost his words when his gaze settled on someone across the restaurant.

His brother-in-law was sitting next to someone other than Asher's sister, and his damn lips were on the woman's cheek. "What the hell?" he said under his breath.

"What's wrong?" Jessica turned in her chair to track Asher's eyes.

Asher shoved away from the table, the crowded place too noisy for anyone to hear the hard scrape of the chair legs against the floor.

He started for Greg, ignoring the swell of chatter and flow of wine all around him.

By the time Greg's brown eyes connected with his, it was too late. Asher grabbed his arm and jerked him off his stool. He bunched his shirt in his hand.

The sudden murmurs from people in the restaurant became dull background noise.

"Are you cheating on Sarah?" The question whooshed out hard and fast.

"What the fuck, man?" Greg surrendered his palms, his brows pinching together. "I'm not cheating on your sister."

Asher's jaw tightened as his gaze darted to the brunette at the bar top table and then back to the two-timing asshole in front of him. "It sure as hell looks like it."

"Let him go." Jessica's fingers splayed at the center of Asher's back.

Her presence caused a momentary lapse of calm before his anger barked back up his spine and he seethed, "What's going on?" His free hand curled into a fist at his side, ready to pummel the guy. "Where's Sarah?"

"How would I know? We split up."

The news was the equivalent to a lead slug from a .30 Win Mag hitting subsonic speed before pinging a target.

Asher released his hold on Greg and backed up a step, bumping into Jessica. He glanced at her over his shoulder, and she lightly shook her head, another plea to get him to calm down. "What are you talking about?" he asked, returning his focus to Greg.

The man smoothed his hands down his crisp dress shirt. "Your sister"—he pointed at his chest—"cheated on *me*. We separated four weeks ago."

"No. I don't believe that. Sarah wouldn't—"

"Well, I guess neither one of us knows her as well as we thought," he cut him off. "It was some guy from her past. Covered in tattoos. Real bad attitude." He slipped back onto his barstool, and the woman he was with reached for his hand. "I walked in on them screwing on top of our kitchen table."

"No. No damn way." Asher clenched his teeth, trying to shake the image Greg had painted from his mind. "You're lying."

"Asher." Jessica gripped his bicep, and her touch had him seizing a breath. "Let's go."

"I bet she's with the prick right now. Apparently, your clean-cut sister likes to get really fucking dirty."

Asher leaned in, his breath touching Greg's face as anger pricked his fingertips, and he fisted his shirt once again.

He'd never liked her husband, and hell, he barely knew the guy. Maybe he deserved to have his ass kicked, anyway.

"Don't," Jessica commanded.

"Asher." It was Owen this time.

Great. Was the whole team going to defend his brother-in-law?

"Jessica's right. Let him go," Owen said slowly as if he knew Asher's mind was working at a shit level right now.

"If you're lying to me, I'll find you and gut you." Asher hesitantly released his shirt and then left the bar in need of fresh air.

"Wait!" Jessica called after him.

On the street, he spun around to find Owen and Jessica there. "What?" He pressed his hands to his eyes, trying to dial down the anger he was hurling at his friends. "Sorry." He edged closer to the building and out of the way of the few passing pedestrians.

"You okay, man?" Owen asked as Asher dropped his arms like weights to his sides, his gaze pinned to the door of the bar as Eva slipped outside.

"I'll be fine." His throat tightened as he thought about who the hell his sister could be with right now.

"No, you're not." Jessica stepped up alongside Owen and crossed her arms, slightly shaking.

"Get inside. You'll freeze." Asher jerked his chin toward the bar.

"I don't think you should go back inside right now," Owen said. "But you shouldn't be alone."

"Here." Eva handed out their coats and offered Jessica her purse. "Can't help myself. I'm a mother now." She smiled.

"Thanks." Owen clutched his jacket and waited for Eva to head back inside before speaking again. "I know what you're thinking, and I'd advise against it."

"Sarah didn't tell you for a reason," Jessica added. "Leave it alone."

He faked a laugh. "She's my sister. I need to know she's safe. What if this guy she's with is—" His words died as an idea rolled to mind. *No. Hell, no.* It couldn't be, could it? "I gotta go." He put on his jacket and whirled around and started in the other direction.

"Don't kill anyone," Owen called out from behind.

Asher kept on the move.

"Wait for me," Jessica said a few beats later, breathy from the cool air.

"Get back inside the bar," he hollered without looking her way. "Where I'm going isn't safe for you." *Or my sister.*

"Asher, please." She was at his nine o'clock now, and he knew she was too stubborn to back down, so he halted and spun to face her.

"Go back." He stabbed at the air, pointing toward the bar. "Tonight is about Marcus. You need to be with the team."

"You should be with us then." When he didn't speak, she said, "I have to go with you. Someone has to make sure you don't get hurt, or hurt someone else." She angled her head. "We're still in charge. I can't let my partner get into trouble."

He stepped so close it had her back up against the building behind her. With a lift of her chin, she zeroed in on his eyes with her take-no-prisoners look he knew all too well.

"You and me." She pressed a finger to his chest. "We're a team."

He cocked a brow and mounted a hand on the brick wall over her shoulder. "Since when is there an *us*?" His breaths quickened as his gaze darted to her mouth.

"Don't hunt your sister down," she said instead. "If she didn't tell you what's going on, there's a reason."

"If she's with who I think she's with, I have to go," he rushed out.

"She's over thirty. Sarah can handle herself." Her palm flattened on his chest.

He dropped his eyes to her fingers, and a strange fluttering sensation grew in his stomach. "I don't give a shit about age. She's my sister. She doesn't have a dad to watch over her." His boots shifted back, and it had Jessica lowering her hand. "I'm responsible for her."

The topic of his father had always been a hard limit for him.

No discussions. No mention of his existence in the world.

This was a first.

"Then I'm coming with you."

"No."

"Too bad," she said casually and shifted past him.

He caught her by the arm, and she peered back at him. "Why do you love to piss me off?"

"I could ask you the same thing." She lightly shook her head. "Let's take my car. It'll get us there faster."

He considered her words. Her known stubbornness. "Fine," he ground out. "But I'm driving."

"Like hell you are." She shook her head. "No one drives my car." She shot him a pointed look, then a slow whisper of a smile ghosted her lips. "Follow me."

He eyed the back of her jeans as she moved in front of him down the street, and he tried to look away. Tried damn hard.

No luck.

She was a distraction, and even though he wanted to latch onto his anger, maybe it was a good idea to cool off before he murdered someone tonight.

Once he buckled up inside her Maserati, he pressed his palms to his thighs and tipped his chin toward the roof.

"Where are we going?"

He peered over at her. "To where you found me three years ago."

CHAPTER THREE

THE SKY ROARED AS IF ZEUS AND POSEIDON WERE BATTLING for world domination. Thunder. Lightning bolts. Pelting rain as they rushed from the car and to the side of the building beneath an overhang for protection. Rain in January was worse than snow, but she still wanted to jab Asher in the ribs for holding his jacket over her head.

She combed her fingers through her messy locks, observing him as he tucked his coat into the crook of his arm. His hair was still irritatingly perfect, swept tight into a man-bun—a look she'd always detested. Until him. Why did everything about him have to turn her on? It made things . . . difficult. "Don't do shit like that, okay?"

"What? Keep you from getting wet?"

Soaking frigging wet. All the time. Her thighs squeezed as the familiar but unwanted burn of desire zinged inside of her. "Don't freeze your ass off for me. I can handle myself."

He clutched the door handle but didn't open it, catching her gaze from over his shoulder. Even in the shitty street lighting the depth of his eyes managed to drill right through her.

"Let's just find Sarah." She pointed toward the door, anxious to get the night over with so she could board her plane tomorrow and get away from him for a few days. Working so close to him over the past few months had screwed with her head.

Every morning. Afternoon. And night. Even on the weekends, Asher had been there.

Kicking his untied boots up atop her desk as he leaned back with his hands behind his head—purposefully irritating her.

Watching her. Poking fun at her. Pulling his bottom lip between his teeth as he studied her. Stripping her with his eyes.

Wash. Rinse. Repeat.

Day in and day out, she'd had to alleviate the lust by running like she was training for a triathlon.

Going into the compound in France had been evidence she needed a system reboot. She'd never made a mistake like that, but when she'd heard the explosion and lost Asher on comms—she'd also lost her mind apparently.

"Stay at my side." His tone was rough, and yet it glided over her skin and had her nipples straining against the fabric of her bra. She hated her body's betrayal. "If anyone touches you, then I'll end up beating the shit out of someone tonight. Maybe even commit murder."

"Enough with the chivalry already." She tipped her chin toward the door as a smile touched his lips.

"Your idea of chivalry is violence?"

She rolled her eyes. "I was kidding."

He swung open the door, and she moved past him, brushing against him in the process, and another unwanted sizzle snapped up her spine.

As they traversed the building, cutting through a crowd

surging toward a cage at the center of the room, Asher surprised her by reaching for her hand, lacing his fingers with hers.

She remained at his side, telling herself it was okay for him to lead since she was in foreign territory.

But as they walked, their united hands stirred something deep inside of her, making her heart ache.

Her only one-night stand with a man in uniform, and it had to be *him.* Of all people. The best orgasms of her life delivered over the course of those six hours. Six unforgettable hours.

She preferred the chauvinistic and cocky jerk—even if it was a façade—to this Asher. Because *this* Asher made her vulnerable, a feeling she couldn't handle.

As they rounded a side of one of the cage walls, her pulse spiked at the sight of Asher's sister. She stood alongside a guy who seemed vaguely familiar. They were watching the current fight in progress, and the guy had his arm draped around Sarah's shoulder.

She'd never met Sarah, but she recognized her from Asher's work file. A lot of blank spaces and dodgy details on his paperwork had led her to try and fill in the facts.

Asher's hold on her hand tightened. He must've spied his sister, too. *Please, don't kill anyone.*

She'd seen Asher fight before. He'd taken down a lot of bad guys in their time together. And she'd witnessed him throw down with the team to train. But three years ago, when she and Luke had walked into this very building, it'd been different. Another level.

She'd never forget the hard look in Asher's eyes that night. The darkness that had consumed his face as he'd landed punch after punch.

Ohhh. The man with Sarah was the guy Asher had been fighting that night. *Shit.*

Jessica kept her right elbow up to afford her space in the crowd as they walked, bumping into spectators.

Asher glanced at her, a look of anger, determination, in the set of his jaw. The nostrils of his Romanesque nose flared, his naturally semi-arched brows lowered, and the corners of his full lips depressed into a hard line.

The man was built like a truck, and he could probably smash anything and anyone in his way. But she needed to prevent that from happening tonight.

They closed in on the couple, and Sarah's eyes landed on them.

"Asher-Mother-Fucking-Hayes." The man at Sarah's side kept her close to him but glanced at his other arm as if checking a watch, even though he wasn't wearing one. "Is this the new thing? A visit every few years?" His voice was hardly audible over the sounds of the fight and the crowd, but she'd always been good at reading lips.

Sarah stepped forward and stood in front of Asher as if prepared to protect the man from her brother.

"What the hell are you doing here?" Asher's voice was like a roar over the cheers from an apparent knockout Jessica caught in her peripheral view.

"Leave," Sarah demanded. Her dark brown eyes whipped briefly to Jessica before settling on her brother.

"You don't belong here. It's not safe." Asher released his hold of Jessica and stepped closer to his sister, reaching for her arm, his coat falling to the ground in the process.

She shook her head and yanked her arm back before he could even touch her.

"It was safe for you, once upon a time." The bitter bite of

Sarah's words couldn't be missed, even with the competition of the surrounding noise.

"Why are you with Angelo?" Asher's arms locked at his sides and Jessica caught the familiar bunching of his fists. "Why'd you cheat on Greg?"

Sarah's pink lips parted, and she brushed her fingers through her long, silky brown hair. There was a twin-like resemblance between Sarah and her Sicilian mother.

"Greg's an asshole. Sarah found him pounding some woman in the ass in her kitchen." Angelo smoothed his hand down his neck, enveloped by inked flames. "I wanted to kill the bastard, but she wouldn't let me."

Asher's arms folded across his chest, and she noticed the tension in his chiseled jaw, even beneath his thick beard, as he eyed the pair in front of them. Jessica's fingers swept to his bicep, hoping to somehow remind him of, well, something.

He glanced at her, and his breathing slowed ever so slightly.

"Greg told me it was you who cheated," he said in a calmer voice as he faced his sister again.

"He's lying," Sarah shouted over the sudden cheers from the crowd. "Three years of marriage down the drain." She dialed up her volume even more. "Banging his coworker because he couldn't think of anything more original. He thought I was working at the restaurant, and then—" She clamped a hand over her mouth to stifle emotions, and one thing was for sure: Sarah was telling the truth. A woman burned was hard to miss.

Angelo wrapped a hand over Sarah's shoulder, and his dark brows drew inward. "I'm not the enemy."

"I still don't understand why you're here." Asher's stance relaxed a hair, but not by much.

"Because Angelo kept me from falling to pieces." A small hint of a smile graced Sarah's lips. "He saved me."

Asher's head dropped forward as if pained by the idea of them together. It was never easy for a brother to cope with his little sister and another guy. Well, at least from her experience, it wasn't.

Luke scared off any guy who ever came near Jessica, which probably was one of the reasons why she'd rarely lasted for more than a date or two with guys in the past. And Teamguys Luke had declared off-limits; although, it'd already been one of her own rules.

She had no idea how Luke would react if he discovered she'd had hot, sweaty sex with one of his right-hand men . . . even if it was before Asher had known she was Luke's sister.

"Angelo and I have been friends for years. He looked after me when you took off for the Navy." Jessica heard the squeeze of emotion in her tone, despite the booming sounds from all around. "You've been absent from my life for a long time aside from occasional texts and calls."

"You didn't touch—"

Angelo held up a palm. "She was fifteen when you left. So, no."

"What the hell changed, then?" Asher's arms fell to his sides as if they were anchored to the concrete.

"Greg screwing his coworker changed things," Sarah rushed out. "Angelo was there for me. He's still here for me."

"No," Asher bit out. "I'm your brother. I'm here. You don't need someone like him in your life. He's—"

Sarah poked Asher in the chest, the muscle straining in her jaw. "But you're not here for me. You've been in New York for the last two months, and how many times have you visited me?" Her index finger flipped up. "One time. For like an hour on Christmas." She huffed. "You should go."

"I'm not leaving here without you."

Angelo took a step forward. "Listen, things have changed. I'm not the same man I was three years ago."

Asher faked a laugh and then spread open his arms, palms up. "Could've fooled me."

"I run fights, but that's it. Nothing else." Angelo's eyes focused on Asher and then flitted over to Jessica. "If you're not here to watch a fight, or to fight someone yourself . . . you should do what your sister wants and go."

"Please, Ash. I can't leave with you. I'm happy. And if you care about me, you'll walk away." Sarah's voice broke, and the crowd boomed again.

Asher snatched his coat off the floor and held it between his palms. "I'll fight. If I win, you leave with me."

Sarah immediately shook her head.

At the same time, Jessica gripped his forearm. "Don't be an ass," she spurted out. "You don't own your sister's choices. You're better than that."

Asher let out a heavy breath and stared deep into her eyes, anger pooling in his browns. "Jessica . . ." It was his warning shot, but she wouldn't stand down. They were a team. They had to have each other's backs, even if most days she wanted to drop him on his.

"Thank you," Sarah said from behind, and it had her pivoting to face the woman.

"Don't thank me." Jessica's spine stiffened. "Your brother's a good man. A goddamn hero." Her stomach muscles tightened as memories breezed through her mind with all the times Asher had come through for the country. For the team. For her. "If he thinks this place is bad for you, then it is. But you're an independent woman, and you'll have to come to that realization on your own. Hopefully, it won't be too late."

Sarah dropped her brown eyes to the floor.

"We're leaving." Jessica looked back at Asher and pressed her hand to his chest, the heavy beats of his heart like vibrations against her palm.

His gaze cut over her shoulder to his sister and Angelo. "Please," he tried one more time.

"I'm sorry." Sarah's words had his shoulders slumping ever so slightly.

"If anything happens to her, you're dead," Asher warned. Then he reached for Jessica's elbow and motioned toward the exit with his chin.

"I'm proud of you," Jessica said once they were on the street.

The rain was still falling, but Asher didn't seem to notice. He kept his jacket clenched between his palms as he stared at the sidewalk in a daze.

"Asher?" She crossed her arms and stood before him, trying to fight the chill from the mix of cold air and rain. "Let's get in my car. I'll take you to your hotel."

He didn't say anything, so she reached out for him. He caught her wrist and seized her eyes, the water gliding down his face as he stared at her. "I should go back in there."

"No. You don't belong in there."

"Sarah doesn't belong in there. She's not supposed to be mixed up with a guy like him." He dropped his hold and looked up into the night sky as if suddenly noticing it was raining. "You'll freeze." He directed her toward her car at the curb.

In the passenger seat, he swiped his hands over his face.

She turned on the heated seats and jacked up the temperature, trying to prevent her teeth from clattering together. "Maybe he's changed." Although throwing illegal fights didn't exactly paint a rosy picture. She gripped the wheel but didn't drive. "His father is the one who got into trouble with your dad?"

Angelo Moretti. She remembered the name from Asher's file now.

His hands fell to his lap atop his coat, resting on his thighs. "Yeah."

"How many more years does your dad have?"

He shook his head. "No idea, and I don't care. He's a murderer, so . . ." He looked out the tinted window and back at the old factory building.

"Sarah can handle herself." She forced herself to drive, afraid he'd hop out of the car and head back inside for his sister otherwise.

"My mom's brother should have never introduced my dad to the life. Dad's not even Italian." He faked a laugh and gripped the bridge of his nose. "Dad tried to protect Sarah, to keep her from knowing about all of the illegal shit he was into. He kept her safe and in the Upper East Side with Mom."

His admission arrested her attention. Her gaze darted to him as they stopped at a red light. "But he didn't protect you," she whispered.

Asher pressed back into the seat and closed his eyes.

Their open line of communication was officially closed. She could feel the door slamming in her face. He had a door, though; whereas, she was fairly certain her walls lacked any entranceway.

"What time's your flight?" he asked as they neared his hotel after a ten-minute bone-chilling silence.

"Early."

"I'm not a fan of you traveling there alone."

"It's Berlin, not Baghdad. And it's for four days. We need a break from each other." She pulled up in front of the hotel.

He lifted his shoulders, a smile in his eyes. "I don't know. Who else will call me on my bullshit while you're gone?"

"Liam's pretty good at that." She looked over at the valet approaching. "Do I need to worry you'll do something stupid while I'm gone?" *Like go back to that fight club?*

He unbuckled. "When have you ever *not* worried about me?"

"True," she said as the valet opened his door. "But, if you feel the urge to do anything crazy, call me first?" Her heart leaped into her throat when he reached across the gears and touched her thigh.

He lifted his brown eyes to her face. "Define *crazy*." He waggled his brows, and like that, the Asher she knew was back. Mask in place.

And that's what she wanted. To get back to the way things were before Luke went on paternity leave, and she and Asher had become way too damn close. So close she'd worried she'd break her rules and sleep with him. It'd nearly happened around Christmas, too. All because of a carriage ride and some mistletoe.

"Get out of my car," she said and couldn't resist the smile stretching her lips.

"You know you love me." He winked and then stepped out of her car, clutching his coat. "And, Jessica?" He braced a hand atop the Maserati and leaned down to find her eyes as the valet held an umbrella over his head.

"Yeah?" she mouthed, a tight knot forming in her stomach.

"Be safe over there. I, uh, the team needs you."

CHAPTER FOUR

"Hey, Nahla, it's . . ." Jessica's eyes dropped closed; she nearly sputtered her real identity over the voicemail, exhaustion settling in. "It's Stephanie." She cleared her throat. "Just checking to see where you are. Hope everything's okay."

Nahla had been a no-show at the airport, which wasn't like her. The last-minute text to meet at Jessica's hotel bar instead officially had her on edge.

Her gaze drifted out the window overlooking the city center of Berlin. Her eyes captured the sliver of the moon making its debut in the dark blue sky as the night ate up the rest of the day.

She was looking forward to seeing the girls tomorrow. Lately, her online teaching sessions had become far too infrequent, with her work schedule exploding from the seams. Apparently, bad guys didn't take time off, so neither could she.

Jessica owed the girls a visit, though. It shouldn't have taken an email from Nahla to get her to come, either.

Guilt. Five letters heavier than boulders weighing down on her shoulders.

She'd been teaching the girls for nearly six years. Some had already gone off to college. She couldn't believe how much time had passed since she'd first met them in Aleppo—the same time she'd met Asher.

Asher. God, she hoped he wouldn't go to the fight club tonight. She'd given Knox and Liam a heads-up to keep an eye on him since Owen and Echo Team had left the city around the same time she had this morning.

The last thing she needed to worry about was Asher getting arrested for knocking the shit out of his sister's new boyfriend.

She blinked away her thoughts, nearly missing the vibration from a text on her phone.

A change of plans. Again.

After reading the instructions, she grabbed enough euros from her purse to cover the wine and then slipped on her brown leather gloves, wrapped her pink scarf around her neck, and tightened her coat before heading out into the freeze-your-ass-off cold. It wasn't snowing, at least.

A taxi delivered her to Pariser Platz. She strode toward the gate where tourists were snapping photos. Brandenburg Gate had once divided the country, but now it served as a beacon of unity and peace.

Another vibration from her purse had her shoulders sagging. Was Nahla canceling again?

Jessica retrieved her phone and eyed the text.

Asher: *Checking on you.*

She removed a glove to type back, a smile skirting her lips. A smile a text shouldn't be able to provoke so easily.

Jessica: *I should be the one checking on you. You good?*

Asher: *If you're wondering if I've damaged anyone's face today, that'd be a negative.*

Asher: *. . . Unfortunately.*

Her smile broadened, and she lifted her chin to observe the crowd, checking to see if Nahla had arrived. No sign of her yet.

Jessica: *Good. Do you think you can stay out of trouble until I'm home?*

Asher: *This is me we're talking about.*

Jessica: *Exactly.*

Asher: *Where are you right now?*

She looked at the neoclassical monument before directing her focus back to the screen.

Jessica: *In front of the Goddess of Victory.*

She'd see how good his German history was.

He didn't answer, and she figured he was busy Googling to determine her location. Of course, he could ping her cell and triangulate her position if he wanted to get tactical on her.

Jessica: *You enjoying your break from me?*

Three little dots popped then disappeared.

When the dots appeared again, her mind drifted back to the Christmas party last month, to the kiss with Asher that night. A mistletoe-inspired one, but still.

In the weeks that followed, Asher had tried to raise the topic of that night, but she'd always brought down the hammer and killed the conversation not even five words in.

"Stephanie!" Nahla's voice stole her attention as she moved toward her through the crowd.

Jessica quickly stowed her phone and slipped on her glove before slinging her arms around her friend, pulling her in for a hug.

"It's so good to see you." Jessica edged back to catch her friend's eyes.

51

Nahla looked left and then right, and her hand settled on Jessica's shoulder. "I'm sorry I had to change the plans, but . . . someone was following me."

Her words had Jessica's hand sweeping over Nahla's arm. "What are you talking about?"

"I think I lost them on my way here," she said, her voice breathy as if she'd been running.

Jessica scanned the plaza now. "We need to get you out of here so we can talk."

"No, we should stay in a public place. The more people, the better." Nahla's hand fell to her side, and she clenched the strap of her purse tight to her body.

"What's going on?" Her heart raced as she blew through a dozen potential scenarios. "Who would be following you?"

A blast of frigid wind picked up and whipped her long, dark hair in front of her. "I-I made a mistake. Someone figured out who I am." Nahla's eyes closed and then opened. "The real me."

"Oh, God." She scrolled through contingency plans in her head. "We've got to get you out of here. I'll arrange a safe house until I can figure out what's going on." She hated being without her team if shit were about to hit the fan. It felt like being naked in the cold.

"I'm so sorry." Her teeth clicked together like a chill of fear had blustered up her spine. "I lied to you. I asked you to come for the girls, but—"

"No, don't be sorry." Jessica shook her head as she tucked her gloved hand in her purse and grabbed her cell. "If your cover is blown, it was smart not to say anything over an unsecured line." She'd taught Nahla how to send encrypted messages, but even then, someone with enough cyber skills could crack them. "Let's go." She pointed toward the road where taxis were assembled.

They'd barely taken a few steps when a crack burst through the air, followed by a snap—a bullet breaking the sound barrier as it zinged past them.

The crowd scattered.

Another slug soared so close to Jessica she could practically feel the sting of the bullet. She crouched, the phone clattering to the ground in the process. She forced Nahla down next to her.

Nahla gasped, her eyes flaring.

Jessica didn't think the bullets had been meant as kill shots. No, they were intended to disseminate the crowd. To try and get to . . . *shit.*

"Stay by my side," she ordered.

Nahla peered at her. Fear darkened her eyes, but she nodded. "Okay."

"I'll keep you safe," Jessica tried to assure her once they were on their feet, even though she wasn't strapped.

She considered their options. If they stayed with the fleeing crowd, she'd put more lives at risk. But if they didn't have the cover of others, they'd be putting a bull's-eye on their heads.

"Let's move." She held onto Nahla's elbow and raced in a zigzag pattern in the direction of the Goddess of Victory, keeping her head low.

A shot whooshed over her shoulder a moment later, and it had her instinctively pulling Nahla down and to her side. She cupped Nahla's head to her chest, offering the best protection she could.

"Stay there!" a hard voice broke through the surrounding screams.

Jessica remained in a squatted position but looked back over her shoulder to observe the gunman on approach.

Tall. All black from head to toe. A mask with eyes visible through slits.

A duffel bag clutched in his right hand.

A bomb?

In front of them, he discharged his weapon again, but the bullet didn't come close.

Jessica looked back to see a Polizei officer take a hit.

"What do you want?" she demanded, facing him again, her defiance a soft echo.

Sirens wailed in the distance.

But they'd never make it in time.

Her heart stuttered as she stared at the masked shooter.

Nahla pivoted out of Jessica's reach and rose, standing her ground before the man. "Please, don't do this."

"Get behind me!" Jessica lurched to her feet to grab hold of Nahla's wrist, but her heart leaped into her throat as the man squeezed the trigger. "Nooooo!"

She immediately sank to her knees, falling to Nahla's side and pressed her gloved hands over the chest wound, blood smearing the leather.

Jessica's throat contracted as she cried, a broken sob releasing from deep within her chest.

"I-I . . ." Gasping breaths left Nahla as her eyes pinned to Jessica before the life drifted free of her in a split second.

"No," she whispered in grief. "No. No. No!" She added pressure to the wound. She had to save her. It couldn't end like this.

"Come. Now," the man said from over her shoulder, but she couldn't take her eyes off Nahla.

She growled the words, "I won't go any—" But agony bloomed on the side of her head and everything went black.

CHAPTER FIVE

"AT LEAST THE FREAK STORM HIT ONCE JESSICA WAS SAFE over the Atlantic," Liam said, walking alongside Knox and Asher down the sidewalk.

The snow was tapering off, drifting lazily as if it was exhausted of blanketing the city.

Asher's boots sunk into the white powder, the sidewalk not yet cleared, as the guys made their way to Asher's mom's home.

"Jessica would've told Mother Nature to go to hell before canceling her trip." Asher reached into his jeans pocket for his phone, checking to see if Jessica had returned the text he'd sent earlier, even though he hadn't received an alert. It'd been hours since he'd sent his message: *I miss you.*

She always replied to his texts, even when he sent dumbass messages to her when he was shit-faced. But this text was different. Something she wouldn't expect from him without his words being swaddled in sarcasm.

"You still waiting for your sister to return your calls?" Knox interrupted his thoughts.

"Jessica talked, huh?"

"Barely," Knox replied. "Only enough details so we can keep you out of trouble."

No one other than Jessica and Luke knew about Asher's past, about the man he'd been before joining the SEALs.

They knew he'd been a fighter, but that was it. Of course, he'd come close to going pro, and then he'd found himself staring at jail bars instead.

"Who is this guy your sister is with you hate so much?" Liam asked as they crossed the street.

"Not someone you'd ever want near your sister; that's all that matters." A burn of betrayal singed Asher's words.

His once-upon-a-time-ago best friend was now hooking up with his little sis. What world was he living in? And how could he ever leave New York now? He had to keep Sarah safe.

"Thank God I don't have a sister." Knox shook his head. "You have any?" he asked Liam once they were outside Asher's mom's building.

They rarely talked about family. Asher had his reasons, as did Knox, but he didn't know why Liam always remained tight-lipped about his.

"No, but I have three annoying-as-fuck brothers back in Sydney."

"What's wrong with them?" Knox asked, smiling.

"That's a story for another day." Liam rubbed his palms together once Asher used his key fob to enter the building.

"Man, I could use some home cooking," Knox said once they'd entered the elevator. He lifted his chin and closed his eyes, taking a whiff of the air. "Especially since she's a legit Italian."

"Legit?" Liam laughed.

"You know, actually born and raised there," Knox answered as they began to ascend.

"She'll be happy to have the company," Asher said once they exited and made their way to his mom's place.

"What does your stepdad do, anyway?" Knox asked.

"Defense attorney." He left out the part about how Bill had been his *dad's* defense attorney.

"Good man to have if you ever get yourself in trouble." Knox slapped him on the back.

"Yeah. He's the reason I joined the Navy." He hadn't meant for the words to slip from his lips, but shit, there they went. He'd been hell-bent over the years to keep his past to himself, like a dirty secret.

Outside the front door, Liam's gaze veered to Knox and then cut back to Asher. "I'm thinking we'll need to hear more about this later."

"Sure, you can read all about it when they print my obituary," Asher said while he rang the bell, deciding not to use his key. He'd learned his lesson the hard way after walking in on his mom and Bill rolling around on the floor half-naked.

He cringed at the memory, but then his stomach folded in at the sight of his sister in the now-open doorway. "Sarah." His brows slanted in. "Mom didn't say you'd be here."

She looked at Knox and Liam before stepping back to allow them entrance. "Yeah, she, uh, didn't mention you'd be showing up either. Intervention, I guess?"

Asher didn't budge. "Angelo's not here, is he?"

Her mouth rounded, and she slipped out into the hall, a hand to Asher's chest to try and push him back. She pulled the door closed behind her and folded her arms. "Mom and Bill don't know about him. Please—"

"Do they know you and Greg split?" Anger flared inside of him at the idea of her getting mixed up with a modern-day gangbanger. No way had Angelo become a new man.

"Yeah, and it took all of my energy to prevent Bill from going to his safe for his gun." She sidestepped Asher and extended her hand to Knox. "I'm Sarah. You must work with my brother based on all those muscles."

Knox smiled and shook her hand. "Yeah, I'm Charlie, but you can call me Knox."

"And I'm Liam." He took her hand next and flipped it over to kiss the top. "Pleasure to meet you, darlin'."

"Don't even think about it," Asher hissed.

Liam held his hands in the air with a knowing smile.

"You guys can go on in. I need a minute with Sarah." He waited for the door to close as he gathered his thoughts, his heart pounding wildly, his lungs burning. "If Mom doesn't know about Angelo, why does she think you and I need an 'intervention'?"

"Because I told her we were in a fight, but I didn't tell her why." Her dark eyes pinned to his, defiance glinting in her irises.

He'd missed so much of her life. Even though they'd stayed in touch through emails and texts, maybe he'd been a shit brother. Maybe what she'd said to him last night had been right. He'd turned his back—not just on his past, but on her.

"After you left, Angelo told me what happened back in the day." Her eyes lowered to the floor as if she couldn't stand to meet his gaze. "He told me he was the one who'd assaulted that guy, but you took the fall and ended up in jail." Her fingers swept to her collarbone. "Why didn't you ever tell me?"

"Would it have mattered?"

Her eyes jerked up to find his. "Yes. Maybe I wouldn't have blamed you for leaving. I wouldn't have been so pissed at you for disappearing not too long after Dad . . ." She dropped her words, her throat catching with emotion. "You're happy doing what you do?"

He wrapped a hand around the nape of his neck and eyed his sister, trying to understand he was now looking at a woman instead of a kid. "Yeah. I'm doing what I was meant to do."

She gave a light nod. "Then you should know I'm finally happy, too. Angelo makes me happy. Despite his faults, I finally feel like I can be me." She paused for a moment. "You don't have to like it, but it won't change the fact I want to be with him."

"You don't know him like I do."

She took a small step back. "I know him a lot better than you do. And people do change."

"He's a criminal, Sarah," he said as steadily as possible. "He'll hurt you in one way or another. I promise."

"Fortunately for me, it's not for you to decide." She turned and opened the door, and he caught her arm.

"Please. Think about this."

"I already have. I'm sorry." She disappeared inside, leaving him in the hall with his thoughts.

He dragged his hands down his face, and a frustrated groan left his mouth before joining everyone in the dining room.

His mom wiped her hands on her apron. "There's my boy." She reached up to squeeze both his cheeks before planting a kiss on the left, and then the right.

"Mama," he said, a touch of embarrassment lacing his tone.

"I'm thrilled you've finally brought some friends." She shifted her focus to the long, oval table lit with candlesticks in the purposefully dim room.

Ambiance. His mother had a thing about setting the mood for every one of her meals.

"Turn that thing off!" she called out to Bill in the other room.

Asher entered the living room and found Bill watching the news.

"Hey, Asher." He rose from his leather armchair, but Asher couldn't reply.

His stomach dropped at the sight on the TV, the headline: *Berlin Under Attack.* His heart stammered, yet his pulse raced. "What's going on?" He grabbed the remote off the coffee table and turned up the volume.

"There was a shooting followed by an explosion in Berlin a few hours ago."

"Fuck. The Brandenburg Gate." Asher reached into his pocket for his phone and dialed Jessica. *Pick up, damn it.* Her line went straight to voicemail.

He called again. Nothing.

"Someone filmed everything on their phone before the blast. Looks like a woman and officer were shot by a lone gunman. Then the guy dropped a bag and dragged another woman away with him, just before the explosion."

Asher slowly lowered his phone to his side as his booted feet strode toward the screen. The footage wasn't great, but it was a blonde with the gunman . . . a blonde with the same build as Jessica.

Her face wasn't visible, but . . .

"Liam! Knox!" Their names roared from his lips. "There's been an incident in Berlin." He checked the time on his phone when he'd sent his text earlier to Jessica and compared it to the report on the news. "I can't get ahold of Jessica, and—"

Liam entered the room and caught sight of the TV. "I'm sure she's fine."

Asher faced him and held his phone in the air. "Have you ever known Jessica not to answer a call from us?" His muscles bunched tight as bands of tension grabbed hold of him—everything inside of him in gridlock. "What if she was the woman taken?" He pivoted back toward the screen and observed the footage play over and over again.

"Let's get to the office and make some calls," Knox said. "I'm sure it's not her, but we'll all feel better when we know for sure."

Asher's phone rang. "It's Luke," he said, numbness hijacking his body.

"What's wrong?" His mom, removing her apron, entered the room alongside Sarah.

"I, uh, have to take this call." He brought the phone to his ear.

"Director Rutherford needs to talk to us over a secure feed," Luke cut straight to the point. "Can you meet me at the office?"

"This is about Jessica, isn't it?" Asher asked, his voice low and barely audible.

There was a moment of silence. "What do you mean? What about Jessica?"

Shit. "You haven't seen the news?"

"No." More silence. "What the hell aren't you telling me?"

Asher hung his head and squeezed his eyes closed, not sure how he'd level Luke with the news.

Jessica was their person. Their go-to. Their rock.

Athena, Aphrodite, and Hera all rolled into one amazing woman. A woman none of them could live without.

"There was a shooting. And an explosion. In Berlin."

Vivid scenarios percolated in his mind, one worse than the other. "Someone was taken. It may have been Jessica." He heard his words—his fragmented thoughts. He'd be broken until he heard Jessica was okay.

"No," Luke whispered over the line. "No," he said again, and the line disconnected.

Asher knew exactly what Luke was going to do. Look for answers. He needed someone to tell him Asher was wrong.

But deep in his gut, Asher knew. Jessica was in trouble.

CHAPTER SIX

WATER POURED OVER THE CLOTH COVERING JESSICA'S FACE as she laid atop the bed.

She couldn't take a breath.

When the man removed the fabric from her face and jerked her into a seated position, she lifted her chin and gasped while glaring at him.

When she'd joined the CIA over thirteen years ago, she'd been subjected to different forms of torture to see whether she could withstand it without giving up intel.

She could handle almost anything. She'd been reminding herself this for the last few hours, at least.

The Farm had beaten the weakness out of her, and by the time she'd become an officer, she'd been hardened into someone she'd barely recognized. She'd become a block of ice the agency had shaped into what they wanted.

Her captor's eyes thinned beneath his mask. He shoved her flat onto the bed again in the vine-covered and graffiti-walled room. From what she could gather, she was in an old hospital probably dating back to the days of the Nazis and eugenics.

More water splashed over the cloth, creating the sensation of drowning.

She tried to go back to her training in her head, to stay focused and not give in to him . . . but her thoughts drifted to the past.

Don't you think we should help Ara and the others? Jessica had asked Asher. Her body had been sweaty and pressed tight against his on the small bed in the barracks.

You're asking me? I don't usually deal with the aftermath of what I do. I just get the job done and then—

Move on? Hadn't she always moved on, too, though?

Her thoughts scattered. Breaking into fragments as she regained her focus and made her way back to the moment. A moment she didn't want to be in.

Ara.

And, *oh . . . the water.*

She was growing dizzy.

Stay strong, she commanded herself as her captor jerked her upright, freeing her of the cloth.

She sucked in slow and deliberate breaths, so she didn't become more light-headed.

He set down the empty jug and tossed the cloth onto a medical rolling table.

He had two portable heaters on the right and left sides of her bed. It was clear he planned on keeping her there for a while, and he didn't want her to die from the cold since the room lacked central heating.

"Who do you work for?"

She refused to give him anything, not even her tears. No, she'd save crying for when she made it out of there.

He turned his back to her when she remained quiet, and she checked her shackled hands before sweeping her focus to her roped feet. Maybe she could escape? She wasn't attached to the bed, so if she could knock him out somehow?

"Your passport says you're Stephanie Patterson." He thumbed through the pages of her alias. "But we both know that's not your real name. The girls call you *Stephanie*, though."

He was trying to bait her. To scare her into giving up information by bringing up the girls. But this man had no idea whom he was dealing with.

"Fuck you." It was the first time she'd spoken.

He faced her again. "There you are." His accent was German. Austrian German, maybe.

She cataloged the few details about him, in case—

"What do you do for work?" he asked, interrupting her thoughts.

She remained quiet.

He set her passport down. "You helped Ara become Nahla. You smuggled her to Berlin. Why?"

Nahla, in Arabic, meant *drink of water*, and now . . .

He turned to grab another water jug from the line of ten on the dirty concrete floor.

He'd given her too much recovery time. A dumb idea on his part.

She shifted off the bed and, as he turned to face her, flung the weight of her arms at the jug, knocking it from his grasp, splashing water everywhere.

"You're a feisty one, aren't you?"

She attempted to shuffle in the direction of a black duffel bag—it had to house his guns. If only she could—

He knocked her to the ground.

Her cheek smashed into the concrete, and he pressed the heel of his hand to her face against the grimy floor.

His knee went to her back. She was forced to take the

brunt of his weight with her cuffs beneath her, digging into her stomach.

"I don't normally deal with the living." His hot breath, even through the mask, had her skin crawling and her eyes sealing tight.

He shifted off her a few seconds later and dragged her to her feet, jerking her around to face him.

With open eyes, she managed not to blink as his fist came straight at her face, knocking her momentarily back to the past.

Again! her instructor had shouted during her training at the Farm. *If you get hit, suck it up and take it like a man. Don't let them sense weakness.*

What if I can't? What if he's too strong? Jessica had scrambled to her feet and lifted her fists on the boxing mat.

Your only weakness right now is in here, he'd said while tapping at his skull. *If he can't get in here, he can't get to you anywhere.*

Jessica took another punch from her captor—this time to her left cheek.

She raised her cuffed hands to deflect his next punch, but he forced her arms down and elbowed her in the face.

"CIA? FBI? Who else knows about Ara?"

This time, a hard punch to the stomach had her stumbling back, losing her footing. Her tailbone slammed hard against the concrete.

She tipped her chin to the ceiling and closed her eyes, trying to remember the rest of her training.

Stick to the cover. Speak to the story. *Be* the alias. Live and breathe it.

She'd forgotten. Failed.

She'd acted too strong. Too tough.

But maybe it didn't matter. He somehow knew of her connection to Ara.

"Who do you work for?" He grabbed the cuffs and yanked on them, forcing her upright again, the metal scraping against her flesh. "Who are you?"

"I'm somebody who will make you pay for what you did to her," she said through gritted teeth, trying not to lose the fight inside of her.

He cocked his head, wrapped a hand around her throat, and squeezed.

She lifted her arms between them to clutch at his wrist, trying not to resist too much to save her energy and breath.

"Tell me what you know, or I will kill you, just as I killed her."

You'll kill me anyway.

"Are you willing to let the girls die, too?"

His fingertips dug harder, and she could feel the rise of her pulse fighting for life in her neck.

For the second time that night, everything went black.

CHAPTER SEVEN

"THERE'S NO EASY WAY TO PUT THIS." CIA DIRECTOR Rutherford's face filled the screen on the wall in the conference room.

Luke, Knox, Liam, and Asher stood at attention, waiting for news they knew would come and didn't want to hear.

"At seven p.m. in Berlin, a lone shooter took out two people and abducted a third just before plastic explosives were detonated. The BND phoned an hour ago to let us know they got a positive match on the woman taken." There was a pause as his light-blue eyes narrowed. "Stephanie Patterson."

"No," Asher said between barely parted lips.

"Jessica's alias," Luke whispered.

The director leaned back in his desk chair. "The Germans don't seem to know Jessica's true identity, and they wouldn't divulge the name of the female victim gunned down who'd been with Jessica at the time. I'm guessing they haven't yet ID'd the victim, given the site of the blast was ten feet away from the body."

"Her phone must've been destroyed in the blast, which is why I couldn't track her location," Luke said in a low voice.

Asher glanced at Luke, the color in the man's face deepening to a reddish hue, anger slicing through him.

"What else do we know?" Knox spoke up since it was clear Luke was in shock.

Asher couldn't get his lips to move either, though. He turned his back to the screen and stormed over to the conference table and braced himself against it with balled hands.

His thoughts began to derail.

A loss of focus had him remembering . . .

You'd look good sprawled naked across this table. The words had accidentally slipped out a few months after Asher had first begun working with Jessica.

Her face had heated. Those walls of ice melted, but only for a moment, as her long lashes batted a few times. *You promised not to even think about me naked.*

In my defense, I spoke the words instead of thinking them. He winked and circumvented the table to get closer to her.

Her arms folded, which only accentuated her breasts in her silky white blouse. Defense 101.

Luke is on his way in here, she rushed out. *Are you in the mood for an ass-kicking?*

He won't—

What makes you think I was talking about him? She arched a brow, and her confidence and attitude had his dick stirring in his pants. *You can't have me again,* she said a moment later, but her eyes lowered to his jeans.

He didn't think she'd even realized she'd swept her luscious red lip between her white teeth, a signal she still wanted him as much as he wanted her.

Now, she was gone.

Gone. "No," Asher said under his breath. He whirled toward the guys as a realization slammed into him, and he regained his focus. "I think I know who the victim is," he rushed out.

His team faced him. Eyes wide and waiting for more.

"Every time Jessica goes to Berlin, she sees Nahla Assi." Asher's spine straightened, and he rubbed his hands down his jaw before blowing out a breath. "Formerly known as Ara Hadeed, the niece to Yasser Hadeed. Hadeed was the former leader of the al-Nusra Front."

The director's eyes connected with Asher's. When he didn't say anything else, Rutherford looked to Luke for more information.

But Luke wouldn't have the answers. He didn't know the truth.

"Jessica was under strict orders to abstain from any contact with her," Rutherford said. "What the hell aren't you telling me?"

Liam and Knox glanced Asher's way, concern flickering across their faces. He couldn't get himself to find Luke's eyes, to risk the look of betrayal he'd find there.

So he glanced skyward for a moment, trying to corral his thoughts. "The CIA may have turned its back on Ara Hadeed and those girls, but Jessica didn't." He couldn't say more because they didn't have time to waste. "We need to focus on getting her back."

"There's no way I'm going to sit around and let the BND or BKA handle this, not with Jessica's life on the line," Luke rasped.

The director shook his head. "This isn't your fight. I'm sorry. The president is turning this over to German officials and the CIA."

"What?" Asher stalked closer to the screen. "No damn way. She's one of us. We can't—"

"First of all," he began, cutting Asher off, "you know the

rules about what happens if one of you are captured." He loosened the tie around his neck. "And second of all, Jessica should never have been in contact with Ara Hadeed." Air filled his cheeks for a moment. A battle between being worried and pissed flared in his eyes. "Stand down. That's a direct order."

The second the line was killed, Knox asked, "We're not backing off, are we?"

Everyone faced Luke for the directive.

"Hell, no." Luke shook his head. "Liam, I want you on surveillance. Get me better footage from the scene in Berlin. I want access to every CCTV camera within the area."

Owen was the next best thing to Jessica when it came to cyber skills, but Liam was a close runner-up.

Liam nodded and hurried out of the conference room, leaving Asher alone with Luke and Knox.

"With a lot of roads being closed and the airport still shut down, it's going to take the rest of the boys longer to get here," Knox said while glancing out the window. The snow, taunting them, had picked back up again.

"I want everything we can get on the Hadeeds." Luke's jaw tensed, the muscle twitching beneath his stubble as he turned to Asher. "You were on the op that took down Yasser Hadeed six years ago, I'm guessing?" he asked, a rough texture to his tone. "Jessica, too."

Asher tried to ignore the feeling of intense pain that burrowed its way into the pit of his stomach. He had to focus. But it was damn useless.

He blinked, a slight blur to his vision as he eyed Luke.

It took him a moment to realize it was unshed tears distorting his view.

"Yeah, she was the CIA liaison." He finally found his

voice. A rawness in his throat. Lacerations to his heart at the thought of losing Jessica.

"Give us the rundown, then. We need to know what we're dealing with so we can find out who has her," Luke gritted out. He was burying his emotions better than Asher at the moment.

He had to remain strong for the team, though, Asher realized. It may have killed Luke to do it, but he was in command for a reason.

Asher's hands swept to prayer position, and his fingers tapped at his mouth for a second to get a grip. "Jessica had been tracking down the Hadeeds' compound for months. When she discovered where Yasser Hadeed was hiding, she provided the military with the coordinates for a drone strike against an al-Nusra Front location in Syria."

"I didn't think the strike took out Yasser Hadeed," Luke said.

Asher allowed his arms to fall to his sides. "The compound was wiped out, but Hadeed wasn't inside. And that was when a girl showed up at the base, offering up the location of Yasser."

"Ara," Knox whispered.

Asher nodded. "Her mom was Yasser's older sister. Her parents had been killed earlier that year by the Assad regime during the war. Ara was forced to live with her uncle, but she didn't approve of what he did, and so she came to us with his location on a silver fucking platter." He took a breath. "My team was brought in to handle the mission. After we took down Yasser, Jessica wanted to provide safe passage for those who wanted out of Syria, particularly Ara."

He didn't usually remember every detail, but that was the op where he'd met Jessica, and every moment had somehow imprinted in his mind.

"The CIA didn't help Ara in return, though," Knox said, picking up on what Asher had told the director.

He took a sobering breath. "No, the brass turned down Jessica's request."

"Is that the real reason she wanted to leave the CIA?" Knox asked when Luke continued to remain silent, his chest simply rising and falling with slow breaths.

"Maybe in part." Asher scratched at his jaw. "Jessica decided to help Ara and the girls, anyway. She paid for their passage to Berlin."

"That's why she teaches them." Knox put the pieces together. "They're the girls from Syria. Shit."

"Yeah. And with Ara she was worried if anyone discovered her identity they'd come after her for betraying her uncle. So, she arranged for a new identity. She's kept in touch with her all of these years but under her original alias Stephanie."

"Why'd you keep this from me? Why would Jessica risk so much—" Luke cut himself off.

Asher knew Luke was discovering a side of his sister he hadn't known—a side she kept hidden beneath boulders.

The so-called cold-hearted woman was anything but, even if she wouldn't truly share that part of herself with anyone.

"I'm sorry, man. I didn't even know she'd helped Ara until last summer. I stumbled upon them chatting over Skype. I tried to talk her out of staying in touch, but then I felt like a dick, so I let it go."

Luke looked to the floor. "That doesn't explain why you didn't let me know you had an operational history together when you joined the team."

Shit. He didn't know what to say about that.

Luke's blue eyes swerved up to Asher's face. "Is there

something else you're not telling me?" His brow arched as he tilted his head to the side, trying to get a read on him.

Asher fought the urge to close his eyes when he released the lie, "No. Nothing else."

* * *

"WE NEED TO BE AT THE AIRPORT IN AN HOUR. IT'S ALREADY almost nine," Luke announced when he came into the room. "Owen's ten minutes out. Wyatt and the rest of the guys should arrive in New York by the afternoon. Hopefully, they can dig up more intel while we're flying."

Asher looked at Luke, but a weighted pressure flattened him, and his lungs struggled to allow for the movement of breath as he considered the possible truth he'd never see Jessica again.

They'd been working nonstop since last night in Jessica's lab, aka her tech room.

Thank God the airports had re-opened that morning. "How are we getting there without Rutherford or POTUS catching wind of it?"

"I have it covered." Luke tossed a handful of passports onto the desk near where Knox sat. "Emergency IDs in case anyone ever tried to screw us over."

"A contingency plan." Knox nodded. "Good thinking."

"They won't know we're gone," Luke said.

"I, uh, think I have something." Liam tapped at the keys on the wireless keyboard and approached the screen that occupied a large portion of the wall. "I have a better angle of the shooter." He zoomed in on the screen, and Asher could clearly identify Jessica, her gloved hands pressed atop the chest of the woman on the ground.

"That's definitely Nahla." His throat grew thick as he tried to keep his eyes on the screen. "Ara," he corrected.

"Here's the interesting part," Liam said as Luke and Knox gathered closer to the screen. "See what the shooter's doing?" He changed camera angles to offer different vantage points of the crime scene. "He took a photo of the victim, and then it looks like he's getting a blood sample."

Crime scene. Asher's lungs burned again as he thought about Jessica. *She's tough,* he reminded himself. He'd have to continue to repeat that thought if he wanted to keep it together.

Teammates had been in danger before, but this was Jessica.

Jessica was different.

"Someone wanted proof of death, especially since the blast would have destroyed her body." Luke turned to face the guys when the footage showed the gunman dragging Jessica away—no one there to stop him. Moments later . . . the blast.

"If this guy was after Ara," Liam began, "why'd he take Jessica?"

"Maybe he saw it as an opportunity. Ransom? Or pump her for intel about Ara?" Knox proposed.

"They left in a black BMW X3." Liam switched to a different camera angle to show the man shoving her body into the trunk of the vehicle before the blast. "He probably ditched it, but this is what we have to work with right now." He zoomed in on the SUV. No plate number.

"There are way too many black Beamers to try and isolate this one on any cams, but I'll keep looking," Liam said, disappointment in his tone.

"The guy killed two people in a public place. He could've taken Ara out at her home or somewhere less visible. Why'd he want an audience?" Asher voiced his thoughts.

"Same reason he took the blood sample and photo," Liam said.

"Evidence the job was done? Worldwide attention? Plus, the blast sure as hell made a statement," Asher continued Liam's line of thought.

"He may have used the blast as a way to escape, too," Liam noted.

Luke positioned his hands on his hips. "I want to know everywhere Ara's been in the last few months. Every phone call. Message. Who she's been in contact with . . ."

"I can think of maybe six or seven assassins who'd be willing to take someone out so publicly. Plus, the use of plastic explosives narrows it down even more," Liam said. "Unless we're looking at a new player."

"Show me the list," Luke said.

Liam deftly worked at the keys and brought up three images with a laundry list of known kills on screen. "The killer wouldn't have used any known aliases to fly in, so let's upload their images into Jessica's program and see if any of them have appeared in Berlin recently."

The room grew silent for a moment, and then Luke cleared his throat. "Hopefully, by the time we get to Berlin something will pop up." He grabbed his phone from his pocket and gave a slight nod. "As soon as Owen gets here, and we catch him up, we'll head for the airport."

"Did we secure a safe house to work out of once we're there?" Asher sat in front of his laptop.

They had a few locations set up around the world, but their office in Munich wouldn't work for this op—and any site associated with their black-ops team would be off-limits since they were going on an unsanctioned mission.

"Yeah. My guy in Berlin pulled some strings for us, and don't worry, he's got our six," Luke answered. "I'm going to call him and see if he's heard chatter about any of our three assassins being in Germany."

Asher's fists settled atop the desk on each side of the keyboard as Luke left the room.

"You okay, man?" Liam came alongside Asher's chair, his keyboard still in hand. "I mean, I know none of us is technically—"

"No. No, I'm not okay." Asher's eyes fell shut.

"There's more you're not telling us, isn't there?" Knox asked. "More to the story between you and Jessica, at least?"

"Nothing that can help bring her back," he said in a low voice.

"She's stubborn as hell, and you know that better than any of us." Knox's words had Asher opening his eyes.

"I, uh, need a second." He left the conference room before the guys could say anything else and went into the men's room.

Bracing his palms against the counter, he stared at his reflection, his heartbeat pulsing in his ears, drowning out the sound of his thoughts.

Slow breaths changed to hard, gasping ones.

And then he dropped his head forward and pounded the marble as rage built inside of him, and his eyes blurred.

This was a nightmare. He felt like he'd been chucked over a high razor-ribbon fence. The sharp metal punctured every part of his body, and he was bleeding out.

The woman drove him nuts, but without her he wasn't sure he'd be able to remember how to breathe.

CHAPTER EIGHT

THE WINDOWLESS ROOM IN THE SAFE HOUSE HAD ASHER wanting to put his fists through the brick-lined walls. Daylight had been killed between the time change and their flight to Berlin. They were running out of time.

She could already be gone.

"Five groups are trying to claim credit for the attack," Knox said, and Asher pivoted to face him. "Al-Nusra has gone through a lot of leadership and name changes in the last six years. They're in the middle of rebranding—again—but they're not on the suspect list."

"That doesn't make sense," Asher murmured. "The group is a bunch of damn shapeshifters. Changing with the times to maintain relevancy." Asher crossed his arms, trying to destroy some of the tension burning in his biceps. "But how can it not be them?"

"Are they pro-ISIS, or . . .?" Liam looked up from his laptop and over at Asher.

"Against. For now, at least," Asher grumbled. "Enemies, regardless. But if they aren't seeking credit for the hit, it could be because they're waiting for something. A second attack, maybe."

Before anyone could say more, Luke's phone buzzed. "It's Owen." He placed him on speaker.

"Egon Becker," Owen announced straight away. "He's our assassin. He used to be part of an Austrian militant group, but then parted ways to work as a freelance killer. He's done a lot of work for nearly every major terrorist organization, and he's known for covering up his kills with explosions."

"Did we catch him on any cameras in Berlin?" Asher asked as Knox displayed the next image onto the screen on the wall.

"Well, we know he's in Germany. We pulled an image of him from a traffic camera about ten kilometers away from the Austrian border. He was in a red BMW X4 at the time. Must've ditched it for the SUV."

"Good work," Luke responded.

"I discovered something else while you guys were flying," Owen said a beat later. "Yasser Hadeed had one other sister. Fatima. She saw a cancer specialist at a hospital in Paris two months ago, and Ara visited her while she was there."

"Any contact before that?" Luke asked.

"Not sure yet. But someone had to have gotten word to her Fatima was in Paris. That or Ara has been keeping an eye on her remaining family back in Syria."

"Where's the aunt now?" Asher followed up.

"Last known location was Aleppo," Owen answered.

"What else do we know about Fatima?" Luke surveyed his team. A mix of anger and fear in his gaze. "I assume she wasn't connected to her brother's terrorist activities, or the military would've taken her out, too."

Asher thought back to the op. "She had two sons. Nothing connected any of them to al-Nusra."

"Her husband?" Luke cocked a brow.

Asher rummaged through his memories from the mission. "He died under the Assad regime as well."

"Okay. Let's put some guys on this," Luke instructed. "Someone must've followed Ara back to Berlin, and then put the hit out on her."

"We're working under the assumption someone killed Ara because of her betrayal to her uncle, are we not?" Owen asked.

Luke looked around at the team. "Yeah, but there has to be more to it than that. Why now?"

"Is it a coincidence the aunt was sick?" Liam scratched at his blond stubble.

Asher's brow rose. "Probably not."

"We still haven't determined why Egon took Jessica," Owen pointed out.

The overwhelming urge to hit something again tore through him, but he kept his arms locked in front of his chest to resist the impulse.

"He may turn her over to whoever hired him." Knox's words were like a blow of reality to the skull.

"We need to narrow down locations. Where would Egon have taken her?" Asher went over to the screen on the wall. He touched the upper right quadrant and expanded it to study the map of Berlin.

Liam sat at the desk and dragged a laptop in front of him.

"See what we're missing." Luke directed the order toward Liam. "Check both Ara's and Jessica's emails."

"She has a separate account for her alias. It's the one she uses to connect with the girls," Asher reminded them.

"You want me to go through your sister's emails?" Liam asked, his voice dropping lower.

"If it means saving her? Hell, yes."

"I'll be in touch once I get more," Owen said. "Since we're not officially working this case I can't ask Rutherford for the operational files from Aleppo, so I've got Echo Team trying to scrounge up what they can find without raising any red flags." He was quiet for a moment, and then he added, "We'll get her back."

Once the call ended, Asher rubbed his bearded chin, thoughts buzzing through his mind. Possible locations where she could be held. "If he expected Jessica to be with Ara last night, that meant he'd already arranged to have a place to bring her to."

"He couldn't have gone too far without catching the attention of the police." Liam observed the map on the screen now.

"Maybe on the outskirts of town, but not too far from the city," Asher suggested. "And I'm sure he has another vehicle ready."

An angry red crawled up Luke's throat and into his cheeks.

"Probably took her to someplace abandoned." Asher zoomed in on the plaza where Jessica had been abducted, and focused on the back roads Egon could've taken to go undetected. "He won't stay wherever he's at for long, though, because he'll know the Germans will be canvassing the city."

Jessica had always claimed to be great at finding people, but now she needed them to find her, and Asher was one of the best trackers—he'd sure as hell not let her down.

"Can I see the keyboard a second?" he asked Liam. "There's a delay on these satellite cams, but maybe . . ." He let his voice trail off as he began working, checking overhead views of various properties.

Twenty minutes later, his heart trekked up into his throat at the sight of a black SUV next to a second dark vehicle parked near a hospital, nearly obscured by trees and the overgrowth of the area. "Here."

The team surrounded him to view the screen. "This is it. No traffic cameras within a five-kilometer radius, and it's been abandoned since World War Two."

"The Germans may have figured this out," Liam said from behind him.

"We would've heard about it." Asher faced the group. "We need to roll out now. She could already be gone."

Luke averted his eyes from the screen and regarded Asher. "You heard him." He nodded. "Gear up. Let's go get our girl."

* * *

"WE'RE TOO LATE." ASHER'S CHEST ROSE AND FELL AS HE gripped his rifle as steadily as possible, staring at the remains of the black Beamer in the midst of the char. Flames licked the sky, wrapping the frame of the SUV like a warm embrace of death. "And the second SUV is gone."

"She could still be inside," Luke said.

If she was . . . she was dead. But no one, especially not Asher, wanted to voice those words aloud.

"Let's move in," Luke commanded as they bypassed the burning car and headed toward the side entrance of the hospital.

"Stay behind me. There could be trip wires." Asher sidestepped Luke without giving him a chance to protest. "We can't lose you both."

Don't be inside. He wanted her back—but alive. He wanted her fucking alive.

His booted feet moved slowly into the hospital.

Death clung to the walls.

A reminder of the atrocities that had once taken place at the site.

His stomach roiled, but he kept moving, kept on the lookout.

Room after room.

Empty.

No wires that he could see. No hidden explosives.

Lead filled his chest when he stumbled upon a hospital room a few minutes later. Two portable heaters and nearly a dozen empty jugs of water scattered all over the floor.

He touched a metal rolling table piled with saturated rags. Still damp.

He winced at the sight of blood on the floor. Fresh blood.

"Waterboarding," he said under his breath, his body growing tenser by the minute. "He was torturing her."

"He didn't want her to freeze. A plus, I guess." Liam tipped his chin toward the heaters.

"We missed her, but not by much." Luke looked over at Asher, a blank look in his eyes.

They hadn't passed any vehicles on the bare roads on their way in, though, which meant Egon had too much of a head start for them to go barreling back outside to comb through foreign territory.

Asher stowed his weapon. He moved to the far side of the room and pressed his hands to the wall alongside a boarded-up window. He bowed his head and reeled his hand back, unable to stop himself.

His gloved fist slammed into the concrete wall.

"Asher." Knox's voice met his ears. "We have to go.

Owen just called. The German Feds are on their way. We can't be found here."

He hadn't even heard the call. His mind had been turned to rubble. Nothing in. Nothing out.

"Come on, man." It was Luke this time, attempting to talk Asher off the proverbial ledge.

He was losing his damn mind.

He was officially showing all of his cards now, and he couldn't give a damn. All he wanted was Jessica back—to hell with everything else.

"We'll get her." Luke rested a hand on his shoulder, but he lost his hold once Asher swiveled to face him.

His jaw locked tight as he swept his gaze to Luke's eyes. "He's passing her off to whoever hired him."

Liam and Knox approached them, still holding their rifles.

"Maybe they'll try taking her to Syria," Knox proposed.

Luke looked back at him from over his shoulder. "No. Too risky." He found Asher's eyes again. "He wouldn't attempt to smuggle her into the Czech Republic or Poland, either."

"They're going to keep her in Berlin," Asher whispered, and his heart raced harder now.

"Another attack," Luke added to Asher's line of thought.

The blood rushed from Asher's face. "We need to get back to the city." He moved past the men, retracing the steps he'd already cleared on the way in.

"You have an idea where she's being held?" Liam asked once they were inside their rental.

Asher strapped into the passenger seat alongside Luke, who sat behind the wheel. "Kreuzberg. If Egon handed Jessica over to someone from the al-Nusra Front—or whatever the hell they call themselves now—they'll be in

Kreuzberg. It's one of the most multicultural places in the city. A lot of refugees live there. They could easily blend in."

"Get Owen back on the phone," Luke instructed. "I need to know if Echo Team found anything on these bastards. I need to know who the hell had the most to gain from killing Ara. Right the fuck now."

CHAPTER NINE

I MADE A MISTAKE. ARA'S WORDS PLAYED IN JESSICA'S MIND over and over again. When she glanced to the left, barely able to move, she'd swear she could see her ghost.

Brown eyes. Golden skin. Long, dark hair. Dimpled chin. Sweet smile.

She'd been twenty-four. Just starting life.

And now she was gone.

"I'm sorry," Jessica whispered as Ara stood before her.

Guilt clawed, nails sharp like a panther's, jabbing into her sides as she waited—as the ticking of a clock that only existed in her mind grew louder and louder.

Her lashes lowered halfway, dizziness starting to overwhelm her. All she could see were little bare feet moving closer to her.

Was the girl a mirage?

Jessica was on her side, she realized. In a new bed.

She opened and closed her eyes again, trying to determine where she was.

Horns. People talking—but she didn't think it was

German. Arabic, maybe. Based on the sounds, she wasn't on the ground floor.

She tried to open her mouth, but it was as if glue kept her lips together. Someone didn't want her screaming, which meant that, if she could be heard, she could be saved.

I'm not in the hospital. The thought sank in as she found herself looking at a pair of brown eyes.

Curly hair framed a girl's face. Her lips were slanted, curiosity in her eyes.

She crouched before the bed, staring at Jessica.

Eight, maybe?

The girl flinched and jerked upright at the sounds of shouting in Arabic from another room. She took off and light filtered in from the half-open door. Jessica's gaze drifted to the table alongside it.

Her heart dropped into her stomach.

An s-vest was already packed with explosives. Alongside it were bottles of chemicals. A few she recognized: hydrogen peroxide and acetone. If the third group of containers housed mineral acid, they'd have what they'd need to make TATP. The white crystalline powder was so sensitive, it could explode under any type of heat or friction. Terrorists called it *the mother of Satan*—and now she was probably in a room with the compound.

Part Two of the act, she realized. Ara had only been the beginning.

"She wouldn't talk." Jessica heard her abductor's voice from a neighboring room.

"It's her. Your job is finished." The second voice was male. The accent was Middle Eastern.

Based on the sounds from the creaky hardwood a man moved farther away from her room.

The hard clank of a door shutting followed.

She was pretty sure her original abductor was gone.

More footsteps, and then her door fully opened.

A man—barely out of his teens—stood in the doorframe now, and she squeezed her eyes closed, dragging up a memory.

Not everyone is an enemy, she'd said to Asher back at the base six years ago when she'd noticed a line of distrust dart through his forehead as they'd walked by a group of Syrian teen boys.

Maybe. But someday, he'd began while pointing, *they could become my enemy. That's the sad truth.*

And now, after she opened her eyes, she realized he'd been right. At least about the man now standing before her.

"Hello, Stephanie," he said. "It's been a long time."

CHAPTER TEN

THE SUN BURNED THE HORIZON AS IT ROSE, AND ASHER slipped on his shades, hiding his tired eyes as Luke and Asher continued to canvass the area of Kreuzberg.

Luke sat behind the wheel with Asher riding shotgun. He patted the cargo pants pocket on the side of his left leg, and the feel of the knife Jessica had given him this past Christmas had his heart steadying a touch.

You got me a knife? For Christmas? He'd been unable to fight the smile on his lips when he'd discovered they were each other's secret Santa.

"We'll find her," Luke said, cutting through his thoughts. It'd probably been the tenth time he'd said those words since driving.

Asher nodded. His own words trapped in his throat.

He should've told Jessica how he felt before she got on that plane—told her the truth. But how could he have known it may have been his last chance?

No. His body tensed. *Fuck that.* He peered back out the window. *I'll find you,* he thought the words, as if she could hear him.

Luke's phone began ringing a beat later, and Asher grabbed it from the dashboard mount to answer, placing it on speaker.

"I just got off the phone with Owen. We're pretty sure we know who we're dealing with. I'm texting you the information now," Liam said.

A sharp breath of air filled Asher's lungs as he steadied his eyes on the screen.

"What do we have?" Luke clutched the wheel so tightly, his knuckles whitened.

"Four terror groups merged in 2017 to form the group Tahrir al-Sham after al-Nusra split ties with al-Qaeda. There appears to be a power struggle for the general military commander now," Liam explained. "The two images I sent are of Bora Nadar and Samir Hadeed. They're the ones who are vying for power."

"Samir's Fatima's son. Ara's cousin," Asher said. "He'd barely been a teenager when I met him in Aleppo." Was he really twenty now?

"So, why the hell is he now claiming to be the heir to a terrorist group? What happened to him?" Luke asked.

"We're still looking into it. But maybe he had Ara killed to show his commitment to the organization. And I'm betting he's not done," Liam said.

Asher's shoulder blades pinched together as he gripped the bridge of his nose. "I assume you're already running a list of every known contact of Samir's?"

"Yeah. If anyone is in Berlin right now, we'll get a match," Liam responded. "We also got word the German police found Egon's latest vehicle ditched."

"Where?" Asher's body tensed.

"Twenty kilometers outside Berlin. Looks like he's

heading to Poland, and he's already handed over Jessica," Liam answered.

"My contact tipped off the Germans. They'll be looking for Egon," Luke reminded him. "We need to let the Germans handle him for now."

Asher hated the idea of letting the prick go, but Luke was right. Finding Jessica and stopping a potential attack was all that mattered.

"One sec," Liam said a moment later. "Owen's calling. I'll patch him onto the line."

"Where are you guys?" Owen asked.

"Still in Kreuzberg scoping out the area," Luke responded.

"Good, because facial recognition got a hit on one of Yasser Hadeed's enforcers from back in the day. He lives under an alias in Berlin. I also got him on camera with Ara a day before she emailed Jessica."

Had Ara really baited Jessica into coming to Berlin? Had this guy forced her to send the email? It was a hard pill to swallow, but if she had done it there had to have been a reason for it. Asher stuffed the thoughts away. He needed to focus on the danger at hand. "He must now work with Samir," he said.

"Looks that way," Owen replied. "He's been quiet since Yasser died, but he's our only lead at the moment, and he just hopped onto the U6."

Asher sat straighter at the news.

"My best guess is he'll get off at Mehringdamm," Owen said. "I'm sending you his image now."

"How long of a ride does he have?" Asher asked.

"Six minutes, give or take. Can you make it to the station?" Owen asked.

Luke input the address into the GPS. "We're four minutes out."

"I'm monitoring every stop in between in case he gets off early," Owen said.

"Any ideas as to where he may have been coming from?" Asher's free hand tightened into a hard fist atop his thigh.

"One idea," Liam joined the line. "He was within walking distance to where Jessica was taken on Sunday. There's still a lot of police and media camped out in that area, though."

"I'm scanning the cams over there now to see if I can get any hits," Owen added.

"Okay. Good work. We'll call once we're in position." Luke ended the call and glanced at Asher.

Asher's mouth tightened, and he looked back at the screen, his veins pulsing with fury as he studied the man on the phone.

Medium height and build. Long dark hair and a beard. Early forties, maybe.

He tapped at the screen and zoomed in on the guy to get a better look at his face and clothes. "Black jeans. A worn-out brown jacket to his knees. He shouldn't be too hard to miss in that get-up."

"Let's hope not." Luke parallel parked a few minutes later. "You take the back. I'll get Liam on the phone and head to the front."

"Plan of attack? Engage or wait for backup?" He wasn't sure he'd be able to wait if the target led them to Jessica, though. But they had no idea how many enemy combatants they'd be up against, and if they made one wrong move it could risk Jessica's life.

"We'll keep it fluid," Luke answered before getting out of the car, which meant he hadn't made up his mind yet.

Asher zipped up his fleece jacket, which concealed his sidearm, and stepped out of the SUV.

It was a Tuesday morning, a work day, and the streets were crowded. People spilled out of the train station and flooded the area, but he kept his eyes sharp on the crowd, scanning every face.

He hung back far enough away from the exit, holding his phone as if checking messages to avoid suspicion. The smell of currywurst from the nearby restaurant hit his nose, and he took a step back to dodge a woman and her baby stroller as they passed.

His eyes journeyed back to the exit of the station, and his pulse spiked at the sight of a man coming up the steps alongside a group of teens.

Brown jacket and black jeans. Check. Check.

Got you, motherfucker. He phoned Luke and gave him the location as he trailed him, keeping a few paces behind.

A moment later, he locked eyes with Luke, who'd rounded the corner up ahead, and tipped his chin in the direction of their target.

Luke joined the flow of pedestrians, keeping the man in his sights.

A few minutes passed before the target stopped outside a three-story brown building that looked like it belonged in the Cold War era with its run-down exterior and peeling paint.

Luke held a closed fist, signaling for Asher to stay back.

He gave a hesitant nod, hating to wait, but he followed orders and watched as Luke entered through the door.

No code to get in, which made things easier.

After a few minutes, though, he decided to head in.

There were five apartments on the first floor, and he assumed the same would be true on the second and third levels.

Where the hell are you? At the sound of something breaking from above, he rushed up the flight of steps and followed the noise.

A partially open door.

He drew his weapon and clung to the shadows in the hall outside the apartment.

"Where the fuck is she?" Luke roared.

Asher moved into the apartment and found Luke in the kitchen, pointing the barrel of his gun at the target. The man was sprawled with his back on the tiled floor and his palms in the air.

A woman clutched a girl to her body and stood pressed against the refrigerator, watching the scene in horror.

"The place is secure. No sign of her," Luke said without looking at Asher.

"What happened?" He moved to stand alongside Luke and kept his weapon drawn.

The muscle in Luke's jaw tightened as he stared down at the man on the floor. "I'm trying to find out."

Asher placed one palm in the air and stepped around the man to get to the woman and child.

"Sprechen Sie Deutsch?" Luke asked from behind.

No answer from the woman or child, and nothing from the man on the floor, either.

Asher lowered the gun to his side. "English?" He crouched to eye level with the girl. "Was there a woman here? A pretty blonde?" He was grasping at straws, but . . .

Luke repeated Asher's question, but in German, and then Asher did his best to string the question together in Arabic. He was rusty, but it was worth a shot.

Still nothing.

The little girl's eyes widened a moment later, though, and

she gently lifted her chin, and her gaze veered toward the hall at the back end of the kitchen.

Asher gave a slight nod in understanding and turned to find Luke leaning in closer to the target, burying his knee deep into his chest, adding pressure.

"I'm going to look around." Asher followed the direction of the girl's gaze and found a hall that split off to the left and right.

After searching the right side and coming up empty, he went and checked the left side and found one room.

He flicked on the light and glanced at the mattress, more like a cot, beneath the window. Then his gaze swung over to an empty table off to his left.

He started to turn but slowed and lifted his booted foot carefully, then pressed it down harder. A hollow feel.

He crouched, lifted the decorative carpets, and shoved them out of the way. Within moments, his fingers were pulling at the loose floorboards.

"Christ," he said under his breath as he gazed at a cache of weapons, explosive materials, and a few cans of paint.

He shoved upright and went back to the kitchen. "We've got a problem."

Luke still had the son of a bitch pinned beneath him, the gun trained on the man. "What'd you find?"

"Explosive materials. Weapons. I think they're planning another attack." Asher looked at the woman and girl, his heart breaking. The girl had been dragged into this world and never given a chance. "We're talking some unstable shit, too. Chemicals that can make triacetone triperoxide."

"Fuck. You thinking an s-vest or something bigger?" Luke's Adam's apple moved in his throat.

"Maybe."

"Where the hell did they take her?" He shoved the barrel

of the gun into the man's mouth, and the guy dropped his eyes closed.

He used to be an enforcer for a terrorist organization, but now he looked like a man on the verge of breaking. Maybe he'd been out of the terrorist game for a while. Asher assumed the woman and child were his wife and daughter, but he wasn't about to hold a gun to them to get answers. He had his limits.

"There was paint hidden. Why hide paint?" His mind rummaged through ideas. "Shit. I think I know where they'd go."

Luke pulled the gun from the man's mouth and stood. The woman remained in the corner with the girl, and the guy started to rise, but Luke shook his head and aimed the gun at him.

Asher retrieved his phone, dialed up the team, and placed the call on speakerphone. "We have to alert the police," he said once the line connected. "We need them to jam all radio frequencies and cell towers within a twenty-kilometer range of the Brandenburg Gate. I think they're planning on setting off another bomb there."

The man's brown eyes narrowed, and he looked away from Asher the moment he'd finished speaking.

He was right. He could feel it.

"They may have a timer and not a remote detonator, but if—"

"The press and police are still all over the place," Luke interrupted.

"Exactly." He took a breath. "I think these assholes are on their way there now. Maybe under the guise of the media." Asher held the phone in his palm as steadily as possible, trying to fight the tremble in his hand. "I don't know how much time we have."

"Especially if this cocksucker was just over there." Luke shifted his attention back to the man. "What time are they planning to attack?"

Asher's heart squeezed at the sight of the girl. Maybe she did speak English. Maybe she understood everything because . . . he was pretty sure she was signaling something to him.

His gaze fell to her hand at her side.

Her closed palm opened, and she extended her fingers to show five before retracting her hand to show another three fingers.

Eight o'clock? "We have twenty minutes," he hissed in alarm after checking his watch.

Luke looked over at him. "I'll get ahold of my contact. He can phone this in for us. We need someone to stay with them, though. We can't let them tip off whoever has her."

Asher stepped closer to him, hating the idea one of them would have to stay.

"Go," Luke said as if reading his thoughts. "You're better at dealing with explosives."

Asher knew it pained him to make that call.

"We'll meet you there," Liam said over the line.

"Just get to her," Luke rushed out. "Don't let the police kill her. If she's strapped—"

"I won't let anything happen to her," Asher said, his voice rough. "I promise."

* * *

Twelve minutes later

"I don't see her yet." Asher checked his watch. They had eight minutes. Eight fucking minutes until Jessica could

97

be blown up. He had to trust the girl. He didn't have a choice.

"Any media vans look different than the others?" Liam asked over comms once he and Knox had arrived at the scene and scattered to surveil the area.

"There's a lot of them," Knox answered.

"Bravo One is five minutes out," Liam announced, which meant Luke had turned the target over to his contact along with the woman and child.

"Why the hell are our comms still working?" Knox asked a minute later. "The police haven't killed the frequencies yet."

"They will," Asher said. "They have to." Of course, if there was a timer, killing the signals wouldn't stop an attack.

"I've got her in my sights," Liam's voice came hard over the lines. "It's Jessica, but—"

"She's strapped," Asher finished. He'd spotted Jessica being shoved out of the back of a van. Her mouth was covered, and the detonator was taped around her hand. She was on her side now, on the ground, struggling to stand.

"Knox, go after the van," Asher ordered. "Don't let the driver get away."

"Copy that," he responded.

Asher started toward Jessica, his heart pumping hard in his chest, trying to suffocate the fear of seeing her in trouble. "We need to get to her before the police see . . ."

But it was too late.

Screams ripped through the air. Jessica had been spotted.

"Approach on the left," he told Liam. "We have to get to her before the police take her out by mistake."

"I've lost visual," Liam said as the press rushed his way.

"She's on her feet now." Asher sucked in a sharp breath,

his eyes connecting with hers. Everything inside him dying at the moment.

The police set themselves up like a human barricade to the public. They pushed everyone back to the standard range from an s-vest.

Nothing was standard about this moment, though, not with Jessica there.

Commands for Asher to leave barked from behind, but he ignored them.

"They won't shoot her and risk the bomb detonating," Liam said. "Right?"

His throat thickened at the sight of Jessica shaking her head, and it had Asher pausing mid-step.

"The police are backing farther away from her." Panic crept into Asher's tone. "They're going to take the shot."

Jessica stood frozen in place, hands still up, but she turned her head to the side, and he followed her gaze.

"You see the cameraman alone about a hundred meters to your left?" Liam asked over the comms.

"Yeah." Asher swallowed. Time stood still. A hard knot fisted in his stomach. "I think that's what Jessica wants me to notice. She's letting us know she's a diversion."

CHAPTER ELEVEN

TEARS BUILT IN HER EYES, BUT SHE REFUSED TO UNLEASH them. She couldn't give in to these assholes who were using her to make a statement and kill others.

Her heart worked into her throat at the sight of Asher in the crowd, and everything inside of her hurt that much more.

He wasn't a dream. He was real. Her team had come for her.

Of course, they'd come, but would they be able to wrap their minds around the fact they might not be able to save her?

She squeezed her emotions away as best she could and slowly skirted her focus off to the left, toward a cameraman standing alone amidst the media equipment abandoned by the other outlets.

Her brows drew together as she fixed her attention back on Asher, hoping he would get the message.

The explosives on her vest were nothing compared to the unstable weapon inside that man's backpack.

The bomber was on the move now, heading toward the crowd. Onlookers stood off in the distance behind police barricades, watching her. Waiting to see what would happen. Trying to capture the moment on their phones.

Go. Her eyes pleaded with Asher. *Stop him.*

The police started to edge away from her, no longer shouting angry threats in both German and English. And she knew what they were planning to do next.

A head shot. A clean kill.

They were going to risk her setting off the vest now that everyone was far enough away.

Asher stood locked in place as if he couldn't decide what to do—a moment of indecision she had never witnessed with him before.

She tried to keep her body still, to kill the trembling, so her thumb didn't slip and hit the detonator taped to the palm of her hand.

Even if her team killed the RFs and cell signals, it wouldn't do any good. The bomb in the backpack was on a timer.

Samir Hadeed wanted Jessica dead, but he wouldn't care if the vest detonated, or she was taken out by the police.

Samir. God, how could he have become this man? How had this happened? He was so young. Too young to be behind all of this.

She ignored the bubbling rise of bile at the back of her throat and dropped her lids closed. She refused to race through her thoughts—to think about everything she'd ever wanted to do but never had.

Her heart was bleeding, though. At least, it felt like there was a gaping hole, and blood was leaking into her chest cavity.

When her lids slowly lifted, she spotted one police officer with a rifle in hand, observing her through a scope. He'd be the man to take her out. But behind him . . . *Luke.*

He was talking to the sniper. *And, oh God, he has Max with him.* He'd been a German Fed before retiring and working in private security. Of course, Luke would reach out to him. But was there time to stop this?

Max moved in front of the man who was close to stealing her last breath, blocking his shot.

A small flicker of hope grew inside of her. She searched for Asher and found him off in the distance with Liam.

Liam stood alongside the German officers, and he and the Feds were motioning for the bystanders to move back.

The bomber was out of sight, but Asher had found the backpack and crouched before it. Brave like always. Made of steel on the days they needed it, and every day in between.

Her head rolled skyward, and she stared up at the bright sun kissing the sky as if everything in the world was okay, and she wasn't standing close to where Ara had died about to follow along with her.

"Hey." Luke's voice had her dropping her gaze. He was approaching her. Alone.

The police were keeping a safe distance; she was almost surprised they'd let her brother approach. *Almost surprised* because this was Luke—and he always came through. Against all odds.

"The signals have been jammed." Luke's eyes were hollow, a shell. He'd probably been through hell since she'd been taken.

She shook her head, letting him know it didn't matter.

He edged closer and peeled the tape from her mouth before eying the vest.

"It's on a timer," she rasped.

His fingers trailed over the stopwatch. "Forty-five seconds." He glanced back over his shoulder, and she tracked his gaze to find Asher running toward them.

The police blocked him, but he started to shove and push against them, through them, one by one. He was going to get himself killed if he didn't stop.

But Max intervened, and Asher charged her way.

"Let me do it!" he called out as he closed in on them.

"The other bomb?" she rushed out, finding his eyes.

"It's diffused." He nodded.

Thank God.

"There's not much time." Tears touched her cheeks. She couldn't hold them back, not with her brother and Asher so close. "If you cut the wrong wire, you could both die. Ju-just go."

"No. We're not going anywhere." Luke shook his head. "Down to twenty seconds."

Asher's fingertips buzzed down the center of her vest, and he carefully shifted a few wires around. He retrieved a knife from his pocket. The knife she'd given him for Christmas.

"I need you to get back," Asher rasped to Luke, his breathing labored.

Luke didn't budge.

Jessica looked back and forth between the two. She didn't want to die like this, but more than that, she didn't want anything happening to them.

She tucked her chin down to try and observe what Asher was doing. He shifted a red wire to the side to get to the blue.

"Back. The. Fuck. Up," Asher commanded. "You're a father!"

Luke didn't move. Stubborn as hell.

"Please," Jessica pleaded, her voice breaking. "Go, the both of you. I don't know which wire—"

"If you stay," Asher began, "I stay." He captured her eyes as he held the blade to the blue wire. "A team, remember?" And then he cut it.

CHAPTER TWELVE

"You shouldn't have done that." Jessica glanced at the IV and morphine drip off to her right before looking back at her guys. "If your faces end up on the news because of me . . ."

"We'll worry about our asses later. Let's focus on getting you better." A faint line appeared on Knox's forehead. Concern practically radiated from his pores. "You look like shit, though." He faked a laugh as if hoping to lighten the mood.

Usually, Asher was the one cracking jokes at shit times to alleviate tension. But right now, he stood off to the side of the room, his back to the wall, a dark, grim look to his face.

She could barely breathe the moment his brown eyes landed on hers.

Her fingers swept to her collarbone, and she forced her eyes closed.

A lump gathered in her throat when she allowed the darkness to swallow her—only to see Ara's face in her mind.

"We need to catch Samir. We need to stop whatever else he's planning." The deep breath she took made her chest ache. It was the kind of pain that couldn't be dulled by morphine. She hadn't wanted the drugs, but the doctors and her overbearing brother had insisted after seeing her bruises.

"We got the cameraman and driver. We'll find Samir." Luke edged closer to the bed and lightly squeezed her shoulder. "The Germans are searching everywhere for him and the assassin."

Assassin. The word spun around in her mind, and she swallowed the hard truth Samir had hired an assassin to kill his cousin. To kill her.

"We'd be looking, too, if the Feds would let us," Liam said.

The German Feds had already questioned them all, and she was sure there'd be several more rounds before anyone would be heading back to the States.

"We're lucky Max came through for us," Luke responded. "The police could've . . ." He dropped his words, probably not wanting to say Jessica had come close to having a bullet to the head.

"You talk to the president yet?" Jessica fisted the white blanket with her right hand and tipped her chin toward the ceiling, unable to look her team in the eyes.

She had done this. She had lied to them about Ara, and now—*what if this is all my fault?*

"No, but I spoke with Director Rutherford a few minutes ago," Luke answered.

"I'm assuming he told you to back down and not come find me." An attempted brow raise had pain darting through her skull, but she hid the groan that tried to escape.

"We stopped an attack," Knox said before Luke could respond. "Everything will be okay."

But would it?

"I'm so sorry about Ara," Luke said, tucking his hands into his pockets.

She waited for a lecture to follow, a lecture she deserved, but he didn't deliver it. Instead, he cocked his head to the side and swept his gaze across the room. She tracked his eyes to find him looking at Asher.

Still quiet.

Not a single damn word from Asher since he'd diffused the bombs.

"She's dead because of me." She had to fight the tears—to battle the emotions trying to break her.

"No."

Her head rolled to the side to observe Asher who'd finally spoken.

That simple word gutted her.

"She's gone because her cousin used her to try and gain control over a terrorist group," Knox said when the rest of Asher's words seemed to die on his tongue.

"What? Why?" A million other questions crashed through her mind, but she held them back.

Asher stepped away from the wall. "We don't know why, but we do know how he found Ara." He arched his shoulders back, and his hands disappeared into his pockets. "She visited Samir's mom in Paris two months ago, and it looks like he had her followed back to Berlin."

"And?" Her eyes narrowed.

"A day before she emailed you, Yasser Hadeed's enforcer from back in the day approached her. It was his house in the city where you were taken to earlier today." Asher appeared to take a hard swallow. Gathered a breath. "We think they threatened Ara. They probably wanted to know who had helped her get away from Aleppo. Who had helped take down Yasser six years ago."

Me. "She wouldn't betray me like that."

"Would she give you up to save the girls?" Knox asked, his voice weighed down as if stones were piled atop his chest.

"You know this for a fact?" she asked, trying to keep her voice as steady as possible.

"No, but it's a fairly safe assumption," Knox answered.

Her eyes fell shut at the memory of her last conversation with Ara. "She said she'd made a mistake." Her throat thickened, emotion trying to leak again.

Contain.

Contain.

She couldn't let her team see her break down.

But . . . what if she couldn't keep it together?

A dull throb in her chest had her gasping for a breath. "If the girls were in danger it's possible she gave me up, but she'd said she was being tailed and had tried to lose someone."

"Maybe she changed her mind. I don't know." Luke's words were soft. Almost delicate. Like he was afraid he'd break her.

Jessica blinked and tried to sit, but failed. The drugs were overpowering her, making her weight feel as if it'd been tripled. "The girls," she sputtered at the realization they could be in danger. "What if Samir tries to use them again?"

"He has too much heat on him," Luke was quick to respond. "Director Rutherford decided to take the girls into CIA custody, though. Agents are picking them up as we speak."

"The Germans don't know about this." Liam's words captured her attention.

"Why would Rutherford interject Langley into the situation?" She tried to keep her eyes open as the drugs lulled her into a foggier state.

"I have a hard time believing Rutherford grew a conscience today," Knox said. "But we'll find out what's really going on."

"At least you know the girls are safe." Luke nodded.

"I need to be the one to tell them about Ara. They should hear it from me."

The room went quiet for a moment. "I don't think that's possible. I'm sorry." Luke shifted his eyes to the floor for a beat, giving her a minute to process everything.

She'd need a lot more than a minute, though.

She glanced at Liam standing alongside Luke now. He wrapped a hand around the nape of his neck. Discomfort. Pained by looking at her. The desperate desire for revenge in his eyes.

Her gaze fell upon Asher again.

He was looking away from her. Even beneath his beard, she could see the hard clench of his jaw.

"I never would've expected this of Samir." She thought back to Syria, to when she'd first met him.

"People change," Asher said, still not looking at her.

"You were right," she whispered, knowing only Asher would understand the past tense meaning of her words.

And before anyone could say anything else, the door opened and an officer stepped into the room. "The captain needs a word."

Luke patted her on the arm and then bent forward and kissed her forehead. "We'll get this all straightened out. I don't want you to worry." Her brother's eyes welled, and it had her heart squeezing.

"Okay," she mouthed and lowered her lids.

At the sound of the door closing, she opened her eyes. Her heart stammered in her chest at the sight of Asher still in the room.

His arms were pinned to his sides, the back of his head resting against the door.

"Shouldn't you be with the team?" She attempted to sit again, but her body resisted the movement. She contemplated trying one more time—damned if she would quit. But . . . something inside of her did want to give in, to break. To shut down.

"I'll go, but, I, uh"—he scratched at his beard, and then his booted feet moved slowly to her bedside—"I needed a minute alone with you."

"I'm okay if you're going to ask that." She sniffled. She needed him to go before he witnessed her breakdown. She couldn't expose a chink in her armor, not even to him. "Go." *Shit.* She heard the break in her voice. And she knew the quiver in her bottom lip was now exposed.

"Jessica." Her name was like water pouring from his lips, and it had her stomach tightening, a desperate attempt to keep it together.

"Please. Go. I need to be alone." Her eyes blurred. "Go," she cried, her chest shaky. A sob threatening.

"No." His voice was firm. Commanding. And it had her looking at him, straight in the eyes. "I almost lost you. I . . ." He smoothed his thumb over her cheek and dragged in a lungful of air as if he were in as much pain as she was.

"I'm okay."

The weight of the bed lightly shifted as he pressed one hand down next to her, and his free hand swept the stray tear from her face. He kept his palm there, cupping her cheek. "I'm just so damn glad you're all right. I don't know what I would've done if we didn't get to you in time. Leaving you to go to the other bomb—"

"Was what I wanted, and I would've never forgiven you if you hadn't saved those people."

She pressed her lips into a tight line, willing away the tears.

A moment later, he whispered, "No one has to know." His thumb swept lightly over her skin in small circles. "No one has to know you cried but me." His brows slanted in. "I won't tell anyone. I promise."

And when he lowered his forehead gently to hers, her lids closed again, and a broken cry fled her mouth.

He remained there against her, still cupping her cheek. She reached up to grip his bicep . . . and she cried.

CHAPTER THIRTEEN

"SUSPENSION UNTIL FURTHER NOTICE." LUKE BRACED HIS palms against the table in the conference room.

"Even Owen and Echo Team? They weren't even there." Asher gripped the back of the rolling chair in front of him and surveyed the guys from Echo and Bravo who were gathered around the table in their New York office.

"One takes a hit. We all fall," Luke said.

"And Jessica?" Asher's knuckles whitened with his firm hold of the chair, and he glanced out the wall of windows, observing the sun disappearing behind the buildings off in the distance.

"She's suspended, too." Luke shook his head. "Not that she should be working anytime soon, anyway."

Wyatt's head jerked back in surprise. "Why her?" His palms slapped the table in front of him.

"Because of Ara?" Asher asked. "Punishment for ever helping her in the first place." He looked back to Luke at the head of the table.

He simply nodded. "We can handle ops for the company until we're cleared to operate for POTUS again."

"*If* we're ever cleared," Owen noted.

"Don't worry," Luke said. "We'll work this out."

Liam rose from the table, his shoulders sagging ever so slightly. "Does this mean we're not allowed to look for Samir?"

"Or Egon since he slipped the Germans?" Asher released the chair and crossed his arms, trying to fight the angry bite of tension roping up and into his biceps. The need to hit something surged fiercer than ever. A soft hiss left his lips.

"We're under strict orders not to further pursue anyone connected to Berlin." Luke hung his head. "Since we stopped the second attack, POTUS managed to cover for our presence in Germany with the police, but we need to lie low for a bit. The security footage was scrubbed, so IDs won't be made on us, thanks to the CIA, but Jessica . . ."

"The media," Asher grumbled under his breath.

Luke straightened and looked at him. "Her alias is sticking with the media so far. The interviews she gave over the phone with them should get everyone off her back."

"I don't think Samir will come looking for her with heat on him. Not now, at least." Owen's hazel eyes met Asher's. "But we're not going to let this go, are we?" He directed his question back to Luke.

Luke's mouth tightened, and he shook his head. "Just stay under the radar, okay? I have a feeling there's more going on that we're not being told."

"Because Rutherford took an interest in the girls?" Wyatt sat taller, and Asher's gaze journeyed from him to Luke.

"Maybe. I don't know, but I've got a gut feeling we're being kept in the dark, and I don't like it." Luke rubbed his jaw. "Thanks for all of your help in getting Jessica home," he added after a moment of silence seized the room.

"She's one of us," Knox said. "No other outcome

would've been acceptable." He stood, and the rest of the guys followed suit.

"One other thing." Luke's hands rested on his hips. "Jessica's asked not to have any visitors right now. She's, uh"—he looked at the ceiling and took a breath—"going through a lot, and she's just not up for it."

The guys nodded in understanding, even if they didn't like it. Since they'd gotten back yesterday, they'd pretty much emptied the shops in the area and flooded her home with every type of flower imaginable.

Asher waited for the room to clear before heading over to Luke. "What else did POTUS say?"

"It's more what he didn't say, to be honest." Luke leaned forward, resting his forearms on the back of the rolling chair in front of him.

"That's why you think there's more to this?" Asher squared his stance, and Luke nodded. "You know Jessica won't be able to let go. She's like us."

Luke touched his mouth, his brows pulling together. He stood up straight and lightly shook his head. "She needs to recover is what she needs to do."

"This is Jessica we're talking about." Asher arched a brow.

"Well, my parents just flew in, so hopefully they can keep her in bed while they're here."

He'd planned on going to her place to check on her regardless of her no-visitors-allowed rule, but at that news . . . "I'm glad they're here."

"I'll have Eva stop by with Lara, too."

Their baby was only ten weeks old, and some days he still couldn't believe Luke was a father. But the reminder had been slammed into him hard on Luke's first mission back from paternity—a mission to rescue his sister.

"You sticking around the city?" Luke asked as they moved into the hall and headed toward the lobby.

"Yeah, of course." He glanced at him when Luke stopped walking.

"Can I ask you something?" He smoothed a hand over his jaw.

"Sure."

"Is there something going on with you and my sister?"

Asher cleared his throat, his eyes widening a fraction. "We're friends, and she was just put through the wringer."

"That's all it is?" Luke raised a brow. "You guys worked together on an op I didn't know about, and you kept her secret about Ara from me. And—"

"I'd stop there." He released a slow breath, trying to steady his pulse. "This probably isn't the best time to get into this conversation. We just got her back."

"There will never be a good time to talk about you and my sister." He angled his head. Eyes thinning. "Are we clear?"

For the first time in his life, he wanted to deck Luke. Hell, he wanted to do more than just hit him.

"Fuck." Luke placed a hand on Asher's shoulder. "I'm sorry. I, uh, think I'm projecting my anger toward Samir onto you."

"It's fine." He was itching to unleash on someone, too, since he hadn't had a chance to physically hurt the bastards who'd taken Jessica.

"No." Luke shook his head. "I was out of line. To accuse you of going behind my back with my sister . . ." His hand dropped to his side. "I know you'd never do that. I'm sorry."

Asher's stomach muscles tightened at Luke's words. Knives of guilt plunged into his chest.

He'd had his tongue shoved down Jessica's throat after

their first op together. He'd had his cock buried so deep inside of her, he hadn't been sure if he'd ever break free, or ever want to.

Sex with Luke's sister. A secret he'd carried for six-plus years.

"I should probably go hit something. Maybe the bag at the gym downstairs before I head home. You want to join me?"

"Aren't your parents flying in soon?"

"Shit. You're right." He glanced at his watch. "I gotta pick them up at the airport in an hour. Rain check?"

"Sure. Tell your folks *hi*. Let me know when Jessica is up for visitors." He rolled his eyes skyward, trying to fight the awkwardness that spanned between them again. "The guys and I will want to stop by."

"Of course."

Asher waited for Luke to leave before he blew out a heavy breath.

"Asher. Hold up, man."

He glanced back to find Owen heading his way from the other side of the hall. "What's up?"

"I wanted to check on you. See if you're okay."

"Why wouldn't I be? Jessica is back, and we were just given a vacation from POTUS."

Owen smirked. "You're such a bad liar."

Asher sighed and propped a hand on the hall wall at his side. "What are you really trying to ask me?"

Owen's smile faded. "We all love Jessica." He was quiet for a moment. "Like a sister."

"And?" Irritation crawled up his spine.

"Except you." His arms crossed his chest.

"What the hell are you talking about?"

"She's not like a sister to *you*. And everyone, except maybe Luke, knows how you really feel about—"

"Stop." Asher shoved off the wall. "I don't know what you're planning to say, but I don't need this from you." His boots inched a hair closer to Owen, and he angled his head. A tightness stretched through his chest, making it harder to breathe. "She's alive. And we'll bring down the sons of bitches who did this to her whether Command wants us to or not."

Owen surrendered his palms. "Fine, but when you get your head out of your ass, I'm here if you want to talk." He headed back to his office.

Maybe Luke had the right idea, he realized.

Maybe hitting something, or someone, was exactly what he needed right now.

And damn, he knew where he shouldn't go but sure as hell wanted to.

CHAPTER FOURTEEN

ASHER PEELED OFF HIS LONG-SLEEVED BLACK SHIRT AND tightened the string of his black sweatpants. Socks and shoes off. He rolled his shoulders, trying to loosen up.

"Just so we're clear, this doesn't mean I'm okay with you and my sister." Asher taped his hands, preparing to enter the octagon.

A smile touched Angelo's face. "Got it."

Thank God, his sister was working at her restaurant tonight. He needed to fight, but he wouldn't have been able to get into the ring with Sarah's eyes on him.

A memory of Jessica with the vest strapped to her body blew back to his mind like fire burning his skin. Eating at him.

Bruises. Waterboarding. A damn s-vest.

Inside the cage, he snapped his hands into fists and cracked his neck.

Egon. Samir.

If he had lost Jessica . . .

His opponent in the ring wasn't big enough. Not tall enough. Asher could kill him.

He stared at the guy and lowered his arms to his sides, inviting him to swing.

The first punch was harder than he'd expected. A blow to his left cheek.

The pain felt good. Like penance for ever allowing Jessica to get hurt. For allowing Egon and Samir to get away.

He let another punch land beneath his chin. A swift uppercut.

The crowd cheered, and Asher focused on the fighter as he walked the perimeter of the cage, arrogance flowing. His dark blond cornrows tight, a too-soon smile of victory on his face.

A left hook touched Asher's mouth next. The taste of blood on his tongue.

Good. Asher flicked his wrist for the guy to re-approach. He wanted to feel more pain. He needed it. He hadn't realized that until now.

"What's wrong?" Angelo asked after the first round ended, and Asher hadn't even swung once. "You're letting him get the drop on you."

Asher took a swig of the water Angelo handed him.

"You come to get your ass whooped?" Angelo folded his arms, his eyes steady on him.

"I need someone bigger to fight," Asher said after a beat. "This guy won't be able to handle me."

Angelo laughed. "He's the one doing all the damage."

Asher grumbled. "If I take him out right now, will you bring in someone else?" He didn't want to murder the kid accidentally.

"Sure, if you think you can get your head back in the game."

Asher smiled. "My head is right where it needs to be," he said before the second round began.

Eight seconds in, Asher knocked the blond guy unconscious. He glanced to Angelo, standing outside the cage. "Now?" he mouthed.

Angelo laughed and held his palms in the air. "Okay. Okay." He disappeared into the crowd and returned a few minutes later. He waited for the blond guy to be removed from the cage and then joined Asher in the ring. "You want to tell me what's going on while we wait for the next fight?"

Asher spit out some blood. No mouth guard tonight. Probably a shit idea. He happened to like his teeth. "Nah, I don't want to talk. Especially not with the man who is screwing my sister."

Angelo glanced off to his right as the room began to fill with even more people. Word had gotten out Asher was in the ring. Plenty of people would be jonesing to fight him.

"I care about Sarah." Angelo pressed his lips into a tight line for a moment, and gravity filled his dark eyes. "I love her."

Asher lightly shook his head, unable to process his words. "Please, don't tell me that."

"You should know the truth." He was quiet for a moment. "And Sarah's worried about you. She said you disappeared from your mom's place last Sunday, and she hasn't been able to get ahold of you since."

Yeah, I was diffusing bombs in Berlin and saving someone I care about. But he couldn't lead with that. "I'll call her later."

"You owe her a lot more than a call."

Asher fisted Angelo's gray V-neck. "Don't ever fucking tell me what I need to do, especially when it comes to my sister."

Two jacked-up security guys entered the cage, but Angelo

waved them off. "I get it." He nodded, his eyes thinning. "But I'm not the same person you once knew."

"You said as much." He let go of him and edged back.

"I don't run the crew anymore. I just run these fights, and hell, I pay taxes on what I make." He pressed his palms down his shirt, smoothing it out. "I'd never do anything to hurt her. You need to believe me."

Asher considered his words for a moment, but there was so much on his mind he wasn't sure if he'd be able to handle anything else right now. Too damn much had happened in the last week.

"I just want to fight," he found himself saying.

Angelo nodded. "Yeah. Okay." He flicked his wrist toward security and motioned for the next fighter to enter the cage.

The guy had a few inches on Asher's height of six-four. He was beefier. Not so much muscle, though. But he was a tank, nevertheless. Exactly what Asher had wanted.

Images torched his mind. Memories from Berlin fueled his rage.

Every punch connected with Egon. With Samir.

Each time Asher pounded the fighter, all he could visualize was what he'd do when he found the cocksucker who thought it would be okay to go after Jessica.

CHAPTER FIFTEEN

"WHAT HAPPENED TO YOUR FACE?" LIAM POINTED HIS FINGER in Asher's direction.

Asher mumbled a few curses under his breath and moved past him to grab his laptop out of the office he shared with Owen. They were three doors down from Jessica's room.

Still no word from her. No response to any of the texts he'd sent since their return to the States.

Radio fucking silence.

And it made everything inside of him hurt. He wanted to be there for her. Needed to. But if he interjected himself into her life when she didn't want his help, he'd be selfish, he guessed.

Jessica was the strongest woman he'd ever met. She'd be okay. He sure as hell hoped so, at least.

"I've never seen a bruise on you, mate. I thought you were made of steel or something." Liam wasn't planning on letting this go, apparently.

"I got into a fight." He slumped down into his chair and powered on the laptop. "Why are you here so early?"

"Looking for the wanker who took our girl. Why are *you* at the office before the sun is up?" Liam eyed him.

"Same." He glanced out toward the hall at the sound of other voices. "Who else is here?"

"The rest of Bravo." He lifted his palms and tucked his hands beneath the armpits of his white tee.

"Where's Echo?" He leaned back into his seat and rubbed his face, the area swollen from the free shots he'd allowed the first fighter to get off last night.

What had he been thinking, going to Angelo's club?

He hadn't been thinking, he supposed.

"Luke sent Echo Team to Detroit an hour ago."

"What the fuck is in Detroit?"

"An old al-Nusra cell the Feds thought died off when Yasser Hadeed was killed. The FBI are staked out there now, so something must be up."

Asher shoved back from his desk. "Why aren't we going instead?"

"We've been grounded. Luke didn't tell you?" Liam's light-green eyes narrowed.

"I was busy," he nearly growled out.

"Yeah, uh, getting the shit kicked out of you?" He faked a laugh. "Was that on purpose? Because like I said, I've never known you to walk away from a fight banged up."

He didn't know what to say. He'd sound like he'd lost his mind if he explained he'd purposefully gotten hit to relieve some of his stress.

"Back to Detroit—why are we grounded? What do I need to know?" He veered his focus to Luke, now in the doorway.

"Rutherford called. He doesn't want us leaving New York. Stuck here until further notice. He's worried we won't be able to sit on the sidelines." Luke leaned into the doorframe with folded arms.

Not a big surprise, considering their team's history.

"Where were you last night?" he asked. "I called after I dropped my parents off at Jessica's."

Fighting.

"Yeah, mate, where were you?" Liam smirked, his eyes swerving to Asher's knuckles. They had gotten banged up when he'd rammed his fist against the concrete wall back at the hospital in Berlin, but now they were a hell of a lot worse despite having them taped last night.

"You weren't where I think you were?" Luke strode into the room and moved up alongside Liam, studying Asher the way Liam had.

"Can we focus on what's going on?" Asher rose, uneasy. Maybe he shouldn't have come into the office this morning.

He'd fought until his knuckles had bled, and then he'd found himself parked on a barstool, drinking until they closed.

Now it was six, still dark out, and he hadn't slept at all.

He rubbed his eyes. "What do we know about this cell in Detroit?"

"More than twenty guys were arrested around the time Yasser Hadeed was taken out, but the Feds couldn't get the charges to stick on five of them," Luke began. "Since Samir reached out to one of Yasser's enforcers, the FBI started tracking all of the remaining people connected to Yasser."

"They have any credible intel these five guys are back in the game?" Asher asked.

"My buddy told me this intel as a courtesy because of Jessica, but surely he's under orders not to tell anyone jack shit about Germany. So, other than this lead, I don't know anything else." Luke's brows lowered at the mention of Berlin. The memory still clinging to his eyes like a dark, hovering shadow. "But if you'd answered your phone last night, you would've known all this."

"And if you'd left a message, maybe I would've called back," Asher snapped, too tired to go to bat with Luke.

"Never needed to before." Luke scratched at his stubble.

And Asher had never mixed it up with his past since joining the team three years ago. Fighting was his drug, and last night might have been the gateway to more to come.

A cold bristle of air—*was that a fucking shiver?*—blew up his spine. "I'm square. Talk to me."

"The boys are going to stay in Detroit. Keep a low profile so the Feds don't sniff them out. I don't want to be left in the dark." Luke briefly glanced at Liam. "If these guys are working for Samir, we should know within a few weeks."

Weeks?

Luke rounded the desk and slapped a hand to his shoulder, and Asher expelled a breath. He could smell the alcohol floating with it.

"You've been drinking, too?" Luke cocked his head to the side. "Maybe you should get some rest and come back later."

"No. I need to be here. I need to make myself useful." Asher fell back into his chair and scooted closer to his desk. "A thought crossed my mind, though, which is why I came in so early."

"Yeah?" Luke asked.

"When I was on that op in Aleppo, Ara didn't have much money. Jessica paid Ara's way for years to help her get on her feet with her new identity." The word *sorry* hung on the edge of his tongue again at the mention of the op—sorry for keeping his past with Jessica a secret. Sorry for other things he'd never be able to say. "I was going to check it out now, but I'm betting Samir didn't have much, either."

"You thinking Ara funneled some of the cash to her family back in Syria? To Samir?" Liam asked.

"No, or else he would've found her sooner," Asher replied.

"Unless he already knew about her, but he didn't have a reason to hurt her before," Luke interjected.

Asher tapped at his computer keys. "I'm doubting Samir or his mom fell into a pile of money in the last six years. Not enough to afford a trip to a Paris hospital."

"We have a lot to try and figure out," Luke said. "You think you can trace the money trail from the hospital and see who footed the bill?"

Asher turned to Liam. "You or Owen might have more luck looking into it since we have to go through back channels without Command noticing."

"I'll get Owen. Knox and I are still working on ideas to track down Egon."

Asher's mind went back to Berlin, to the hospital—to the water jugs scattered on the floor. His raw knuckles burned with the need to hit again. "The Feds get Samir's men to say anything?"

"They're not talking. We expected that, though. Guys like them never roll on their group. They'd rather die." Luke hissed a low breath. "But I'm following up on a few leads. We'll figure this out." Luke knocked on the desk two times. "I promise."

"How's Jessica?" Asher asked after Liam left the office to speak with Owen.

He shook his head. "I've never seen her like this."

His spine bowed at the news. "She in pain?"

"Pretty sure it's more mental than physical. But, uh, Eva will keep bringing Lara over to her place and, hopefully, it'll lift her spirits to see her niece."

"She needs time," he recited the words he'd been repeating in his head. "She'll be back to herself once she's recovered."

"Yeah, I hope so."

There was more Luke wasn't telling him. He could feel it.

Once Luke left his office, Asher grabbed his phone to message Jessica.

His fingers hovered over the screen, but he couldn't bring himself to type. She hadn't responded to his drunken texts yet, and it was still pretty damn early in the morning to be messaging her now.

He'd wait. Give her the time he knew she needed.

She'd been through a lot, but she'd be back barking orders at the office in no time.

CHAPTER SIXTEEN

SHE STARED AT HER HANDS, AT THE SMATTER OF BLOOD ON her palms.

Her eyes fell to the ground, to the pool of dark crimson atop the snow beneath her boots. More blood dripped from her fingertips, like red dye drizzling onto a snow cone.

Her stomach roiled. Her heartbeat slowed.

She extended her arm, reaching for Ara off in the distance, a backdrop of shining light nearly absorbing her. Her wide eyes stared back at Jessica. Scared, tired eyes.

"I'm sorry," Jessica choked out.

Her eyelids lifted a moment later, and she inhaled a sharp breath when she found herself staring at her ceiling in her bedroom. Her third nightmare of the day. At least she hadn't broken into a sweat this time.

She slowly dropped her feet off the side of the bed at the sound of the door buzzer.

"Jessica," her mother said through the bedroom door a few moments later. "Your brother is here. He needs to talk to you."

Her body protested the movement as she stood, her knees weak, her heart now racing.

She carefully shrugged on a cotton robe and tightened the belt, wincing from the bruises along her abdomen.

It'd only been a couple days since she'd been back from Berlin. Not quite enough recovery time.

Her jaw hurt the most. The rest of her body was like one giant, achy bruise—like a soreness from doing one too many reps at the gym, only magnified.

She gathered a breath and left the room, but paused midway down the hall when she caught sight of herself out of her peripheral view in the mirror.

Pivoting to face her reflection she found a woman she barely recognized staring back at her. A broken version of the person she'd forced herself to become over the years, a woman her team needed: strong, dependable, able to make tough choices.

All that was left of her now were haunted blue eyes, dry lips, and faint bruises like smudges of dirt beneath her eyes and on her neck.

No confidence. No strength.

"There you are," her dad said. She followed his voice to find him standing a few feet away, his hands tucked into his jeans pockets, a grim look of discomfort etched on his face.

He'd been military for thirty years, shaped by his experiences, the same as her. He understood what she was going through far better than her mother could.

Of course, her father still didn't know all the details of her work—it was safer that way—but he now knew enough to worry a parent to death. But the man also bled red, white, and blue—he'd never hold her back if her actions meant helping the country.

He cocked his head to the side, and his eyes thinned as

she slowly ate up the space between them. "Luke has some news about your friend."

My friend. The friend I let down. Her stomach burned like acid swished around, eating at her.

She caught sight of Luke talking to their mom in the kitchen. He was leaning against the center island with crossed arms, a hard look on his face as their mom spoke to him in her native German tongue.

Their father had met their mom when he'd been stationed in Germany almost forty years ago.

"Hey." The whispered word had Luke redirecting his focus to Jessica, and he pushed away from the counter to approach. "Thanks for having Eva and Lara stop by earlier. It was good to see them." Of course, she'd only held her niece for all of five minutes before she'd rushed to her bedroom to lock herself away and cry in secret.

"They'll be back again tomorrow." Luke came to stand before her.

As much as she wanted to refuse the offer, she simply nodded, and then she surveyed the living room off to her left, the bouquets adorning the area like she was at a funeral, as if someone had died.

Ara died, she reminded herself. Guilt butchered her, tearing her apart, making her feel like a branch swaying in the wind, ready to snap.

"Her body has been buried. She's back home in Syria," Luke said.

She knew he was leaving out the words *what was left of her body*. Despite his announcement, she couldn't get herself to look away from the roses.

Bloodred.   Bright-as-fucking-sunshine-yellow.   Snowy white.

"I want them out of here," she cried as her hands pressed

to her abdomen. "All of them. Get all of the flowers out. Please."

She turned on her heel, hurried back to her bedroom, and slammed the door shut.

She ignored the knocks on her door. The requests for her to come back out.

At the sound of a text, she padded to the end table by the bed and lifted her phone.

Asher: *Hope you're okay. Worried about you.*

With a slightly trembling hand, she set the phone back down. She'd been surprised he hadn't come over, ignoring her request for no visitors. Some part of her wished he had. But the other part of her was terrified of him seeing her this way.

She could barely look her family in the eyes, and so she wasn't sure when the hell she'd be able to suck it up and get back to normal so she could see her team again. So she could work again.

And damned if she wasn't scared she might never crawl out of the hole she felt like someone was burying her in—especially since that someone was her.

"You shouldn't have come." Jessica stared at her best friend, Grace Dalton, who stood on the other side of the door, holding wine and a brown shopping bag. She resisted the urge to do something strange, something she rarely did—hug. "Come in."

"I knew the wine would work," Grace said once Jessica locked up behind them. "Your parents gone for the night?"

"They left thirty minutes ago. I forced them to head to the

hotel." The perks of having a one-bedroom meant she could be alone, at least at night.

Grace set a bag on the dining table off to the side of the kitchen island and pulled out about five different types of slippers. "I had a feeling you didn't own any, and these bad boys always make me feel a little better."

She handed her two of the pairs. Fuzzy, pink slip-ons. And navy blue slipper boots with two white balls dangling off to the sides.

"I couldn't decide, so I got a few options."

Jessica forced her lips to curve at the edges as best she could and set the slippers back on the table. "Thank you."

"Why is there so much uneaten food sitting here?"

"My mom's been trying to comfort me with her favorite German cuisine: all the dishes her mom used to make." She thought back to her grandmother's funeral in Munich four years ago, to all the food shoved at her by relatives. "My family cooks to cope," she said softly.

Jessica hadn't found a way to cope this time, though.

She'd barely eaten, so that hadn't worked.

Binge-watching Netflix hadn't amounted to much of anything other than blurry eyes.

And sleeping had resulted in waking up with high blood pressure from nightmares.

Fail. Fail. Fail.

"The bruises are starting to fade. How are you feeling?"

"I'm okay." Jessica motioned for her to head to the living area, and she followed behind.

Grace sat next to her on the couch and reached for her hand. "Luke didn't tell Noah everything that happened, but you were the woman in Berlin I saw on the news?"

She'd be wearing a wig when she left her apartment for a few weeks, that was for sure.

Well, if she ever left.

"Yeah, that was me."

"Don't worry. I don't think people will recognize you," she said, reading her thoughts. "But maybe you could go out as a redhead for a bit." She hid her emotions with a shaky smile, her tongue scraping along her bottom lip as if fighting a tremble there.

Grace, who used to be nearly as cold as Jessica, was about to cry. She'd changed after she'd fallen in love with Noah, a good friend of Jessica and Luke, and a former Teamguy.

"I don't know how you do this job." She covered her quivering lip with her hand and dropped her eyes closed. "If we lost you . . ." She sniffled but reopened her eyes. "I'm sorry. I came here to make you feel better—not for you to comfort me."

She didn't know what to say. Because, hell, she wasn't great at comforting someone, or talking about feelings. "Thank you for coming." She reached for her forearm and pressed her palm over the sleeve of Grace's blouse. "Thank you for caring, too." She meant the words, even if they'd been hard to say.

Grace had always been in the dark about her job up until Luke had asked Noah and Grace to be godparents to Lara. Luke knew better than to ask anyone on the team since they all worked in a dangerous profession.

"Of course I care." She blinked back more tears. "Sorry. Something about motherhood has softened me." She placed her free hand atop Jessica's. "Is there anything I can do?"

She lifted her eyes heavenward. "Just be here," she whispered. "That's more than enough."

CHAPTER SEVENTEEN

"ARE YOU KIDDING ME?" ASHER BACKED UP AGAINST THE wall at the fight club. "Five." Sarah held up her palm between them. "You've been here five nights in a row, and I had to hear you're back in town from Angelo." She shook her head. "And believe me, he's in a lot of damn trouble for waiting so long to tell me you've been fighting every night."

"Calm down, okay?"

She swatted her hands at his chest. "What happened? You left Mom's place over a week ago like a bat out of hell, and now I find you here?"

They were near the back exit of the club, Angelo's private entrance.

"Tell me what's going on," she hissed.

"I had to go out of town and handle some things." He pulled on his shirt over his head.

Her hands flailed again. Palms smacking his chest. "Why the hell are you here? You hate Angelo and this place."

He wasn't sure how to answer that. He wasn't buddy-buddy again with the guy, but he needed this place. He needed his old friend right now.

The days had blurred by.

Fighting. Drinking. Research.

Repeat.

Not always in that order.

He missed Jessica. He'd never admit it to the guys, but . . .

He missed her smile. Her laugh. Her annoyed look when he said something dumb. The way her bottom lip only tucked between her teeth for him.

Hell, he missed the blue balls he got from her eating cherries.

He was pretty sure her absence was why he was losing his damn mind.

That, and every time he closed his eyes, he remembered her in the s-vest. Seconds from death.

Whenever he slept, he woke up to the same dream— cutting the wrong wire and losing her. His life wasn't like the movies. Nothing was ever like fiction. But his dreams always played out like some major Blockbuster film. Only, in his head, the bad guys won.

Day after day with no word from Jessica and only updates from Luke . . .

He was going stir-crazy. And from what Luke was saying, she wasn't getting any better.

After every fight he attempted a phone call.

No answer. No surprise.

A few more texts would be sent once he was five drinks in. Maker's Mark. The good stuff. Yeah, well, the good stuff also made him eerily vulnerable and had him giving in to his desire to message her like some frat boy with a crush.

No Maker's Mark tonight, he'd already decided.

"You two okay?"

It was maybe the first time he'd ever been relieved to be

rescued by Angelo. Of course, the guy was also the reason his sister had shown up tonight. He didn't like her here, and not just because of Angelo or the fighting—it made him edgy to have her anywhere near violence or violent people.

What am I, though?

He was living two lives lately. It'd been easier back in the day. He'd never walked the fine line. No need to balance.

Now, he was a SEAL by day and an animal by night. A man who turned into a beast in the cage, tearing everyone apart to the near brink of death.

He'd become the man he'd run away from. And all it had taken was nearly losing a woman he cared about, a woman he wasn't even allowed to have.

"I should go." Asher heaved out a deep sigh.

"Damn right, you should!" Sarah hit his chest again and then winced. "You made of titanium or something?" A fraction of a smile touched the edges of her lips.

"Sorry I ratted on ya, but I was worried about you." Angelo shrugged.

"Like I said, I should go." Asher started to turn but then halted. "You shouldn't be here, either."

Sarah stepped closer to Angelo, and he looped an arm around her. "I won't let anything happen to her."

Asher grumbled and rolled his eyes, still hating the idea of them together. But what choice did he have? He couldn't kill Angelo. Could he?

"See you again tomorrow?" Angelo asked.

"What?" Sarah spun out of his grasp and now slammed her palm against Angelo's chest. "No!"

"I don't know. Maybe." *Probably.* His visits to the club had become a welcome routine.

Let the first fighter get in some good shots.

Feel the pain.

Be the pain.

And then unleash.

He needed to leave before his sister hit him again. He'd already taken enough punishment tonight.

Asher grabbed his jacket and boots, and once he was fully dressed he left the club and made his way to the bar he'd been hanging out at every night.

"Damn you, Maker's Mark," he said to his glass before he poured the liquid down his throat an hour later.

"You okay, honey?" A women's voice crawled over the back of his neck and had him flinching as if someone had gotten the drop on him.

He glanced back to see red nails atop his shoulder. "Not interested."

She huffed and flitted away. Thank God for that.

He found his phone in his jacket pocket and scrolled through his messages.

Still nothing from Jessica.

Valentine's Day was in a week, and he hated the idea of Jessica pent up in her apartment on that day.

She deserved better. She deserved the fucking world.

After downing another drink, he tossed his money on the bar and then went out into the night. No snow, but it was the bitter and bone-chilling kind of cold that could freeze a man's balls off.

He hopped into a taxi and, twenty minutes later, found himself parked outside Jessica's.

He paid the driver and then tucked his hands into his jacket pockets and lifted his eyes to the third level. "What am I doing here?"

I should go.

But for some reason, he couldn't get himself to move.

CHAPTER EIGHTEEN

JESSICA ROLLED TO HER SIDE AND TOOK A CALMING BREATH, trying to shake off her nightmare. She caught sight of the time on her alarm clock, but when her phone buzzed from a text alert, she fumbled for it, nearly knocking it off the nightstand in the process.

Asher: *You alone?*

She sat upright, her heart skipping a few beats as she stared at his words.

Her fingers splayed over the screen as she thought about whether or not to answer.

Asher was like water. A vital force. But water had nearly drowned her in Germany, and so . . .

She set the phone back down but kept her eyes locked onto the screen, her thumb wedged between her teeth.

Asher: *I'm on the street outside your place. Tell me to leave, and I will. If you don't respond, I'll just hang out here.*

Her gaze swung over her shoulder to the window, and she stood.

Her heart effectively in her throat, she maneuvered to the

window and peeled the curtains back a hair to see if Asher was joking or not.

Leaning against a streetlight, Asher had his gaze pinned on her window. A quick salute her way had her staggering back and losing her grasp of the curtains.

"Shit." Her phone buzzed again, and she grabbed it.

Asher: *You're awake. But are you alone?*

Damn it. She didn't want him to see her like this, but she couldn't let him stay out in the cold.

Jessica: *I'm buzzing you in.*

After a minute, she heard the heavy sound of a rap at her door.

"Give me a second," she said, her voice weak. Barely used, even when her parents visited. It wasn't like she was going to chat about her feelings with them.

"Of course." The sound of his voice did something to her. It was like a reset button had been pressed, refreshing her.

She gathered a breath and opened the door.

"Hi," he said and his Adam's apple moved with a hard swallow as he eyed her.

Her hand swept to her mouth at the sight of the bruises on his face, and she rushed forward a step, a gasp slipping from her lips. "What happened? Were you on an op I didn't know about?"

Had Luke kept something from her?

She brushed the back of her hand over his cheek, and he swallowed and wrapped his hand over her wrist.

He shook his head, and his gaze narrowed.

Standing so close to him now, she could smell the alcohol.

"You've been fighting," she said, and her lungs felt as if they were going to collapse.

He paused, his brows drawing inward. "It's not what you think."

She retracted her hand from the circle of his loose grip and pivoted out of his reach to face her home. "You've been in New York for months, and you never went to that club. Why now?" She briefly peered at him from over her shoulder. "Don't lie to me, either."

He held his hands up in surrender before closing the door behind him. "I needed to release some tension." He circled her to find her face.

"Oh." She didn't like the idea of him revisiting his past, a past she knew would be hard for him to walk away from again. But she was in no position to criticize.

"I've been worried about you." He removed and tossed his jacket. "Are your parents at a hotel?"

She nodded. "They leave tomorrow. They were going to cancel their cruise in the Bahamas, but I convinced them to go."

"Have they been driving you crazy?" He smiled.

"Of course." She folded her arms as a brush of cold air moved across her skin. Somehow, Asher had brought the outside in with him.

She glanced down, remembering she was only wearing a tee that stopped mid-thigh, along with her slipper boots, one of the pairs Grace had given her.

Asher observed her from head to toe, and his gaze somehow warmed her, eliminating the chill that had brushed up her spine moments ago.

"I wasn't expecting guests."

"Guess not since you banned us from coming by." His forehead creased, a touch of frustration gathering in his eyes.

"I'm sorry. I didn't want you guys to see me like this."

"Like what?" He cocked his head to the side, studying

her. "I see a beautiful woman in front of me." His voice lowered. "A strong-as-fuck woman."

She lightly shook her head. "How is *fuck* strong?"

He cracked a smile. "Back to busting my balls already?"

His brown eyes found hers, pinning her in place. He felt like home.

"Maybe I should've had you come over sooner." She said the words without allowing her typical filter to hold them in.

Being near him, even for a minute, already had her feet touching the ground again—he was like a magnet, pulling her back to where she needed to be. To *who* she needed to be.

"I'd ask you how you're doing," he began, "but it'd be a stupid question, I'm guessing."

Not sure how to respond, she sidestepped him, strode into her living room, and dropped down on the couch.

He followed slowly, glancing around the room. "Did you not get any of the flowers we sent?"

She looked at him as he sat in the armchair opposite her. "I did, but flowers die, and I couldn't handle watching that happen."

His mouth rounded in understanding, and he was quiet for a minute before asking, "You want to get out of here? Go for a drive?"

She nearly laughed. "You don't have a car in New York, and you've been drinking." She pressed a pillow to her lap when she realized he could probably see her underwear. "And I'm not ready to drive."

"Right." He nodded. "Next idea."

"It's late, Asher." Her stomach muscles tightened as she eyed him. She didn't want him to leave, though. Not yet.

"I know. I'm sorry." He started to stand, but she patted the air, and he slouched back into the chair and pressed his palms to his thighs. His gaze drifted across the room as if he didn't know where to look. "You're healing."

"Yeah, on the surface, I suppose." *Shit.* More words she hadn't meant to say slipped through.

He shifted in the seat. He was about as good at dealing with emotions as she was. They both sucked, to put it mildly. But he was trying to be there for her, and so, she'd do her best not to muck it up.

"My friend is dead," she said a moment later and blinked a few times. "I've lost people before. It should be a been-there-done-that thing, right? Why isn't it?"

He was on his feet in an instant, and she found him sitting next to her. She shifted to better face him.

His hair was tied back, a few of the lighter amber-colored strands out of place, and she instinctively reached out and touched them, smoothing them down.

There was a cut above his eye and another on his lip. A few bruises on his cheek, too.

"Are you trying to look like me, to make me feel better?" A lame attempt at a joke, but she was doing her best. Unchartered territory and all. "How'd someone manage to hit you?" When he didn't speak, she lowered her hand atop the pillow on her lap. "You *let* someone hit you, didn't you?"

His gaze dropped, and he reached out and brushed his knuckles across the top of her hand. "You consider talking to someone about what happened?" he deflected.

"You're serious?"

"It could be the alcohol talking because I know you're as stubborn as me."

"You're much more stubborn than me."

"True. We're both fighters, I guess."

"I'm not a fighter." Her jaw clenched tight. "Not anymore. I failed."

"No." He covered her hand with his, and the gesture had her closing her eyes. "You're the strongest woman I know." He paused. "But everyone needs help once in a while." At the sound of a subtle throat clear, she blinked her eyes open. "I could try and help if you'll let me." He shrugged, trying to play off the show of emotions. "I mean, we're a team. You. Me. Right?"

She let go of a deep breath. "Luke's back now. You don't need to—"

"I *do* need to . . ." He lifted his hand and rubbed his jaw before rising to his feet. "Jessica, you could have PTS—"

"I don't," she cut him off. "I know the signs of PTSD, and I don't have them. I have some nightmares, but they're not about what happened to me."

He nodded in understanding. "You'll get through this," he slowly said. "And I'll always have your back, and not just because we're—"

"I know." She fought the rise of tears in her eyes. Unexpected. Unwanted.

"We'll find the men responsible. I promise." Turning his back to her, he squared his hands on his hips. His head dropped forward.

"It won't matter."

He spun to face her in the space of a heartbeat. "What?"

She tossed the pillow off to the side and stood. "There will be another Egon. Another Samir. A string of bad guys to replace them once they're taken out. These unresolved conflicts in the Middle East will keep producing men like them." A tear escaped and touched her cheek. "Maybe we should just let it go. Stop interfering with everyone's problems."

He closed the gap between them to stand directly in front

of her and lowered his head to find her eyes. "You don't mean that."

She'd been thinking about this for days now, but it was the first time she vocalized her thoughts. "Maybe I do."

"Don't quit on me." His hand wrapped over her shoulder, and her lip quivered at his touch.

"Maybe I can't do this anymore." Tears started to burn a trail down her cheeks. "Maybe I can't be this person anymore."

"What person?" He gathered her into his arms and pressed her cheek to his chest, holding her in place.

She'd opened up and cried in front of him in Berlin, but she'd blamed the medicine. What was her excuse now?

"Maybe I want to give up."

He continued to hold her firmly in place, and she could feel his chin resting atop her head. "You're a fighter." He was quiet for a moment. "You're supposed to grieve. To recover. To take time, but you're Jessica Annaliese Scott. And the Jessica I know isn't a quitter."

"I just don't think I can." A sob tore from deep within. "I'm sorry to disappoint you, but—"

"You could never disappoint me." He pulled back, gathered her face in his hands, and focused on her eyes. "But you need to find the fight inside of you. It's in there. I know it."

Her chest hurt.

Everything fricking hurt.

And she wanted to bow down to the pain and let it consume her. Let all of the losses over the years sweep through and take her away. Take her to a place where it wouldn't hurt so much.

She'd spent years honing her ability to remove emotions from her work, to be a woman who wouldn't cave to the pressure of pain and loss. To grieve quickly and then move on for the sake of the job. But now . . .

"I ca-can't. Too many people are gone." Stolen from the world too soon.

"You *can* do it." He dropped his head and pressed his forehead to hers. "I've got you, okay?"

She pulled back a moment later to find his eyes, his warm hands still on her cheeks. "I don't know if I can do it. I don't know if I want to."

"Maybe it's too soon to talk about this." He wet his lips, hesitating to say more.

The words from the CIA officer who'd recruited her from MIT blew to the forefront of her mind.

People will die. Good people. Because you won't be able to save them all. You won't be able to help everyone. Probably not even one percent. But that doesn't mean what you're going to do won't make a difference.

Those had been the words that had won her over, convinced her to join the agency.

One percent. Screw that, she'd whispered to herself before stepping into Langley.

"Jessica?" Asher brought her focus back to the room. "I'm sorry if coming here was a mistake." He released her cheeks and moved back a few feet. "I should've given you space."

"No." She sniffled. "I'm glad you came." Two steps was all it took for her to be back in front of him. For her hands to land on the hard planes of his chest.

His heartbeat quickened beneath her palm, and he dropped his head forward a touch as if he wanted to kiss her. As if he wanted to steal her pain and make it his. And he would if he could—she knew it in her heart.

He'd always have her six, wouldn't he? "Most days you

drive me crazy," she whispered. "But I never want . . . to know what it's like . . ."

"You'll never have to know." His words brushed across her lips; he'd received her message even though she wasn't able to fully deliver it.

"Let's get you to bed." He lifted her into his arms, and she didn't protest.

How could she?

He placed her beneath the covers of her bed—a place where she'd guiltily fantasized about him for years, force-feeding herself the lie that the only thing between them was lust. An insatiable need to fulfill desires and nothing more.

"Goodnight," he whispered and pressed his lips to the top of her head.

CHAPTER NINETEEN

A HARD-HITTING ELECTRONIC SONG POUNDED THROUGH THE room, hiding the heavy swipes Jessica was taking at the punching bag. The surround sound was so loud he could feel the vibrations pulse through him.

He stared at Jessica in her black yoga pants and black sports bra, sweat dripping down her spine as she worked her gloves at the bag.

What the hell are you doing?

He lowered the music, and it had her whirling to face him. "Good. You made it." She propped her gloved hands to her hips and sucked in a sharp breath.

As he made his way through the gym, which was hidden in the basement of the skyscraper of their office building, he couldn't help but notice the light marks still on her stomach from the motherfucker who'd hurt her.

"Last night, when I said you should fight," he said, stopping in front of her, "I didn't mean literally."

Her chest rose and fell with heavy breaths.

Waking up to a text to meet at the gym had been about the

last thing he'd expected when he'd rolled out of bed that morning.

"You were right. I've been hiding out at my place, and I needed to get out. To remember who I am." She wet her lips and touched a glove to her forehead, pushing back some of the blonde hairs that had escaped her ponytail. "You made me realize I need to do what I did when Marcus died."

"And what was that?" He hadn't witnessed what happened to her back then, and he was beginning to wonder if maybe he'd screwed up with what he'd said to her last night.

"I need to focus on work. To fight."

He cocked a brow. "Killing our punching bag is your solution?"

"Better than pummeling people, like you've been doing," she shot right back.

And now he knew how she'd coped with Marcus's death: burying emotions and redirecting her anger and focus elsewhere. He'd been guilty of the same, but maybe what worked for him wasn't necessarily the best route for recovery.

"Listen, I think I misspoke last night. I want you to fight but maybe—"

"No," she said and edged closer. "You were right. I need this. But it's been a while since I've trained. I mostly sit safely behind my computer while you guys do all the work. Maybe I wasn't prepared in Berlin."

"You shouldn't be in the field."

She balked. "Because I'm a woman?"

Normally, he'd say some stupid remark to piss her off; he loved to drive her crazy. But today wasn't a typical day. What happened to her had changed things. Hell, it had changed everything. He just hadn't figured out what that meant yet.

"I got you shot in France," she said softly. "If I'm in the field, I distract you?"

Yes, but . . . "When you're on comms, I feel safer. You have my back, and it helps me get the job done knowing you're there, looking out for us."

Her mouth pinched briefly.

"But you should be able to defend yourself." Not that he ever wanted her going anywhere alone ever again, but he doubted he'd be able to chain her to his side for all of eternity, even if he liked that idea.

Maybe he could insert a tracking device into the back of her neck or arm?

"Well, that's why I asked you here. Will you train with me? I need to get better."

He allowed his lungs to fill with air as he processed her question.

"I don't want you going back to Angelo's club, though," she said a beat later. "Fight with me, instead."

"Let you hit *me*, you mean?" He cracked a smile. "Because you know I'd never lay a hand on you. Not even with gloves."

She moved closer, her chest practically touching his, and she lifted her chin. "You'd never touch me, huh?" Her glove skated up his chest, and he swallowed hard at the proximity.

She'd had a bomb strapped to her chest less than ten days ago.

Why the hell was his dick stirring in his pants right now?

"Promise me you won't go back." She held his eyes. "Be with me instead."

Be with you? That's all he'd wanted, even though he knew it was impossible. "Okay," he rasped, not sure how he got sucked into doing something he may regret later.

He went to the stereo and turned up the music, and then

kicked off his boots and removed his shirt. "Let me grab some other pants from my locker. Be right back."

She nodded, but he could feel the heat of her stare on his back as he left.

When he returned, wearing only his dark drawstring sweats, he found her standing at the center of the fighting cage.

He thought back to last night, to the fight before his sister had shown up. The fight before he'd found himself drinking and then going to Jessica's place.

His body itched for it—the feel of control fighting gave him.

Control. Fighting could empower Jessica, he supposed. But would it also make her like him? Dodging emotions by way of fists?

Maybe Berlin had woken her up to the fact there was more to life than work, but now he'd single-handedly encouraged her to shield her feelings once again.

Fuck. He blew a sigh from his lips as he ducked under the rope, and she tossed a pair of gloves at him. "I won't be needing these. I'm not hitting you, remember?" He shook his head lightly as he dropped them off to the side. "Are you sure you should be doing this right now?" He had to at least try again. "Maybe you should talk through your—"

"Unless you're Oprah or Dr. Phil, that'll be a hard pass from me." She cleared her throat. "Besides, I did about all the talking I need to for the next few lifetimes last night."

Titanium walls resurrected.

I'm such an idiot. "Jessica, I meant what I said about not wanting you to quit or give up, but that doesn't mean I think you need to be hard as—"

"Ice?" She stepped in closer, her eyes possessing him, sucking him into her universe. "A rock?" She removed her gloves and tossed them next to his. "I need this." She snapped her hands into fists in front of her face in a boxing position. "Now that we're done with this wonderful talk, let's fight."

He observed the faint bruises on her skin, and anger bunched in his stomach. But he gave in to her. Like always. He flicked his wrists, motioning for her to step closer, and she followed his command.

"Don't hold back. I need to be better prepared. Stronger than the enemy."

His heart was going to break at her words. Hell, it'd already broken a million times over at every reminder of what she'd been through.

But he nodded because he couldn't get himself to say anything.

Over the next hour, they practiced everything from rear-naked chokeholds to the basic karate self-defense moves.

And now, Jessica was boxed beneath him, her back to the floor. She squeezed her eyes closed as he held his body weight above her. "You ready to stop?" A smile flickered over his face when she focused on him again.

Her chest heaved up and down with deep breaths, and her skin glistened with sweat. He'd often envisioned her in this position, but for very different reasons.

She tipped her chin and found the ceiling. "I'm not done. No."

"I think you should be done. For today, at least." He angled his head, not wanting to get up yet.

"Ten more minutes?" Her tongue swept over her bottom lip as she steadied the rhythm of her breathing.

God, he shouldn't want to suck that bottom lip. To pull it between his teeth and taste her.

He inwardly groaned.

She pressed a hand to his sweat-covered chest. "Angel

wings are very fitting since you think you're my guardian angel." She stared at the ink. "And the Irish fighter on your right arm—"

"What's going on?" a voice called out, killing her words.

Asher's eyes widened, and he pushed off her and rose. He extended a palm to help her stand before his gaze veered to Luke heading their way from the elevator.

"Let me handle this," she said with a nod, and then started for her brother. "We were training."

Asher left the ring, snatched his shirt from where he'd tossed it, and pulled it on. Talk about an erection killer. Then again . . . maybe he needed a cock block to keep his mind from diving into dangerous waters. Waters he'd probably drown in given the woman he was with.

He turned off the music and started toward them.

"Why are you here? And training? Really?" Luke folded his arms, tucking his hands beneath the armpits of his army-green long-sleeved shirt. His blue eyes ripped straight to Asher.

"I asked him to train with me. I needed to get out of my apartment. To get my head back together," she said, crossing her arms to match Luke's defensive stance.

"You should be resting. You were in Berlin only—"

"I remember exactly where I was," she interrupted. "You don't need to remind me."

Luke's brows pinched together. "You should've asked me to help you. I could've trained with you."

"You need to focus on Eva and Lara," she said. "How'd you know we were down here?"

"I saw you on the security cameras when I came into the office."

Of course, he'd be there at the crack of dawn. They'd all been arriving before the sun rose to get in extra work time.

Asher had been so distracted he'd nearly forgotten about the security cams and how it might look to Luke if he saw Asher on top of his sister.

"You should get back home and rest." Luke's voice had a soft plea to it, and he pressed a hand to her shoulder.

"I've got to take a shower." She peered over her shoulder to glance at Asher. "Thank you," she mouthed and then started for the women's locker room.

"Sorry, man," Asher said once she was out of earshot. "She texted me and asked me to meet her here."

"Does she know you've been fighting again?"

Asher gripped the back of his neck. "I'm not going to fight anymore."

Luke's mouth tightened, and he sighed. "Get cleaned up and then meet me upstairs. The rest of Bravo is on their way." He headed toward the elevators, his back muscles pinched tight.

Asher dragged his hands down his face and then went into the men's locker room. He saw the text from Luke asking him to meet at the office—the message he hadn't gotten since he'd been in the ring with Jessica.

He set his phone down and removed his sweatpants.

"Thanks for not telling him about last night."

Asher pivoted to face Jessica in the doorway, only wearing his boxers. "What if I was buck naked in here?"

"Nothing I haven't seen before." A white towel was wrapped around her body. Her hair not yet touched by water. "I just wanted to catch you before we showered and went upstairs."

"And you thought coming in here in only a towel and with me in my boxers would be the perfect time?" He hoped to hell he'd keep his dick from leaping to attention at the sight of her.

She remained near the door, which was probably a good idea, and he leaned his shoulder against the wall of lockers.

"I need this to just be between us. I don't want anyone to know what I said last night. I don't want them to know I got . . . *weak*."

He pushed away from the lockers, unable to stop himself from striding closer to her. "To let the guys know you're human?"

"Luke has enough on his plate. I don't want him to worry about me."

"Too late for that." He stopped a few inches away, focusing on the hand that clutched the white towel to her body. "He's your brother. It's in the job description."

"Well, I . . ."

"I can't keep secrets from him. He's already on my case about not telling him about Aleppo and—"

"That's my fault. I'm sorry."

He tipped her chin with his fist to focus on her eyes.

"I'm not asking you to keep a secret, but I am asking you to protect my privacy. When we go upstairs, I don't want them looking at me like some broken China doll. I can't deal with them being fragile with me, and if they know what I said to you last night—"

"Okay." He lowered his hand from her chin, and her gaze dipped to his chest.

"Same time tomorrow?"

He nodded. "Yeah."

"And you're not going to Angelo's tonight?"

He let go of a breath. "If you stay in the locker room practically naked for much longer, I can't make any promises. I'll need to relieve some tension." He hadn't meant to answer so honestly, but damn. Did she not know what being in a towel in front of him was doing to him right now? And the guilt at wanting her after what she'd been through was going to shred him.

"You can relieve tension with me instead." A true blush—one he wasn't sure he'd ever seen on her—touched her cheeks.

"Oh, can I?"

"I mean, fighting." She shifted back a step, and he propped a hand on the wall at his side and studied her.

I'm going to hell. "Please, get out of here," he practically growled, unable to hide the bulge in his boxers anymore. His hand converted to a fist on the wall, and he fought the urge to bite into his lip as he studied her.

Her gaze journeyed to his tented boxers.

"Go," he said with a laugh.

"Yeah, okay." She touched his chest, pressed up on her toes, and kissed his cheek. "Thank you for the fight," she whispered and left the room so he could take the coldest shower of his damn life.

* * *

"What do we have?" Jessica dropped her purse onto Luke's desk and joined the team at the conference table where Bravo was gathered. She scooted to the table, placing herself between Owen and Luke and straight across from Asher.

Now, like a damn idiot, all he could think about was her in that towel thirty minutes ago. He cleared his throat and glanced at Luke. There was a visible strain in his throat. He probably had concerns about her being back at work.

"Uh, what are you doing here?" Liam was the first to speak.

When Asher directed his focus back to Jessica, he noticed

the pearl earrings he'd given her for Christmas. It was the first time he'd seen them on her. She'd said she was going to save them for a special occasion.

"You guys need my help." She clasped her hands atop the table, looking strong as hell, her blue eyes sharp and focused again.

The Jessica everyone knew was back, but he couldn't shake the worry that came along with the return of her old self.

"Ah, welcome back, then?" Knox said it as more of a question, his eyes skating over to Luke with concern.

Everyone appeared to be looking to Luke for a clue as to how to handle Jessica's appearance at the office.

"Is it safe for you to be walking the streets?" Owen looked at her.

"I wore a wig to the office this morning."

Asher hadn't seen it, but then again, she'd already stripped to yoga pants and a sports bra before he'd arrived.

"So." She drummed her nails on the table now. "What do we have? Why'd you call everyone here to work so early?"

Knox laughed. "You kidding? We've been rolling up here before the sun even gets her ass out of bed every day since . . ." He dropped his words. No one wanted to mention what had happened to Jessica, not the second she was back.

Her lashes lowered for only a beat before she gathered her focus back on the team.

Luke gave a slight nod as if trying to come to terms with her being present after what had happened to her. "Echo Team's in Detroit. Looks like an old al-Nusra cell may have been recently activated."

Jessica took a slight breath, barely noticeable, when Luke delivered the news. "How'd we find this out if we're not on the case?"

"A tip from one of my guys at the FBI," Luke said. "Since they know Samir went to his uncle's enforcer, they decided to track down everyone still on the streets affiliated with Yasser Hadeed."

She cocked her head, clearly needing more details. "And were they right? Anything turn up in Detroit?"

"Nothing they'll tell us, which is why Echo is there, so we're not kept in the dark." Luke straightened. "Wyatt's working on mirroring the phone of the guy he believes to be in charge. Once we have access to his texts and data, we should be able to determine how Samir has been in contact with him. Maybe we can figure out their next moves."

"I'm sorry. I should've come in sooner." She frowned. "I know more about Yasser Hadeed than anyone, and if Samir is taking any pages from his playbook—I'll be able to help."

"How'd Hadeed make contact with his people in the past?" Liam asked.

She stared at her hand on the desk, her mind possibly skipping back to the past. "Ciphertexts in the classified sections of newspapers. I'm betting Samir utilized the same route."

"Someone, probably the enforcer from Berlin, told Samir the old protocol," Asher said with a shake of the head, disappointed Yasser's enforcer had slipped through the government's fingers six years ago.

"We need to get those phones mirrored and fast." Luke scratched at his neck. "I don't want to be two steps behind the FBI. This is our fight."

"What else do we have?" she asked a beat later.

Luke opened his laptop, tapped at a few keys, and then slid it to her.

Jessica stared at the screen for a few minutes. The room dead quiet.

"Ara was in contact with her aunt for that long?" She looked up from the laptop. "I taught her everything. Selecting a key. Using a cipher to encrypt a message." A few quick blinks later, she added, "Apparently, she taught Fatima."

"You can thank Liam for that find." Luke tipped his head toward him. "The translations from Arabic to English are fairly accurate."

"So, that's how she knew Fatima was in Paris?" Her fingers brushed over her lips as if in thought. "I can't believe she'd take the risk by staying in contact with her old life."

And Asher knew what else she was thinking: how could Ara have lied to her about it? But people didn't always think straight when it came to family. To the ones they loved.

"They emailed each other only a few times a year," Liam said. "But in the more recent messages dating back to the last five months or so, Fatima started to ask Ara where she was living. And she began insisting Ara reach out to her cousin."

"Samir," Jessica whispered. "I still don't understand why Samir would become this person. It doesn't make sense."

"Well," Liam began, "his brother was killed eight months ago."

"By us?" she asked, shock in her eyes.

"No, Samir's brother had joined the rebel fighters against the Assad regime. He was taken out by Assad's military," Liam explained. "But it looks like the event pushed Samir over the edge. Maybe he blamed the US and Europe for allowing Assad to remain in power?"

"The timeline would fit, I guess." She surveyed the team. "What else did you find out?"

"Since I couldn't get the hospital in France to discuss patient records, I had to hack their systems to access Fatima's charts." Liam gave her a lopsided smirk. "You're a good teacher; what can I say?"

"My teaching helped Ara send messages to her aunt—getting her killed." She rubbed her forehead, and Liam winced at her words. "Sorry, go on."

"Fatima didn't have cancer," Liam said. "Her scans were clean, so I think she lied to Ara to get her to visit."

"She lured her out," Jessica said with a shake of the head. "Samir must've put Fatima up to it. Any idea where she is?"

"We may not be on this case, but thankfully, some of our people are keeping us in the loop." Luke took a breath and looked at Jessica. "A DEVGRU team went to Syria after Berlin to try and locate Samir and his mom."

"They were gone, weren't they?" Jessica's lips pursed, and Luke nodded.

Their team had been working this case for a week, and as much as they still felt in the dark—he couldn't imagine the way Jessica was feeling right now. Getting slammed with all of the details at once.

Were they overwhelming her?

Then again, she wanted to get more than her toes wet—she was ready to jump in the deep end and swim right away.

Right or wrong, he knew he wouldn't be able to stop her from going full throttle.

"Without operational authority, it makes what we do on our end tricky." Asher roped a hand around the back of his neck and squeezed at the mounting tension.

"We need to figure out how Samir was able to afford such a high-priced assassin," Knox said.

At his last word, Jessica's hands dropped beneath the table, and she snapped her eyes closed.

"You need a minute?" Asher asked.

"No." A hard breath later, she looked at everyone. "I'll be fine. So, uh, did we catch Samir on camera at the hospital with his mom?"

"No. I don't think he traveled with her. Well, not under his name, anyway," Liam answered.

"Samir's been a ghost since his brother died. He didn't have any ID in Syria. And there are no pictures of him we can run through our facial recognition software to try and get any hits," Luke explained. "Hell, he's barely twenty."

"What about the sketch I gave the Feds in Berlin?" she asked. "My artwork that bad?"

Luke semi-smiled. "Drawing isn't exactly one of your talents, but that image will help authorities if they ever come face-to-face."

"I can try again," she said, and Asher could see a darkness shadow her eyes. The pull of failure attempting to lure her away.

"We'll run your sketch through the systems again. Maybe we'll get something." Luke glanced around the room.

"Samir got to you in Berlin somehow," Knox interjected. "Must've had a fake passport, which means there's a photo of him out there. We'll keep checking all the flights around the time you were taken and see if anyone looks similar to the photo you drew."

Her shoulders slumped. "I'm sorry."

"Not your fault." Asher's brows drew together, and she looked over at him and took what appeared to be a calming breath.

She lightly nodded before focusing on the rest of the team at the table. "What about his mom? How'd she get to Paris?"

"She acquired a visa and passport a few months prior to the trip. It was her first time out of Syria," Liam told her. "When we pulled the flight manifest and checked the cameras at the airport—she appeared to be alone."

She shook her head. "Someone must've been in Paris

159

waiting to see if Ara would show, though. What about the hospital cameras?"

"Aside from Ara visiting—no one else that we noticed," Liam replied.

"There has to be someone funding Samir."

"I think I have an idea how to access Samir's accounts." Knox rose from the table, and all eyes went to him. He braced his palms against the back of the chair and swallowed. "My pops is going to be in Austria soon. Some political thing, I don't know. We'd be in Egon's territory."

"What are you getting at?" Luke leaned back in his chair.

"Egon usually gets his jobs by way of a message board. The new age we live in . . ." He lifted his shoulders. "Hitman for hire, ya know?"

"You want to lure him out by requesting a hit on your dad?" Asher asked in surprise. He knew Knox and his dad had had a falling out, but still.

"No. No." He smiled. "I'll go with him, and we put the hit on me."

"First of all, we're still grounded," Luke began while slowly rising. "And secondly, we don't know if he'll be the one to answer the message."

"How about a third reason," Jessica chimed in. "You could get killed."

Knox shook his head. "This might be our only chance to draw him out, and it wouldn't raise any questioning brows for him if we put a hit out on the son of a politician. That's a normal gig."

He had a point, but there were still a lot of roadblocks.

"You don't even talk to your old man," Liam said.

"I'll do what I have to for the team, and you know that." He swiped a hand down his jaw. "Could you put an encrypted message up? Ask for a public killing since that's Egon's specialty?" Knox briefly closed his eyes. "God, I'm sorry, Jessica. I didn't—"

She held her hand in the air. "It's okay. I want to find this bastard, but I don't want you to risk your neck."

"You guys won't let anything happen to me." Knox semismiled.

Luke was quiet for a moment, stroking his jaw. "Put the message out there. If he takes the bait, then I'll find a way for us to get there."

"If we catch Egon, we can hopefully trace the transaction from Samir to Egon, and then get a handle on Samir's accounts," Luke said. "We need to know who is bankrolling him."

Asher looked over at Jessica. She was already on the laptop. Back to business, so it seemed. Well, she was trying, at least.

"Any word on the girls?" When she looked up from the screen a moment later, he could see fragments of fear and sadness clouding her eyes. A temporary obstruction.

"They're in a CIA safe house in Oslo," Luke answered. "Although getting Rutherford to share that news wasn't easy."

"That's good." She rolled her lips inward briefly. "When this is over I can't see them again. Being close to me is too dangerous."

"Jess." Owen was on his feet and standing behind her now. He placed a hand over her shoulder.

"You don't need to say anything," she said without glancing back at him, her eyes committed to the screen again. "I, uh, should work."

Owen nodded, but his eyes met Asher's, and he cocked his head toward the door, motioning to meet him outside.

"What's up?" Asher asked.

"There's something you should know," he began. "When I was recovering all of Jessica's data from the phone she lost in Berlin"—he scratched at the back of his head—"well, Luke was in the room with me, and he saw her texts. He saw the last message she got before Egon took her."

Asher cursed under his breath. His damn *I miss you* text had now become public to his team. *Just great.*

"When did he see it?" Asher lifted his hands from his pockets, not sure what to do with them.

"Last night."

"The text . . . it isn't what it looks like."

Owen raised his brows, and a slight smile tugged at his mouth. "Sure, man."

Shit.

"Anyway, I thought you should know." Owen reached for the knob to go back into the office, but then paused and looked at Asher from over his shoulder. "If there's something going on between you two, he'll get over it. You'll just have to give him time."

CHAPTER TWENTY

"Harder, Princess."

"That's as hard as I can hit. And don't call me *princess*." She took short gasping breaths and rested her forehead against the black heavy bag.

"You ready to put some gloves on before you mess up your beautiful hands?" He was standing before her with gloves extended. "So damn stubborn."

"I learned how to be that way from the very best." She sidestepped the hanging bag and kissed the air, even if some crazy part of her wanted her lips to land on his.

He handed her the puffy gloves, and her gaze lingered on his body as she fastened them. Well, more like attempted to tie them.

A six-foot-four distraction was two steps away.

His broad shoulders arched back, his eight-pack like eye candy on display. Beads of sweat rolled over his tan skin like drops of water had been airbrushed onto him for a beer bottle commercial.

Strings of guilt for wanting him pulled at her to the point

where she wondered if she'd fray and unravel—and give in to the pulse of need inside of her.

"Pretty sure you were stubborn long before you met me, Peaches."

"So, we really are back to the nicknames, aren't we?"

"Just trying to make you feel at home." He winked his devilish, panty-melting wink.

"I also think you're trying to get me to quit training."

"What? By pushing you so hard?" He grabbed a bottle of water off a nearby bench, and she watched the movement in his throat as he sucked half of it down.

He offered the other half of the water, and she arched a brow and lifted her gloves to remind him she couldn't hold the bottle. "Torturing me now, huh?"

He rolled his tongue over his bottom lip, a devious look etched into the lines of his face—the look of a man who could do sinful things to her with his tongue.

Maybe training wasn't the best idea, not if she wanted to maintain her defenses and keep her lust from bursting out of her like one of those jack-in-the-box toys after being wound up.

Fighting with him had helped take her mind off the heavy stuff, but it'd also built up more sexual tension than normal between them. A sword with its double edges and all.

She'd come close to propositioning him for sex with no strings yesterday. Sex as a cure to what happened in Berlin—that's how off-kilter she'd become.

"Water. Please." She lifted her chin, and he brought the rim of the bottle to her lips, but she couldn't take her eyes off him as he gently poured the cool liquid into her mouth. A few drops splashed onto her chest, cooling her breasts.

"Did I quench your thirst?" He pulled the bottle back. "Or do you need more?"

Holy hell. Desire throbbed hot, hard, and fast straight down to her very wet center. *I shouldn't be thinking about this. About you naked. Me pinned beneath you. This is wrong.* "We need to focus on training."

"Ugh, aren't we doing that?"

Shit, she'd had that conversation in her head and not out loud. *Now I sound like an idiot. Great.* "Let's take a break from the bag and practice that kick you showed me yesterday. I couldn't quite nail it." She removed and tossed the gloves she'd just managed on.

"Of course you want to nail it." He playfully waggled his brows before tossing the now-empty water bottle into the recycling.

"Shut up," she said with a laugh, and the laugh felt good. A nice change from the sorrow constantly trying to entice her back.

Her hand swept down her neck and to the top of her sports bra as she eyed his back while he moved to one of the larger mats off to the side of the ring. "You coming, or what?" He faced her and flicked his wrist.

She blinked out of her stupor. "Yup." A hard nod followed, more for her benefit. A snap-out-of-it kind of nod. "Okay. So, the part where I sweep my leg up before I spin always gets me messed up. You know, falling-on-my-ass messed up."

He grinned, his white teeth flashing. "I remember. Enjoyed it, too."

"Teach me how not to fall, okay?" She wet her lips, doing her best not to allow her eyes to travel down the center of his chest and to the dusting of hair beneath his belly button.

He crouched before her and placed his hand on her thigh, and she startled and almost fell back onto her ass—just the opposite of what she wanted to happen. "What are you doing?"

He looked up at her. "Helping you with the kick. You okay?" A line darted through his forehead. "You wanted to train."

"And we're supposed to be working on removing your tension, too," she sputtered without a filter.

"Yeah, well, that's not exactly happening." He urged her leg up and extended it, and her hands swooped to his shoulders, so she didn't fall.

"Sorry," she whispered, too softly for him to probably hear. "Your hands, um. I can't." Her stomach muscles banded tight when his eyes touched upon hers. "Forget the leg kick. Let's do something that involves more space between us."

He released her leg—thank God—and she removed her hands from his slick shoulders. "Works for me," he said before clearing his throat and turning away.

She knew he was adjusting his pants, and then after he bowed his head and placed his hands on his hips.

They were both in way too deep.

Lust and desire, she could handle. Hell, it was par for the course between the two of them. Days like these were a welcome distraction from the darkness of her situation.

But . . . it was everything else, circling them the way the earth orbits the sun, that had her feeling all screwed up in the head. So out of sorts and conflicted. Feelings she despised.

Working so closely with Asher when Luke had been on paternity leave had done enough damage to her defenses.

But Berlin had been a game-changer, no matter how much she didn't want to admit it.

The floodgates had opened, and now she needed to figure out a way to snap them closed. And fast.

* * *

Her hands still ached from punching the bag earlier. He'd been right about not using gloves. *Maybe I am too stubborn?*

She held the ice to her knuckles and stared at her computer screen. Still no response to her post for a hitman.

If the plan didn't work, they'd have to come up with another way to go after Egon. They needed to track the money trail, but she also wanted him to pay for what he had done to Ara.

Every time her fist had slammed into the bag the past three days, she'd envisioned his face. And then Samir's.

And then, at times, she'd drawn up an image of herself.

Angry at herself for being taken. For letting Ara die. For becoming weak and confused when she'd returned home.

Her gaze floated up to see Luke in the doorway, and she dropped the ice pack to her lap, but it slipped to the floor.

"You okay?" He sat in the chair in front of her desk and leaned forward, elbows on his thighs.

"Uh, yeah." She pressed back into her chair, repositioned her glasses to the bridge of her nose and eyed her brother.

He'd been treating her like glass since she'd come back to the office, but he'd witnessed her meltdown, and so now, she'd have to prove to him she was the same old Jessica. Tough as nails.

"The president called." He dropped the words into the air. "We're off suspension."

"Really? So soon? How'd you convince him?"

"I didn't have to. He needs us on an op."

Her lids lowered halfway, and she stared at her hand on her lap, a slight tremble there. "When? Where?"

"A quick recon op in Mexico City. Should only take a few

days, but I'll need to bring Bravo with me. I don't like being gone when we have work to be doing here, but this is our chance to get off suspension, so I had to take it. I'm not sure if you're ready to come with us, but the idea of you being alone at your place while we're gone—"

"Samir isn't going to come after me here." She still couldn't wrap her mind around the fact he was behind all of this, capable of such evil.

"Yeah, I don't think you're in danger." He sat upright and scratched at the stubble on his jaw. "But after what happened, you should stay with someone while we're gone."

There was no way she'd ask to stay with her best friend, Grace. She had two kids and a stepdaughter. Way too much on her plate.

"I'll be fine."

"I may not be able to touch base with you while I'm in Mexico. Maybe I should ask Wyatt to come back from Detroit?" He stood, a palpable unease moving through him.

"I don't need a babysitter." She shifted to her feet as well but pressed a palm to the desk to stay grounded. "I'll keep working on tracking Samir. Maybe we'll get a hit on the message board from Egon while you're gone."

He was quiet for a moment. "We'll be back soon." He lowered his head and pinched the bridge of his nose. "Are you sure you'll be okay?"

She circled the desk, and his arm swooshed back to his side. "I'm good." A half-truth, but she couldn't risk the team losing focus because they were worrying about her. "This is a good thing. Now that we're no longer suspended, we might be able to hunt down Egon."

He lightly nodded. "Yeah, okay."

"I'll check in twice a day with Wyatt. That work?"

"Yeah." He smiled, but it dissolved quickly. "You know,

if anything had happened to you back in Berlin I'd never have been able to forgive myself. No more secrets, though. I can't protect you if I don't know everything."

She dragged her hand over her mouth and to the column of her throat before her fingers splayed across her collarbone.

"And now that you're training with Asher every morning, it has me on edge you're considering putting yourself at risk again."

"I'm trying to better protect myself." *While also giving myself a serious case of female blue balls, apparently.* "Er, that's all." She turned, blocking her face from him, worried he'd read her thoughts. "And I don't have any more secrets."

"You're sure?"

"I promise," she snapped out maybe too quickly.

He was quiet for a moment. "I should pack and say bye to Eva and Lara before I head out."

"You don't need to have her check on me, either," she said, knowing exactly what he was going to do.

"Mm-hm." He pressed a hand to her shoulder. "Stay safe. I'll be back before you know it."

She tracked the sound of his steps out of the room before heading to her desk to grab the ice pack that'd fallen to the floor.

"Nice view, Peaches."

Startled, she jerked upright and faced Asher. "Funny." She set the ice pack down and smoothed her hands over the sides of her pencil skirt, ensuring it was back in place. The memory of his hands on her earlier had her tensing.

"I'm guessing Luke let you know we're not grounded anymore?" He came into the room and stood opposite the desk. "I'll miss a few training sessions with you. Sorry about that."

She waved a hand in the air. "I'll be fine on my own."

"But will you be?" He cocked his head. Worry in his eyes.

"I don't need this from you, too." She sat and scooted closer to her desk.

His eyes flipped to the ceiling as if he were biting back the urge to say something. He'd been edgy at the office and only seemed to be his typical playful self when inside the boxing ring. "You know Luke will have a parade of people checking on you while we're gone. You won't be able to stop him."

"And it's not necessary."

He crossed his arms. "Are you still having nightmares?"

Her gaze flicked to his brown eyes, the color of mahogany with a darker rim. "No. I think our fight sessions have helped keep them at bay."

"Then maybe I shouldn't go. I could see about staying here."

"When have you ever backed out of an op? Not for anything or anyone."

"You're not just anyone."

Her cheeks heated at his words, but then frustration burrowed into the pit of her stomach. She needed her thick skin back. Where had it gone, and why was he making it so difficult to maintain the fortified structure she'd built around her heart?

"Stop saying that stuff to me."

"What 'stuff'?" He used air quotes as he circled the desk.

The smell of leather with mint citrus notes and a touch of cinnamon from his cologne touched her nostrils.

She rose and removed her glasses, and then pinched the top of her nose before placing them back on.

"Oh," he said while scratching his throat, and closing one eye, "is this gonna be another one of those times where you say you prefer me to be a jerk?" His tone was light, but she knew he was holding back from delivering more of a punch with his words.

"The playful banter. The jabs." *The desire to screw.* "That's fine. It's given with us." Her hands clenched into fists at her sides, her fingernails biting into her palms. "But these sweet and caring comments . . . you know how I feel about them."

He dropped his eyes to the floor. "Guess I was right. No surprise there."

"We had a moment at my place, and you let me cry on your shoulder. And maybe we had a few moments before Berlin." She paused. "I really do appreciate what you've done for me, but this other thing between us has to stop."

"Define this other thing for me," he said while twirling a finger like a helo blade, "because surely the thing you're referring to can't be my desire to pin you to your desk, lift your skirt, and—"

"Asher, please." She inched closer to him, which maybe wasn't the best idea because she could smell him even more. Feel the tension beating off of him like the crest of a wave on impact.

"I want to hear it from you. For you to say the words this time. No escape. No deflection. Tell me you don't want me. Let me hear you say it."

"We had sex one time." Her index finger flipped up. "*Six* years ago."

His mouth rounded, and his booted feet inched back a step. "You think all I want from you is sex?" The depth of his voice, the sting cutting through his tone—it had her pressing her palms to her abdomen.

She was hurting him and damned if his pain didn't hurt her, too.

It was what the team needed, what the country required of them—to be coworkers. Plain and simple.

Although how could anything ever be easy with them?

He turned his back, his fingers diving through his hair, his corded forearms tightening, and the sleeves of his shirt bunched at the elbows, started to slip.

"I'm just trying to get back to my life," she whispered, fighting the break in her voice. "To be who I was before I lost my mind."

"And you want the wall back up between us?" he asked softly and slowly eased back around to find her eyes, shoving his sleeves back to his elbows.

"The wall should never have come down." He'd been working at her with a chisel and blow torch before Berlin. But now all he had to do was hug her, and she turned into someone she didn't recognize. How was that possible?

"Jessica, I know that's what you think you want, but—"

"But nothing." Her eyes fell shut because she couldn't possibly look at him and say what she needed to. "Don't you get it? I'm trying to be me again. We have to go back to the way things were before everything became so hard between us."

"You can't keep doing this," he said, and she opened her eyes. "Pretending to be okay." His pupils dilated a touch, and he remained quietly observing her as he waited for her to speak.

"I'm not pretending," she responded once she found her voice.

"I call bullshit, and you know how I know?" He stabbed the air. "I was like you before joining the team."

She swallowed, her chest feeling as if her lungs were collapsing. "Yeah, and what changed?"

"You," he whisper-said. "You changed me." He took a

breath and mumbled, "Whether I like it or not." He focused on her mouth before his brown eyes flicked back to hers.

"You're still a Teamguy," she sputtered, willing her tone not to waver. "And I'll always be Luke's sister. Plus, there are about a million other reasons why there can never be more between us, even if . . ." Now it was her lower lip quivering.

"Even if what?" He edged closer, eating up almost all the free space between them, and she knew she'd come far too close to revealing the truth. The truth she wouldn't even confess to herself.

"After Berlin, this is the last thing we should be discussing."

He turned his head as if he didn't have the stomach to look her in the eyes while she attempted to deflect. "You could've died without ever . . ." It was him dropping his words this time, and maybe he realized they'd be wasted on her.

"Go to Mexico, and when you come back, can we please go back to normal?"

"Normal?" He faked a laugh. "Sure. As normal as us kissing in Central Park at Christmas? As normal as the way you make me feel every time we're in the same room together?" He surrendered both palms in the air. "That's the only normal I know." The room grew quiet, so quiet she could hear the beats of her heart, and he turned and started for the door. "See you later, Jessica."

Jessica. Not Peaches.

Part of her wanted to crumble to the floor, but no, she'd done this to herself. She deserved whatever punishment came along with hurting the man she cared about.

When he was out of sight, the past catapulted to the front of her mind, a reminder as to why she had to sacrifice her wants and needs.

You're like Superwoman, Ara had said when she'd first arrived in Berlin over six years ago.

Nah, I'm no one special, Jessica had responded.

You are to me. You're my hero. Ara had hugged her, and she'd let her do it. She had even hugged her back.

She'd realized then she needed to do more.

And right now, she needed to be the woman Ara had thought her to be.

She needed to be a hero.

And heroes didn't have time for love.

CHAPTER TWENTY-ONE

"Luke made you come, didn't he?" Jessica glared at Eva and rolled her eyes.

"It's Valentine's Day, and we're going to have a girls' night out. Samantha's in New York while she waits for Owen to get home, and she brought her friend Emily with her." Eva waved a finger in the air with a quick smirk. "Friends don't let friends spend Valentine's Day alone."

"I'm not going clubbing. I've only been home for a few weeks." She shook her head. "Going out for a night on the town after what happened would be crazy."

"What you need is to take your mind off everything." Eva stepped inside Jessica's walk-in closet and disappeared from sight. "We don't know when the guys will be back, so you get to be my plus one tonight."

"I don't want to be a plus anything." Jessica dropped onto her bed at the sight of Eva carrying an armful of dresses out of the closet.

She set them on the bed and began sifting through them. "Well, I need to celebrate the fact I can fit into my old clothes," she said with a laugh.

"Yeah, your boobs don't, though."

"Perks of breastfeeding, and Luke certainly isn't complaining."

Jessica held up her hand. "Woman . . . this is my brother we're talking about."

"Right." She smiled. "Okay, which will it be? Classic black? Or red?" She narrowed one eye and held the two choices in the air, and then diverted her eyes to Jessica's legs, clad in pajama pants. "You've been shaving?"

"I haven't let myself go." Okay, maybe the first week after Berlin she had, but she was slowly finding her rhythm again. "You know, two weeks isn't that much of a recovery for most people." She shot her friend a pointed look.

Eva tsked. "Since when are you 'most people'?" She tossed her the black dress, which would have Jessica's breasts spilling out of the top.

"I cannot go clubbing. I have work to do, and—"

"And punching bags to hit?"

Jessica processed Eva's words. "Luke told you, huh?"

Eva's lips pursed, and her lashes lowered briefly. A light shade of red inched up her throat and to her ears. "Yeah, uh, Luke told me everything," she softly admitted. "He mentioned you've been training with Asher. Until they left for Mexico three days ago, anyway."

Asher was the last person she wanted to talk about, especially with Eva. "He's the best fighter, so . . ."

"I know." She cleared her throat. "And he's probably good at a bunch of other things, too."

"Yeah, so, can we go back to talking about your boobs?"

Eva pointed a finger at her. "There you are. I missed you."

Jessica stood and eyed the black dress. "And what's that

supposed to mean?" She wished Luke hadn't told Eva everything.

"Just get dressed," Eva ordered. "And wear the red lipstick, okay?"

"Are you trying to score me a date tonight, or what? I thought I was your plus one." She reluctantly walked toward the en suite, dress in hand.

"When was the last time you had sex?" Eva's arms crossed.

"You're marrying my brother." She pivoted to face her. "I probably shouldn't be talking about this stuff with you."

"You honestly think I'd share your secrets with him?"

"I don't have any secrets."

"Mm. Sure." Eva's eyes narrowed.

"The last thing I need right now is sex, anyway." *Even if I want it with Asher. Only him.*

"Are you sure?" She arched a brow. "Maybe you need to let loose."

She silently contemplated the notion.

"Or is it that you already found someone you want?" Eva asked.

"Don't start." She already knew what was coming.

"Luke saw Asher's message to you just before . . ." She found Jessica's eyes and took a breath. "When Owen was syncing all your data after your phone got destroyed in Berlin, Luke saw the text from Asher."

"What text?" Jessica tossed the dress onto the bed and went to her nightstand to grab her phone.

"Asher told you he missed you. It's not on your phone now?" Eva stood next to her as Jessica scrolled through the messages to and from Asher right before Egon had tried to destroy her life.

"The last message on here is from me." She blinked and put her phone down. "Why would Luke delete the text?"

Eva dragged a palm down her face.

"And why'd Luke tell you about it in the first place?"

Eva slumped onto the bed and pressed her palms atop her red pressed slacks. "He's been venting to me. You know how hard it is for him to open up, but—"

"What is it?" Jessica sat next to her.

"He thinks there's something going on between the two of you, and I'm honestly surprised it's taken him this long to figure it out."

Jessica's brows scrunched. "But there's nothing going on." *Never can be.* And she'd told Asher that before he'd left for Mexico.

"You'll always be Luke's little sister, even though you're this powerhouse of a woman." She shifted on the bed to better face her. "It won't matter what guy you end up with in the future—Luke's not going to like him. Well, not at first."

"There's nothing for Luke to worry about." But her mind breezed back to the supposed *I miss you* text from Asher.

It wouldn't have been a big deal to most people, but it was a huge-ass step for Asher. He didn't do *I miss yous* or hugs. He was like her. Practically cut from the same cloth. Well, he used to be, but he had changed, hadn't he? Admitted as much in her office, anyway.

"I think I need a drink." Jessica rose to her feet and grabbed the dress from the bed.

"So, we're going?" Eva's dark brows rose. "No fighting me?"

"Yeah, I guess." She sighed. "But I'd better wear a wig. The image of me in that vest, is, uh, still making its way through the news cycle." Her throat thickened at the memory.

"It's not that clear of an angle." Eva stood. "Maybe I'll wear a wig, too, though."

"The paparazzi still hounding you since you're back in the spotlight?"

Eva was part of the famous Hollywood Reed family, but she'd hidden from her name for years until she met Luke.

"Unfortunately. And the last thing we need tonight is to draw attention to me, only for them to discover you."

"Good call." Jessica went into the bathroom and shut the door behind her and then peeled off her pajamas.

As she went through the motions of getting changed, Asher's text continued to batter her mind: words she hadn't even read because her control-freak brother had deleted them.

She'd have to deal with Luke's invasion of privacy at some point. But she wasn't itching to talk about the subject matter: Asher.

Right now, she just wanted her team back home safe. Not being with them on an op had driven her nuts the past three days, but she also knew it'd been best to stay behind. She couldn't risk their lives with a bad call if she lost her focus.

Two weeks ago, she'd had a bomb strapped to her chest.

Yet somehow, right now, all she could think about was a simple *I miss you.*

* * *

JESSICA STUDIED THE GLITZY CLUB, BUT SHE WASN'T FOCUSED on the flashy lights, the people dressed to the nines, or the music. No, she was scanning every door to note possible escape routes and checking for anyone who looked dangerous.

She'd let her guard down in Berlin. She wouldn't make the same mistake again.

"You look tense," Samantha's best friend, Emily, commented.

The woman bore a striking resemblance to Jennifer Garner, who'd starred as a CIA spy in the old show *Alias*—a show Luke had teased Jessica about watching when they were younger.

"How's your brother doing? Stopping that massive attack back in 2017 like he did—he's an incredible guy." Jessica thanked the bartender for her martini and refaced the group.

Emily tucked her golden-brown locks behind her ear and gave a light shrug. "Jake's good. He thinks he needs to be Superman, though, I swear. Trying to save everyone. Kind of like you and your team, huh?"

Jessica wondered how much Owen's fiancée, Samantha, had told Emily about her team, but her thoughts faded as they clinked their glasses together in a toast.

"Happy Valentine's Day, ladies," Eva said.

"You, too," Samantha and Emily said at the same time.

Jessica inhaled a breath and followed it with a large gulp of liquor, hoping it would settle her nerves.

"Think the boys are okay?" Samantha asked, stress lines appearing between her eyes.

"They'll be fine," Eva said, but she was unable to hide the crease of worry in her forehead.

"Sorry about what happened to you," Emily said shortly after in a low voice. "And I'm so sorry about your friend."

Jessica's heartbeat ramped up, but she managed to utter, "Thank you."

Despite the loud house music pumping through the room —an interesting remix of a Charlie Puth song—the silence between them became deafening.

Eva reached out for her arm. "I'm glad you came out with

us. I know this can't be easy, and maybe I shouldn't have pushed, but—"

"No, you were right." A total lie, but what could she say? She didn't want her future sister-in-law feeling bad. "Why don't you guys have some fun. Hit the dance floor."

"I'm thinking Luke and Owen wouldn't be thrilled with you grinding up against any guys. We should probably stick close together if we do go out there," Emily said with a chuckle.

"Owen's progressive and all," Samantha began, "but not when it comes to men groping me."

"Yeah, Luke, too. But we can protect each other on the dance floor." Eva looked to Jessica, but before she could reply, Jessica's gaze snapped to a familiar face at a booth in the back of the club.

"I'll, um, be right back." She slipped her glass back onto the bar and, before anyone could ask questions, maneuvered through the crowd.

Asher's sister sat alongside a few other women. Bottles of expensive champagne crowded the table. Angelo wasn't in sight, though.

Sarah's long dark hair, a reminder of Asher's, was swept into a high ponytail, and the dress she wore—well, Asher would've had a brotherly heart attack.

"Uh, hi." Sarah shifted off the leather to stand. "What's with the hair?"

Jessica touched her long black wig. "Right. Um, it's a Valentine's Day thing," she sputtered. "Don't ask." A quick, forced laugh tumbled free. "So, you're here with friends?"

When Sarah pointed to someone behind Jessica, she glanced back. Angelo stood off to the side of the club, talking to some guy. A guy who was poking his finger at his chest. How had she missed him before?

Maybe her radar was still off. *Shit.*

"That doesn't look good," she said, turning to face Sarah. "Everything okay?"

"An old acquaintance of his, I think."

Acquaintance, sure.

"Asher's not with you?" She blinked her long dark lashes a few times. "No, he wouldn't be," she answered herself, shaking her head. "He hates Valentine's Day."

"Does he?" She scratched at her collarbone, not sure what to do or say—or why she'd even chosen to approach her.

"Our pops was arrested that day," she said so low Jessica pretty much had to read her lips, especially with the heavy beats of music all around.

"Oh. Sorry. I didn't remember the date from his file."

"Why would that be in Asher's work file?" Her brows pinched together. Curiosity there.

She was quiet for a moment before hoping to deflect. "So, how's your restaurant? It was your mom's place before you took over, right?"

"Yeah, it was. Things are hectic this time of year, but I needed a night off." She tilted her head and crossed her arms. "Didn't something happen to you recently?"

How much did she know? Asher wouldn't ever share operational details with her, but . . .

"We were together when he saw the news about Germany, and the color drained from his face at the mention of you being in Berlin where the attack happened."

Ohh.

"And then a week later, I found him fighting at Angelo's."

This wasn't news, but the fact that his sister knew so much was surprising.

"Angelo said he hasn't been back in a week, though."

Sarah glanced toward Angelo before her gaze flitted back to Jessica. "I'd rather him not fight."

Me, too. "Is he okay with you and Angelo being together?"

"He's not happy, but he's been off my case about it, at least. Distracted by something or *someone,* I think."

"Hi, beautiful." A voice buzzed from behind.

Angelo.

He reached for Sarah's hand and pulled her into his arms. "Ready to get out of here? I want you all to myself."

Jessica shot them an awkward wave and slipped away.

She found Eva, Samantha, and Emily on the dance floor.

"Hey, who were you talking to?" Eva hollered over the music.

"Ah, no one." She tried to shake her arms loose, to feel the beats of the music splinter throughout her body and take control . . . but her signals were jammed; she couldn't get her body to function properly.

Egon.

Samir.

The bullet to Ara.

She needed to get out of there. It was too crowded. Too . . . everything.

"I can't do this," she rasped, probably not loud enough for them to hear. "I'm sorry." She located one of the exits—an exit that five men had just walked through.

Bravo Team.

"They're back," Samantha shouted.

"How the hell did they find us?" Emily asked as they left the dance floor.

Luke, Owen, Knox, Liam, and . . . *Asher.* The men strode through the crowd, their eyes already pinned in their direction.

Asher was now sporting an entirely new look, and it had her jaw dropping. *What happened in Mexico?*

Luke plastered on a smile as he ate up the distance between them and lifted Eva into his arms.

Owen followed suit with Samantha.

They had their happily-ever-afters. But she couldn't have hers. Not now, at least.

But would it be too late for her to find love once—*if*—she was able to shed her hard exterior and finally let someone in?

She lost her thoughts when Liam and Knox nodded *hello* before greeting Emily.

But Asher didn't say a damn thing. Maybe she didn't deserve anything after their last conversation.

Luke lowered Eva to the ground and kissed her before murmuring, "Happy Valentine's Day, babe."

"You made it just in time." Eva kissed him again.

Luke threaded his fingers through Eva's long blonde wig. "Interesting look," he said with a smile.

Eva diverted her attention to Asher. "It looks like Jessica and I aren't the only ones with new hairdos." She crossed her arms and eyed Asher who was still quiet. "What happened to your hair?"

Knox's lips split into a grin. "He lost a bet." He wrapped a hand over Asher's shoulder. "And a bet is a bet."

You really did it. Asher had chopped off his hair. Tapered on the sides and a little longer, almost spiky, on the top. Similar to Owen's, only darker. His beard trimmed as well.

"What kind of bet?" Samantha asked as they shifted toward a bar top table farther away from the DJ and the flow of traffic.

Jessica peered around the club, searching to see if Sarah had already left. When she didn't see her, her gaze landed back on Asher.

On the *new* Asher. Hell, he looked good no matter what.

"It was about—" Liam cut himself off and coughed into a closed fist when his gaze flitted to Emily. "Anyway." He raised his brows. "Luke and Owen rounded us up when they discovered you ladies had gone out for a night on the town."

"I didn't expect you to be out tonight, though." Luke observed his sister, but his flicker of concern dissipated when Eva tugged at his arm, as if warning him to let it go.

"Whose phone did you track?" Jessica asked her brother.

"Eva's." Luke arched a brow and his lips tightened as he observed Jessica, as if somehow knowing Eva spilled the truth about the *I miss you* text.

But what if Eva hadn't told her?

Maybe she wouldn't feel so torn looking at Asher right now. And her stomach wouldn't hurt so damn much. It'd make keeping him at arm's length easier, at least.

Liam rubbed his palms together and came in for the save. "Well, we're here. Why don't we celebrate now?"

"Celebrate? Does that mean everything went as planned?" Jessica's brow rose as she tried to discreetly gather intel about their recon op for the president.

"It went well," Liam answered, but the man was staring directly at Emily as if she were the only one in the club.

Great. Jessica sidestepped her friends to get closer to Liam. She pressed a hand to his chest so she could whisper in his ear. "Don't even think about taking her to your hotel tonight. Understood?"

From what Samantha had said a few months back, Emily had shit luck when it came to men, and the last thing she needed was Ladies-Man-Liam hurting her with his Aussie charm and disappearing act in the morning.

Liam surrendered his palms but looked back at Emily . . . who was now being pulled away by Knox.

Jessica stifled a groan.

"I'll give Knox the speech," Samantha said with a smile, reading her thoughts. She grabbed Owen's hand, and they followed Knox and Emily out onto the dance floor.

"Do you want to stay, or finish tonight just the two of us?" Luke asked Eva, holding her by the hips.

"Hmm. It was supposed to be ladies' night."

"No, you two should go," Jessica said.

"I don't want to leave you," Eva replied.

"I'll make sure she gets home okay," Liam said before Jessica had a chance to speak.

"No one needs to babysit me." She patted her wig, ensuring it was still secure. For a split second, she'd forgotten why she was wearing it.

Luke let go of Eva and motioned Jessica away from the remaining crew. "How are you?"

She found his eyes. "Nothing yet from Egon."

"That's not what I was asking."

"Well, that's what matters right now."

Luke squared a hand over her shoulder. "Jessica," he hissed. "Talk to me."

She swirled a finger in the air and looked around. "Here?" She brought her hand to her ear now for dramatic emphasis. "I can barely hear anything. Why don't we have a heart-to-heart at the office in the morning?" *Or maybe never.*

"Will you be training with Asher before work?" He lowered his hand.

"I don't know." At least her nightmares hadn't returned, even with him gone. But she wasn't sure if Asher would want to train with her after how she'd treated him before Mexico when she'd stabbed him with her finely pointed ice-like words.

Luke took a hard breath. "Let Liam take you home when you're ready. Okay?"

"Sure." She wasn't in the mood to argue again.

She waited for Eva and Luke to leave, gathered her thoughts, and then returned to the table where Liam and Asher were standing.

Liam drummed his fingers on the table. "Can I at least have one dance with her?" He jerked his thumb in the direction of Emily on the dance floor with Knox. "I should save her from him. The guy can do a lot of things, but dancing isn't one of them."

She couldn't help but smile. "Fine. But be good."

"Will do." He winked and darted off.

Shit—and now she was alone with Asher.

"How are you?" Low. Deep. Hard as a fucking rock. His voice, at least.

"So, you speak? I was beginning to wonder if you'd lost your voice along with your hair." She stood opposite the table from him, hoping the bit of distance would help ease the tension that was stretching her chest like a rubber band on the verge of snapping.

"Funny," he grumbled and lifted his hand to smooth it over his head. He probably missed his hair.

"I can't believe you cut it." In the years they'd worked together, she'd never seen him with short hair.

"Needed a change, anyway," he said without looking at her. "You didn't answer me, though."

She rolled her tongue over her teeth as she deliberated what to say. "Eva made me come here. I, uh, didn't want to." *And I haven't had enough to drink to deal with this moment.* She thought about telling him about seeing Sarah, but what if that only added fuel to an already lit fire?

His dad, she suddenly remembered. Asher probably

didn't want to be there, either. Of course, how much did Sarah still know about her brother? Maybe he'd hated Valentine's Day when he was younger, but surely, he didn't still despise the holiday.

Then again, from what she could remember they were always on ops around this time of year, so he wouldn't have been able to go out on a date with someone, anyway.

"I'm sorry." The unexpected words came out like a short puff of air.

"For what?" He looked at her again, his eyes thinning.

Cue the discomfort. Magnify it by ten.

Deep breath in. And then out.

"For how I treated you in my office. You were just looking out for me, and I'm a bit on edge right now."

"Understandable."

A bluster of nerves traveled up her spine at the gruff texture of his tone. Without thinking, she circled the table and lifted her hand to his chest. The memory of his text seared her mind.

He wrapped a hand over her wrist as if he were going to remove her hand, but when her eyes journeyed to his, she saw a hard depth to his browns.

"Do you want to dance?" she asked, not sure what the hell she was doing right now.

"You think that's a good idea?" His brow furrowed.

"Probably not." Her stomach turned at the idea of leaving the club without him, though. "But I'm not sure if I care right now." This brush with honesty was intoxicating, and she wanted to lean in to it, to give in to the truth. To give in to him.

He lifted his chin and glanced up at the second level of the club. A few people stood near the railing, observing the dancers below.

Without responding, he took hold of her hand and guided her through the pack of people and toward their friends.

Asher said something to Liam she couldn't hear, and then led her off the dance floor and toward the spiral staircase.

He kept his hold on her, never letting go—as if he was afraid she might run—and then they walked side by side up the flight of steps.

The upstairs was less crowded, but the music still pulsed hard, practically rattling her body.

They strode to a dimly lit area. He let go of her hand and motioned to an empty booth. "I need a drink first." She was pretty sure he'd spoken through gritted teeth, his lips barely parting with his words. He gestured for a staff member.

She settled onto the seat and smoothed her dress down.

"I'm good," she said when the cocktail server stopped by their table a beat later.

"Maker's Mark. Straight." He rubbed both his palms down his face and stared at her from across the table once the server had vanished.

An obvious unease spread across his face. She was beginning to wonder if maybe his discomfort wasn't just about her. Maybe Sarah was right about the night.

She didn't want to bring it up, though. So, she pointed a finger in the air at the change in song. "One of my favorites."

He thanked the server after she'd delivered the drink and raised the tumbler to his lips, never taking his eyes off Jessica. "I like it," he said before taking a swig.

"You like rock music, I thought."

"Yeah, well, this house techno stuff is decent."

"'House techno stuff'?" She smiled as he gulped down more of his drink, not even flinching from the straight liquor. "So, what really happened with the bet?"

He set his drink down and rested his forearms on the

table, and she focused on his hands. The knuckles still recovering from the damage he'd done last week at the fight club.

"We were at a nightclub in Mexico City, keeping tabs on a courier for the cartel, and Knox made a bet."

"Yeah, I got that part. What kind of bet?" She leaned back and observed him.

He scratched at his beard. "There was a woman."

Her stomach didn't just drop at his words.

It was a freefall. And no chute. Wind whooshed through her hair, and she was going to crumple upon contact with the ground.

She reached across the table and took a hard swallow of his drink, nearly choking on it.

A smile crossed his lips, the first of the evening. "You okay, Peaches?"

A fluttering sensation blew through her chest. Unwelcome thoughts and feelings raining down over her. A hard case of jealousy. "I'm fine." She pushed the drink back to him. "That's, uh, strong."

"Mm-hm." He drained the glass.

"Since when do you mix business with pleasure on an op?" She forced the words out as steadily as possible, but she wondered if he could see the beats of her heart pumping relentlessly.

He cocked his head to the side. "I don't."

"Well, what happened?"

"Does it matter?"

Yes. No. Damned if she knew what to say. "Why'd you even take his bet?"

"I didn't, which was the problem."

"I don't follow." She straightened a touch and rested her folded arms in front of her on the table.

"He was trying to prove a point, Jessica." The way he said her name sent goose bumps scattering across her skin. "I'd rather cut my hair than entertain a bet involving hitting on some woman in a club."

Her brows drew inward. "So, the forfeit cost you your hair?" She rolled her tongue over her lips, wetting them. "Not very fair of him."

"Like I said, maybe I needed a change." He roped a hand around the back of his neck and looked away from her.

"Well, you had your drink. Do you still want to dance?" She shifted off the seat and stood, and his eyes dropped to her legs.

The mother of all breaths left his lips as he rose in his black boots. "You seem better. *Are* you better?" He didn't touch her yet, though. A foot of space still separated them.

"I don't know what I am," she answered honestly as she stared deep into his eyes, losing herself. Her thoughts. Even the roadblocks between them.

Gone. Gone. Gone.

He kept his eyes on her as if getting a read, and then he did it—he closed the gap. He braced his hands on her hips, and her palms landed on his hard chest.

Her lip quivered as she thought about his text before Egon had taken her in Berlin. The text she'd never had a chance to see.

"Asher, I, uh." She had to fight like hell to get the words out, but a touch of relief raced through her body when she'd managed, "I missed you while you were gone, and I . . ." Her throat thickened. "Be with me tonight." A statement. Not a question.

His head didn't jerk back like she expected. But there was definite surprise in his eyes. Conflict, too. She didn't blame him after their last conversation at her office, but he asked, "*Only* for tonight?"

He wanted more, but would she ever be capable of *more*?

"Could we start with tonight and see where—" His mouth stole her words, and his hands swooped from her hips to her face, holding her in place as his tongue twined with hers.

She groaned against his lips, readying for him hard and fast.

Her body hummed to life, chucking every last negative thought out of her head as she clung to ideas of what was to come.

"Fuuck," he murmured against her lips before pulling away. "We need to get out of here."

She found his eyes, his hands still on her face. "I know all of the exits," she said breathlessly, still reeling from the kiss.

He nodded but pressed his mouth to hers again, hungry for more.

He had her backing up to one of the columns, and he pinned her to it, caging her with his body, not giving a damn who was around. "This dress," he rasped as his hand traveled up her thigh and roamed over her flesh.

"I thought we were leaving," she said with a light laugh when his mouth found her neck and planted sucking kisses there.

"We are. I just need—" He pulled away, his chest rising and falling. His eyes narrowed on hers. The conflict gone now. "I need you," he whispered.

CHAPTER TWENTY-TWO

HE'D RESTRAINED HIMSELF FOR YEARS, SO WHY THE HELL DID a ten-minute ride in the back of an Uber feel like hell on fucking earth?

His gaze skated down her long legs to her red heels, and when his eyes settled back on her face, he saw what he was feeling in her blue irises—years and years of pent-up lust.

She kept quiet, though, her lip between her teeth.

This wouldn't be their first rodeo. But after six years, it sure as hell felt like it.

His cock was so hard it bulged through his pants, and now that he caught her eye-fucking it, his entire body grew tenser than he'd thought possible.

"We're here," the driver said, interrupting thoughts of what he planned to do to her.

Years of fantasies would be coming true.

Was she ready after what had happened to her, though? And was he prepared for what he knew would happen after their time between the sheets? Because it would happen, wouldn't it? She'd close herself off to him. It was inevitable.

He needed to get rid of the doubt trying to infiltrate his defenses. To hell with the consequences.

"You're having second thoughts?" she asked a few minutes later when they stepped inside the elevator.

His hands transformed to fists at his sides as he tried to curtail his desire to take her into his arms and fuck her against the wall right then and there. He'd already come close at the club.

His body was strung so damn tight.

When he was in the cage and about to fight, the adrenaline would burst through his veins, and he'd always feel such an incredible rush.

That rush had nothing on this moment.

A moment he was minutes away from having.

But . . . *damn it*. Doubt settled inside him again like a frustrating checkmate. "Are you sure?"

She stepped in front of him, eliminating the last bit of distance between them. His heart was fast beneath her palm now resting on his chest. "Don't second-guess this, okay? Not tonight." A blonde brow arched.

And he couldn't resist.

He lowered his head, captured her bottom lip, and sucked it. Cherry-flavored gloss. Of course, Cherry.

"Eh-hem."

He hadn't even heard the doors part, but when Jessica staggered back to face whoever was standing outside the elevator, he spotted an old woman with a dog clutched beneath her armpit.

"Oh. Hi, Mrs. Jacobs." Jessica's cheeks bloomed as red as her heels. He'd never taken her as one to get embarrassed, but maybe they were in unchartered territory. He was about to go to her place to have mind-blowing sex, after all.

"Why' is your hair black?" the woman asked. Her gaze

moved straight to Asher's tented pants, and it had him dropping his arms in front of him. He didn't want to give her a heart attack.

"Valentine's Day costume party." She stole a glimpse at Asher from over her shoulder and motioned toward the open doors with a slight tilt of the head. "Have a good night," she told Mrs. Jacobs, and they maneuvered out of the elevator and down the hall as if they had to get cover from a sniper on overwatch.

"Talk about timing," she said with a laugh while digging into her purse.

He wrapped a hand over her shoulder as she fidgeted with her key in the knob, and he brought his nose to the back of her head where her long black wig rested in soft waves atop her wool coat. He shifted the locks to the side with his free hand and brought his mouth near her ear.

At the sound of her groan, he dropped his hand to her hip and pulled her tight against him, his hard length pressing into her.

"You want to take me in the hall, huh?" she breathed over her shoulder.

"I want you everywhere," he answered, maybe more honestly than he'd intended. But hell, after three years of back-and-forth, he just wanted to strip away the lies and deliver the truth.

"Mm, me, too." Her voice was like silk gliding over his skin, and it had his balls tightening.

She pressed the door inward a moment later, and she pivoted to face him. "I'm going to get naked now." She walked backward into her apartment with her eyes on him.

He lost her gaze only for a second to shut and lock the door.

Her purse hit the floor. Jacket next.

She removed her black wig and then her hairpins, unleashing her mass of blonde hair.

He groaned as he watched her, doing his best not to charge at her like the beast he was.

She reached for the zipper at the front of her dress and slowly lowered it and revealed a strapless black bra that barely contained the swell of her flesh.

He kicked off his boots and swallowed as she shimmied out of the dress and toed it out of her way.

Black bra. A black lacey thong. And red heels.

A vision.

And all his tonight.

"Keep the rest on," he said like a rough command, like he'd swallowed sandpaper.

He removed his jacket and shirt and watched as her gaze dropped to his chest.

"You're stunning." He practically breathed the words as he unbuckled his belt and removed everything but his boxers.

"How much do you want me?" Her long lashes lifted, and her blue eyes stole his breath.

"More than you can possibly know." In two steps, he closed the distance between them and lifted her into his arms.

She arched forward, pressing her body tight to his, and held onto him as he peered into her eyes, never wanting to forget the moment. Because knowing Jessica, tomorrow she'd . . .

But he didn't want to think about tomorrow. Not now.

"Fuck me," she said as her eyes dropped to his mouth. "Really, really hard."

"You're going to kill me, woman." He brushed his lips over hers. Soft at first, but when their tongues met, he couldn't hang onto the fine thread of control anymore.

He set her atop the desk, which was up against the living

room wall, and she kept her ankles hooked around him, hands now atop his shoulders. "What are you doing?"

"I'm hungry," he growled out as he ran his finger along her slit over the top of her black lace.

She jerked forward, nearly scooting off the edge.

He arched a brow as he shifted her panties and touched her clit. "You're so wet for me. Aren't you, Peaches?" He gently slid his finger up and down in one stroke before stealing his touch from her.

She groaned. "Ugh. I hate you."

"I know you do." He nipped at her plump, pouty bottom lip.

She started to reach in the direction of his boxers, but he captured both her wrists and slung her arms up and around his neck. "Not yet. You've been torturing me for years." His thighs pressed to the mahogany, and she shifted even closer to him.

He lowered his eyes to her bra, and with each hard and heavy breath she took, her breasts nearly lifted out of it.

As much as he wanted to tear every strip of material off of her, to have her buck naked and quivering beneath him, he needed this to last.

He'd waited too long to rush this night, and he didn't know if it'd happen again. And so, he'd take his time. Even if it killed him.

He unwrapped her legs from around his hips and pulled her to a standing position, but only long enough to tug at the strip of lace between her legs. "This is in my way."

She stepped out of her panties, heels still on, and then he set her back onto the desk. Close to the edge.

He lowered to his knees. The hard wood was cool against his skin, just what he needed. She was in the perfect position for a taste, as if the carpenter had designed her desk in consideration of a six-four guy going down on a woman.

She gripped his shoulders, and he looked up at her. He could never grow tired of bowing before her, like a servant before a queen. She was in his eyes. Always would be.

He guided his hands up the inside of her legs, noting a slight tremble in her thighs as his fingertips skated closer to her smooth center. His tongue traveled along her slit this time, and a hard gasp blew from her mouth. She shoved her hand through his hair as if forgetting he'd cut it.

"We're on my desk," she cried.

He removed his mouth from her and shifted back a touch so their eyes could meet. "And?"

Her lips parted, a hazy look to her eyes now. But a slow nod followed. "We can clean it after."

A lazy smile gathered on his lips before he focused on her sensitive flesh again.

Everything inside of him hurt to be with her—he wanted her more than maybe he'd even realized until that moment.

"You're such a tease, Ash—"

"And you love it," he said before placing sucking kisses on the inside of her thighs. "Now, are you going to be a good girl and come for me?" He darted his tongue over her skin before thrusting two fingers inside of her.

She murmured something he didn't understand before asking, "What makes you think I'm a good girl?"

God, he needed to have his hands, his mouth—his everything—on her.

He shifted upright and scooped her back into his arms, and she shimmied against his body, rubbing her clit against his skin so he could feel her wetness.

"We need to get these tits free." He carried her down the hall to her bedroom.

He lowered her to her feet and kissed her hard as he worked at the clasp of her bra, and then within the space of a heartbeat, he spun her, so her back was to him.

"What are you doing?" she asked from over her shoulder.

"Enjoying the view. Give me a second." He removed his boxers and stroked himself as his gaze landed on the hard slope of her ass and journeyed down her long legs to her heels.

He was going to come just looking at this woman. It'd been a long time. And she wasn't just anyone. No, she was the fucking *one.* If only he could get her to see that.

"God, your body is ridiculous." He wrapped his arms around her waist and pulled her against his chest, enjoying the warmth of her.

Her hands traveled over his arms like a hug when his palms landed on her full breasts. Her nipples were hard as he massaged and gripped her tender flesh.

"You're certainly taking your time. You have more self-control than I do."

Her hips rotated, and the circular motions against his cock had him closing his eyes and taking a much-needed breath. Because, in reality, he needed to fight for control.

"I want to look at you," she said, a heady desire winging through her words.

He stepped back, following her command, and she faced him.

The moment her eyes roamed over his body before settling on his face, he knew he was done for. There was a damn Fourth of July party in his chest. Emotion caught in his voice when he said, "You don't know how long I've been waiting for this."

A smile touched her lips as she reached for his chest, smoothing a palm down the center.

He gathered her in his arms, relinquishing the control he'd fought for.

Her smile, of all things, was his undoing.

Her breasts smashed against his chest, and she held the back of his neck as he kissed her, his hands firmly positioned on her ass cheeks. "Peaches," he whispered against her lips. "Mine," he grunted, pretty sure he sounded like a caveman, but fuck if he cared.

He carried her to the bed a moment later and lightly tossed her onto it.

She propped her hand behind her head, staring at him as if cataloging every inch.

"Condoms?" He hadn't expected this, and so, he hadn't come prepared.

"Nightstand. They've been collecting dust."

He knelt onto the bed and braced himself over her. "Oh yeah? And why is that?"

The back of her hand touched his cheek. "I think you know," she softly said and reached between his thighs to hold his hard length.

It had him clenching his jaw, his back teeth nearly grinding against each other. "Show me how you got yourself off when you were thinking about me." He arched a brow as he raked his gaze over her breasts before finding her eyes again.

"Oh?" She squeezed harder, her nails slightly buried in his skin. "Are you that confident that—"

He thought about their time at the gym before Mexico, when he was close to blowing his load while they'd worked out. "Hell yes."

She cracked another smile. "I used my hand instead of hardware, and I pretended it was you touching me."

"Show me." He shifted back to his knees, forcing her to lose her grip.

He inwardly groaned at the loss, but when her fingertips burned a trail down her body to her already wet center, the blood rushed south, and his cock swelled.

She never let go of his eyes as she touched herself. "I want it to be you," she half-cried, arching her back as if she'd go crazy without him. "I need you." Her voice deepened. "I need you, Asher Hayes."

The truth. Finally.

Her words had him lowering himself on top of her, and he sought entrance between her thighs. He stroked her and guided his fingers inside of her as they kissed.

She didn't need warming up. She was soaked. Ready.

And he couldn't wait any longer.

He retrieved a foil wrapper and rolled the condom on. "How do you want me?" he asked through gritted teeth, staring deep into her eyes.

"With you on top." She wet her lips. "For the first time," she added with a smile, and he positioned his tip at her center.

With their eyes connected, he hooked her leg up to rest over his arm as he braced himself above her. He sank inside of her and bit back a growl as her back arched off the bed at the movement.

He wanted to be as deep and close to her as possible. So close maybe they'd never come apart.

He took slow and deep breaths as he moved, trying to comprehend the onslaught of emotions battering him as she took everything he gave.

He slid almost all the way out before pushing the crown of his shaft back in harder than before, and she squeezed her pussy tight around him.

The feel of her.

The warmth.

She was perfect.

And all his.

He kissed her with a wild hunger, and his entire body blazed hot as if a trail of fire burned down his spine.

His cock pulsed inside of her, and she shifted her mouth from his to release a moan deep from her lungs.

She clung to him, her fingertips digging into his skin as if hanging on for dear life.

But when he lifted his head and found her eyes closed, it had his heart stammering. His body slowing down.

"Look at me," he said gruffly. "Please," he added, because damn it, he needed to see her. To know she felt the same.

He noted the movement in her throat as she swallowed, and her eyelashes fluttered open, revealing a sheen to her blue eyes. Emotion she'd been hiding.

The sight had him moving harder and faster. Maybe a little too rough as his need for her grabbed hold of him like never before.

God, he'd never wanted anyone so much in his life, and he knew he never would.

Her. Always her.

"I'm going to come," she whisper-yelled. "I can't hang on any longer."

He fought the desire to explode inside of her as she trembled beneath him, holding on tight to his frame.

Her blue irises glossed over, and then her fingertips slipped from his shoulders as she climaxed. She relaxed onto the bed and took deep breaths.

He slanted his lips over hers and stole her breath—he wanted to become the very air she breathed.

Everything inside of him grew calm the moment he came. Well, everything except the heavy beats of his heart.

"Jessica." Her name skated from his mouth like a forbidden whisper.

"Yes?" she whispered.

"I missed you, too."

CHAPTER TWENTY-THREE

THE MUSCLED PLANES OF HIS CHEST WERE HARD BENEATH HER fingertips as she rode him.

She gave him everything she had. Every moment. Thought. Feeling.

He made her feel complete in a way she didn't know was possible.

As she moved on top of him, he held her gaze, possessing her with his heated stare.

Her eyes. Her body. Her soul. He owned it all at that moment.

The tension that had built up for years exploded between them tonight like fireworks over the Hudson.

Her throat tightened with emotion as they moved together, and her heartbeat climbed while his remained slow but strong beneath her palm, giving her the energy she never knew she needed.

When Asher's gaze narrowed briefly, and his finger twirled like the blades of a helo, Jessica's lips split into a smile. She shifted off him, eager to follow his request.

He pressed up against the headboard, and she spun around

and positioned herself with her back to him, then sank onto his hardened length.

His hands smoothed over her exposed backside, and she groaned and leaned forward. "I've been dreaming about you in this position for years."

Her insides contracted and pulsed, an orgasm already impending. She squeezed as hard as she could and sighed in ecstasy when he reached around her body to touch her. His deft fingers somehow knew her trigger points. Hell, he seemed to know everything about her.

She dropped her head, and her fingertips continued to bite into his thighs—probably leaving marks—as she tried not to let loose yet.

He stretched her. Filled her completely.

And the anticipation for the climax built until she had nowhere higher to go.

He pressed his chest to her back as he held her tight while her body sputtered, and a hard, shaky tremble left her panting.

He palmed her breasts and squeezed her nipples, which were still tender since he'd spent time sucking and kissing every inch of her.

Tight in his arms, she could feel him come a moment later. She closed her eyes and waited for her breathing to calm down.

"That was incredible," she said once she finally stood to allow him to discard his condom.

What she'd give to be skin-to-skin with him, though.

At the sound of the flush from the other room, followed by the shower water turning on, she padded into the en suite.

She froze, staring at his perfectly sculpted body—like someone from the Renaissance, and since he was half-Italian it was fitting. He managed to rob her of every last breath.

Seeing him in all his naked glory in her bathroom every day was something she could get used to.

"Shower?"

"Your shower is big enough for an orgy." He propped a hand on the glass wall, and his brown eyes greedily took in the sight of her.

How had they held off for so long? Why hadn't they done this sooner?

A million different reasons popped into her head, but when she stepped into his embrace inside the shower a moment later, and he pinned her to the wall, she forgot every last one of them.

* * *

"Don't stop. Don't stop. Don't—" Her body was on the verge of convulsing. "Don't . . . fucking . . . stop." She pressed her fingertips to his head as he went down on her.

Her legs were going to wilt like flower stems in a storm, and he'd have to carry her to the office. That'd be some shock and awe for the team.

"Mm. I love when you talk dirty to me." He shifted to rest alongside her. "Some of the things you said to me."

Yeah, she'd never been a saint. But with Asher, it'd felt right. Everything with him was utterly perfect.

Except for the fact they worked together.

And he was one of Luke's best friends.

And he was also one of *her* best friends.

She caught him stroking his cock. The man was a machine. But was she surprised? Back at the base six years ago they'd gone crazy, too.

Tonight had been different, though. There was a

friendship and trust between them that hadn't existed six years ago.

"There's something I didn't tell you last night," she said a beat later, and it had him releasing his hold of his shaft and turning on his side to better view her.

"What is it?"

"I, uh, saw Sarah and Angelo at the club. They left right before you and the team showed up."

He shifted to his back and peered skyward.

"She told me about your dad and Valentine's Day."

He gripped the bridge of his nose and closed his eyes. "You didn't know?"

"I never looked too deep into the details. I didn't think it was my place." She reached for the crumpled comforter at the bottom of the bed and pulled it up, feeling the need for a shield.

"If only I'd had an upstanding military dad like you and Luke." He sat upright and pulled one knee to his chest, and she sat up with him but kept the bedding clutched to her body.

She didn't know what to say, so she waited. Her heart rate climbing as she wondered if she should never have mentioned his dad.

"Times got tough for my parents when we were kids. The family restaurant was on the brink of closing. And next thing we knew, my dad was acting like Santa Claus every day. Tripping in piles of money."

"What changed?" she softly asked.

He took a sobering breath. "Angelo's dad offered my old man some side gigs to make money."

"Angelo wasn't mob, though. The crew he ran was—"

"Angelo was an angel compared to the circles our dads ran in." He raked a hand over the top of his head.

"How'd a side gig turn into murder?" Maybe she should've read the details of the case so Asher wouldn't have had to explain.

He inhaled through his nose and released the breath through barely parted lips. "Feds had an inside man on some job my dad and Angelo's father took; and the next thing we knew, they were getting pinched on Valentine's Day. My dad murdered the undercover officer. Angelo's dad went along for the ride by accessory. He claims it was an accident, but . . ."

"I'm sorry." She hooked her arm around his and rested her head against his shoulder.

"My mom married Dad's lawyer. Crazy, right?" He faked a laugh. "He wasn't anything like Pops. Did a few tours in the military when he was younger." He shifted out of her reach and maneuvered off the bed to stand. "He used his connections to help get me out of jail for that bogus assault charge, but only if I promised to serve. I owe him for getting me out of that life." He looked her straight in the eyes. "But now Sarah's being roped into that scene, and it's hard for me to believe Angelo is walking some righteous path."

She allowed his admission to stretch between them.

Asher was opening up, doing something she wasn't capable of doing. And she felt a touch of jealousy at his ability to do it.

Why couldn't she do the same? Share her feelings.

He lifted his hand and eyed the sleeve of tattoos, then pointed to the Spartan figures holding swords and weapons on his forearm. The ink spiraled up and merged with his SEAL tattoo: a trident crossing over a lightning bolt with the head of a horse above them—representing his time on Black Squadron, the elite group he'd once been part of before joining their team.

A battle between the past and present raged on his arm.

"We got the ink after our dads were sentenced. Kind of like a promise we'd always be brothers—warriors—and not fuck up our lives like they had." He half-smiled. "Well, not as badly, I should say."

She stood. "But Angelo didn't stick to that."

He slowly nodded. "Fighting started as our way to deal with the upside-down world we were living in. But he took it to another level and started getting involved in other shit."

She took tentative steps his way. "Does fighting still help you feel in control?"

"Maybe, but I've been a good boy until—"

"Berlin," she interrupted, her stomach dropping.

"Don't blame what happened to you for my need to hit someone." He half-grinned. "But, what we did tonight is a much better alternative to release tension."

"Oh, is it?"

He reached for her and braced her hips and held her eyes. "Absolutely."

And as much as she wanted to switch the conversation back to sex—or actually have it, again—she needed to tell him one more thing. "You should know I looked into Angelo while you were in Mexico."

"What?"

A puff of air left her lips. "I made some calls."

"Why?" His brow creased as he crossed his arms.

"Because I'm worried about you and—"

"The fighting?"

"Not just that." Her body tensed, worried he was angry at her for possibly crossing the line. "I don't want anything happening to you. But from what I can tell, Angelo told you the truth. He's trying to get his life back on track."

He blinked a few times and smoothed a hand down his jaw. "Even if that's true—"

"You still don't want him with your sister." She forced a small smile. "Brothers." *Speaking of brothers* . . .

His arms fell to his sides. "What are we telling Luke?" he asked, reading her thoughts.

"I need time to think about it."

"Yeah, sure." A touch of frustration blew through his tone, though.

"Asher." She reached for his chest. "There are still reasons why you and I—"

"Yeah, I know them." He tapped at the side of his skull. "And that's why I've been a choir boy for three years." His hands landed on his hips now. "But guess what, I don't give a fuck about the reasons anymore."

CHAPTER TWENTY-FOUR

ASHER'S JAW TENSED AS HE CHANCED A LOOK AT JESSICA. She hadn't said a word to him in hours, ever since he'd basically announced he wanted to be with her.

He had known it'd be difficult to work together after that, but he hadn't realized it'd be this fucking hard to be in the same room with her.

"How long do you think this will take?" Luke clutched the back of her desk chair and observed her computer screen as she typed.

"It'll be quicker without you breathing down my neck." She glanced at him from over her shoulder, and he surrendered his palms and stepped back.

Asher's gaze shifted to the team scattered throughout the room working, and then he returned his focus to his own screen, trying to force his thoughts off of last night and to the mission.

"I wish you had access to the decryption program you wrote for the CIA. It'd make this a lot easier," Luke grumbled.

"You want to call and ask them for it?" she asked,

sarcasm drenching her words. "The code I wrote was specific for Yasser Hadeed, but I remember it."

Asher glanced at her again to catch a slight smile gathering on her lips as she redirected her focus to her screen.

"This call has to be from Samir. Burner phone traced to Madagascar three weeks before Berlin," Knox said. "No way was Samir actually there, but he damned sure made it look like that. Decent tech skills."

"You really think five guys who used to report to his uncle would up and commit to Samir, a twenty-year-old?" Liam chimed in, his brows raised.

Asher thought back to Samir. To the kid who'd had his life torn apart by war. "It's possible he killed Ara to prove he has what it takes to lead."

"Well, it looks like the men bought in. It can't be a coincidence these Detroit guys started viewing the help wanted section of the *New York Times* a few times a day after Berlin," Liam said.

"I hate being an outsider on an op. Not knowing all the details makes my skin itch." Knox leaned back in his chair at the table and stretched his arms out in front of him.

"Same," Asher said under his breath. Especially when it all related to Jessica.

At least Wyatt had managed to clone a phone belonging to one of the guys in Detroit, so they could hopefully stay on top of this case since they couldn't get any more intel from the Feds without raising red flags.

"Let's just hope Samir's using the same code his uncle did." Luke circled the desk and edged closer to the rest of the team. "Now that we've identified which help wanted ads he wrote, we just—"

"Need to decrypt them." Jessica's words buzzed through the room, but she kept her eyes locked on her screen.

Luke pivoted to Owen. "Where are you on tracking the name associated with the help wanted ads?"

"Samir obviously set up a bogus name and account for the ad, and the IP address he used has been rerouted a million times," Owen answered. "Where the hell did Samir learn to do all of this?"

Asher stood from the table and brushed his hands down his face, wishing he could do more. Cyber wasn't his area of expertise.

"He had to learn this shit from somewhere," Owen said. "And he'd need to have picked it up fast, given that we're looking at a narrow window of time between when his brother died and when he turned into a terrorist."

"Unless he's always been like this," Knox pointed out.

"No." Jessica wet her lips and took a breath. "If only he would've left Syria with Ara."

"He knew you took her and the others out of there, right?" Knox asked.

"Yeah, because I made him the same offer." She blinked a few times. "But Samir's older brother and mom didn't want to leave, and he wouldn't go without them."

"Too bad," Knox said glibly.

Asher couldn't take his eyes off Jessica. She was too close to this case. Her lips were downturned, her breathing slow and controlled, but he could tell she was working harder than normal to keep it together. And sex last night probably hadn't helped her mood or focus.

"I think I'm done," she whispered a few seconds later. "It's not too complex. A polyalphabetic substitution cipher."

She zeroed in on her screen, tapped at a few keys, and then rolled back from her desk and eyed her computer, her gaze narrowed and focused.

Luke went behind her to monitor the progress as her

algorithm worked to identify the pattern of letters that would decrypt Samir's messages in the *New York Times*.

When she lifted her eyes to Asher a moment later, he'd swear the air in the room shifted between them. So much so, he wondered if everyone could feel it.

"There." Luke leaned in and pressed his finger to the screen. "Good work, sis." He braced a hand over her shoulder.

"You think the Feds already know about these ciphertexts?" Asher asked.

"If they're working with the CIA, they'd have access to Jessica's decryption program, but I'll reach out to someone I trust and make sure they're clued in," Luke said.

"Looks like these are just meeting spots and times. Nothing that would help us," Jessica sputtered, a tinge of annoyance in her tone.

"Which means someone has to be providing the men in Detroit with information when they convene," Luke said. "Must be a burner phone because Echo hasn't seen anyone else come and go."

"We'll try and access the mic in their phones the next time they meet," Luke said. "But if they're smart, they'll turn their phones off."

Jessica was quiet for a few moments, and Asher knew what she was thinking. "If Samir's smart enough to pull all of this off, isn't he smart enough to know the first thing the FBI would do is track his uncle's former associates?" She pressed her hands on her desk alongside the computer and glanced around at her teammates, her attention landing last on Asher.

"He didn't anticipate us showing up in Berlin. Or that you'd survive to tell anyone about him," Luke reminded her.

When she stood and crossed her arms, Luke inched a few steps away from her. Her eyes remained connected with

Asher's as if she were drawing energy, or maybe comfort, from his stare.

His arms hung heavy at his sides, his mind completely absorbed by her blue irises. "Jessica's right." He released a hard breath. "Samir reached out to the Detroit cell *before* Berlin, but he started sending the encoded messages after. He may have planned on working with them, but now he's using them as a diversion instead."

"We can't be certain of that." Luke eyed Asher. "We're making a lot of assumptions about some twenty-year-old's capabilities and thought processes."

"I'd rather overestimate him than underestimate him," Asher said, a firm grit to his tone. "It's possible he changed his plans after what happened in Berlin. Both the Feds and our men could waste time looking into Detroit if Samir decided to switch gears."

"But that would mean we have no idea where to look now," Luke said.

Jessica glanced over at her brother. "We're not saying to pull Echo back; let's just keep an open mind."

"We really need this lead with the assassin," Liam said grimly.

"We're running out of time, too," Knox commented. "My dad will be in Austria in two days."

"Maybe Egon's waiting until the last minute?" Liam asked. "I wouldn't be surprised."

"It's possible." Luke surveyed Bravo Team.

Mixing emotions with operations never ended well.

It was reason number one he knew Jessica was worried about being with him. But she worked with Luke, and since he'd decided that morning he wouldn't give up on her without a fight, he'd play that card if he had to.

"Let's regroup in a few hours. I need time to think and

reassess all of the intel." Luke knocked on the desk two times. "I want something new when we get back together."

The guy's nodded and fanned out of the room.

Liam glimpsed Asher from over the shoulder as they walked down the hall. "You good?"

Asher caught sight of Jessica disappearing into her office, and then he tipped his chin toward Liam's room, motioning to talk in private.

"I'm fine," he said once they were behind closed doors, and he fought the curl of tension wrapping tight around his spine.

"What happened with you and Jessica after the club? You took her home, and then what?" Liam dropped into a swivel chair.

"Why is it any of your damn business?" Asher drew an uncomfortable breath and let it out. "We have more pressing shit to worry about right now, don't we?"

Liam leaned back in the chair and cocked his head to the side. "It matters if there's something going on that's getting in the way of your focus."

Hadn't he given the same lecture to Owen last fall? And now, here his buddy was, doing the same damn thing for him.

"What happened with you and Emily last night?" Asher hoped to deflect.

Liam laughed. "Nothing." He shook his head. "You think I want Jessica, Eva, and Samantha killing me?" He scratched at his trimmed blond beard. "Back to you, though. There's still tension between you and Jessica. Hell, you can cut it with a knife. But it's shifted. Something changed, and I'm worried—"

"You don't know anything about Jessica or me." Asher tensed. "You don't do real."

"Not anymore, but . . ." He pinched the bridge of his nose,

a possible brush of truth nearly escaping his normally sealed lips. "Both you and Jessica are like family to me, and damn it, I'm worried that woman will break your heart." He stabbed at the air. "And don't give me shit about you not having one."

Asher almost laughed. "You're worried about me?" Maybe he was right to, though.

"I—" Liam tipped his chin toward the door, and Asher turned to see Jessica through the window about to enter. "We'll talk about this later."

Jessica opened the door, and her eyes darted between Liam and Asher. "We got a hit on the message board."

Liam jumped to his feet. "Egon?"

"Yeah, we're pretty sure it's him," she said as her eyes connected with Asher's, and a red streak crawled up the column of her throat. "It looks like we're going to Vienna."

CHAPTER TWENTY-FIVE

"Are we ever going to talk about what happened?"

Jessica pressed her palm to the scanner on the wall and waited for the doors to part before revealing a weapons cache at their safe house on the outskirts of Vienna.

"You asked to come with me, so I was hoping that meant you wanted a chance to talk."

"I had to come because you don't know the equipment I need."

Total bullshit. Of course, he'd know the tech they'd require for the op. "Jessica." He moved next to her and wrapped his hand over her arm as she reached for a pistol on the wall.

"I may be rusty at hand-to-hand combat, but at least I'm still good with a gun." She clutched the gun in her right hand and batted her lashes a few times before sweeping her gaze to him.

He let go of his hold and wrapped a hand around the nape of his neck. "Fine. You want to be stubborn and not talk about us—that's fine with me."

He shouldn't have expected anything different. The

woman was infuriating, and of course, sex would only complicate things with her. What had he expected? For her to roll out the red carpet for him?

"Should we talk about how much I disagree with you being on this op? Being this close to Egon after what he did to you?" His nostrils flared at the mere mention of the motherfucker's name.

"Let's hope it's him who answered our job request," she said after a cold beat of silence pinged off the walls in the ten-by-ten storage room.

"It will be," he said through gritted teeth, not willing to accept any outcome other than capturing the son of a bitch. They wouldn't let him get away a second time. Not on his watch.

She placed the weapon inside a duffel bag and reached for an FN SCAR assault rifle next. "This should work."

"I hate that we aren't shooting to kill," he rasped. "No way a guy like him will leak any intel, and hell, he probably knows jack shit about Samir. Just like he doesn't know anything about us hiring him for this job."

"As much as I want him dead," she briefly closed her eyes while maintaining her grip on the rifle, "we don't have orders to kill."

"We don't even have permission to be here."

But that sure as hell wouldn't stop them. With the possible old al-Nusra terrorist cell being reactivated, they couldn't bide their time and hope the Feds and CIA were handling things.

Sitting around and hoping had never been their go-to method.

Proactive. Not reactive.

She stowed the rifle, and when she was back on her feet, her hands went to her hips. "Luke deleted the text."

"What are you talking about?"

"He saw the message you sent me in Berlin just before Egon . . ." Her eyes rolled skyward as if she couldn't handle looking at him. "He didn't want me to see it, and so he deleted it. Eva told me."

"I knew he saw it, but I didn't think he'd do that." Asher turned away and rubbed at his forehead, trying to gather his thoughts.

"You knew?"

She circled him.

"Owen told me." He sighed.

She kept her eyes tight on his. "I haven't talked about what happened . . . because I think Luke's right about us."

"Right about what?" His brows pinched tight, and he did his best not to reach up and grab her by the shoulders. His arms weighed heavy at his sides as he fought the compulsion to touch her.

She wet her lips as if biding her time before saying, "It's too dangerous for there to be anything between us." She held up her palm between them when his lips parted. "I know I'm a hypocrite because I work side by side with my brother. But you're different." She lowered her head, stealing her eyes from sight. "It'd be different with you."

"What are you trying to say?" A sharp pain cut down his chest, and his lungs burned.

"You can't do what I do. You can't compartmentalize."

"Hide behind walls, you mean? Act like it's no big deal when one of our own gets hurt? Killed?" His forearms tensed. "Is that why you've become the way you have? Because you think it'll be easier to make the tough calls in the field?" His eyes widened at the realization. "If you remove emotions from the equation you think you're protecting the team. Is that it?" His hand swept over his short hair as his cheeks filled with air.

She was quiet for a moment and lightly shook her head. "You almost let the other bomb go off in the crowd in Berlin to come for me instead."

"But I didn't." He placed a hand over her shoulder, no longer able to hold back.

"That moment of indecision could've cost lives."

"You think the rest of the team wouldn't have felt the same damn way?"

"No. Maybe not even Luke."

He lowered his hand from her shoulder and cupped his mouth as he processed everything. "You're the one who ran into the compound in France last month because you got worried. Or did you forget that?"

"Because I let my emotions get the best of me!" she yelled. "And look what happened to me after Berlin." She stabbed at her chest, her voice breaking now. "I can't be with you for the same reasons you can't be with me. We'll only get each other killed—or worse, innocent people could die. We have to protect the team. The missions."

She swiveled around out of view, offering her back.

"Jessica." He repositioned himself in front of her, and she lowered her hand to expose streaks of liquid sliding down her cheeks. His thumb smoothed over her skin. "There has to be another way."

She swirled her finger in the air. "This is the problem. Do you not see it?"

"See what?" he asked, his voice straining.

"We're in the middle of an op, and we're in a weapons room talking about feelings." She wiped the tears from her face and backed up, bumping into the duffel bag behind her. "The loss of focus is dangerous."

"It doesn't have to be like that."

She remained quiet, allowing his thoughts to diverge into multiple directions. "We had sex," she began, "but there can't be more than that between us. I'm sorry." Her eyes dropped closed before she covered her face with both hands.

God, was she right? Was it truly impossible for them to be together?

He'd had only two thoughts since Valentine's Day: revenge for what had happened to Jessica and *being* with Jessica.

Never before her had he believed he'd lose his mind over a woman. Lose his focus.

But he was on an unsanctioned op, and all he could worry about was the woman standing before him. *What's happened to me?*

He scrubbed his hand over his beard. "You're right." His tone inched into icier territory.

"I am?" An unusual touch of disbelief, like a soft echo, reverberated in her tone.

"Yeah," he mouthed.

They had a job to complete, and he needed to get his shit together.

"Asher."

"What?" he seethed, unable to stop the frosty bite to his words.

"I'm worried you'll start fighting again." Her lip planted between her teeth for a second. "You know, to release tension."

Her words surprised him, and he directed his focus back to her. Back to her pouty pink lips. *Damn you.* "I only know of two ways to handle my stress. Fighting." He paused. "And fucking."

Her bra was too thin because he could see her nipples pressing against the fabric of her long-sleeved black shirt.

"It's not my call, of course, but I'd honestly rather you do the second option than go back to that fight club when we're in New York."

He edged closer to her, eating up the space between them. "You want me hooking up with other people?" He hadn't gone near anyone in . . . hell, he'd forgotten how long it'd been.

"No, I didn't say that." Her fingers touched the column of her throat.

"What are you saying then?" He tilted his head, observing the pulse at the side of her neck.

"What if we used each other for sex?" A tremble swept through her tone. "You know, release tension. But keep it strictly about sex. No emotions."

"You really think we can keep emotions out of it?" He stepped closer and gently gripped her biceps. "You think some screwing-only rule will keep things normal while we work?" A moment later, he pressed his mouth to hers, and she mewled against his lips.

A chisel.

Axe.

Hammer.

The woman didn't need jack shit to chip away at his heart. She already had it. Owned it.

He pulled back but didn't release his hold of her, and she stared at him as she took quick breaths.

"Tell me, Jessica. Tell me how the hell we're supposed to leave emotions out?" He arched a brow and waited for her to find the words. "If you think you can do it, then maybe your heart is made of ice."

She shirked free of his grasp and pressed the back of her hand to her mouth. "Maybe it is."

He shook his head when she turned away from him. "And maybe you're a better liar than I realized."

* * *

"ARE YOU READY FOR THIS REUNION WITH YOUR OLD MAN later?" Liam knelt in front of a black duffel bag and sifted through some of the supplies Asher had provided him once back at the hotel.

"I'd rather take a bullet." Knox turned away from the window in the hotel room overlooking the city and faced the rest of Bravo. "But to be clear," he began with a smile, "I'm counting on you not to let that happen. I can't exactly patch myself up."

Liam winked. "Hopefully, I still remember my training."

"And hopefully, it's Egon waiting in the wings to take the shot," Owen said. "There will already be EOD guys and dogs on location to clear the area before your dad begins his speech."

"Since there's so much security," Knox began, "I think we managed to convince Egon not to use explosives for this job."

"Let's hope so." Owen looked over at Asher. "Luke and I will comb the area, just in case."

"And I'll take the second tower for overwatch." Asher tucked his hands into his pockets and eyed Knox. "If Liam can't get the shot, I've got your back."

Knox nodded.

"How hard was it to convince your dad to bring us along for extra protection?" Jessica asked, looking up from her computer as she sat on the bed with it on her lap.

Her long, denim-clad legs were stretched out in front of

her, her back was to the headboard, and her lips now in a hard line. A million thoughts probably raced through her beautiful brain.

She'd switched to business the moment they'd packed up their SUV and headed to the hotel, as if their sex-with-no-strings discussion had never happened.

He couldn't forget it, though.

And as much as he'd wanted to agree to her ludicrous idea, he knew it'd only make things worse for both of them, whether she'd admit it or not.

"Dad was just happy I'm coming," he said. "He wasn't about to say *no* to me bringing you guys as security and risk me backing out."

"You know POTUS must know we're up to something," Liam said with a smile.

"Yeah, well, since Knox's dad is contemplating making a play for president in the next election, he's not about to intervene," Owen remarked. "And by the way, if your dad gets elected, what the hell does that mean for you?"

President Rydell was coming up to the end of his eight years soon—but Knox's dad as president? That'd be some crazy shit.

"I don't even want to think about it." Knox's palm smoothed over his clean-shaven jaw.

"Yeah, well, it's a bridge we may have to cross someday." Luke rolled up the blueprints and patted them against his thigh. "There's a chance come 2021 we'll all be out of a job if the new president doesn't keep things rolling."

"And if Rydell finds out we're still pursuing Samir—"

"We could be toast even sooner," Liam finished for Owen.

There were way too many things to think about. And

Jessica had been right about one thing: he needed to focus. He had to protect his team out in the field.

Asher crouched in front of the supply bag and retrieved his rifle. His eyes caught Jessica's as he rose to his feet, but he forced his attention away from her.

"Let's run through all the scenarios. I don't want Egon slipping away, and more importantly, I don't want Knox getting shot." Luke moved to the center of the room. "Four hours from now, we're going to nail this son of a bitch."

CHAPTER TWENTY-SIX

"Bravo One, what's your position?" From inside the van, Jessica eyed both laptops in front of her, monitoring all of the feeds, but she'd lost visual on her brother.

Before Luke could answer, he appeared back in her line of sight.

"Bravo One, cancel that. Position confirmed." Jessica switched screens and found Bravo Two—Owen—before confirming Knox's location as he moved through the crowd with his father.

God, that had to be an awkward homecoming. Knox hated the political life, but he'd taken one for the team, and she was grateful. Now, they just had to ensure he didn't take a bullet, too.

She wished she could get eyes on Bravo Three and Four, but Asher and Liam were out of sight and on overwatch.

There were only a few locations where Egon would be able to wait in the wings for the shot, and Bravo Three and Four had them covered from their vantage points.

They couldn't risk scaring Egon off, so they had to wait

until he showed himself—even if that left them with mere seconds before Egon could fire a kill round at Knox.

Beneath Knox's blazer was a bulletproof vest, but that wouldn't do anything to save him from a head shot.

"Bravo Four, any signs of the target?" She shoved the locks of her long black wig to her back and studied the laptop.

"Nothing yet," Liam responded.

"Bravo Three, anything?" she asked.

"No visual contact," Asher said, his voice gritty and hard. "Copy?"

The man was angry at her, and maybe it'd been piss-poor timing to lay the truth between them that morning, but he'd insisted on the conversation, and so . . .

How could he not see the danger a relationship between them could pose to missions, though?

And yet, why did her stomach hurt so bad right now when she thought of their talk? Why did everything inside of her hurt, in fact?

Sex with no strings. Sure.

Maybe she was losing her mind. Because when he'd kissed her that morning she'd never wanted him to stop. Sex would be a gateway to more, and she'd been blinded by desire to make such an offer.

"That's a good copy, Bravo Three," she finally answered, blinking her thoughts back to focus.

"I think I have visual confirmation of the target," Liam said a second later, and the beats of her heart escalated.

"Bravo Four, what do you mean by you 'think'?" Luke asked before she could.

"I have movement in tower three, but I can't confirm if it's our guy," Liam answered.

"Four, hold your position until confirmation," Luke ordered.

"Shit." It was Asher. "I think he knows we're here. He's on the move. I'm going after him."

"Wait," Jessica yelled, worried about an on-foot chase in the midst of a political gathering—in a foreign country, no less. And, more importantly, something could happen to Asher.

She scanned the cameras, but she didn't have a clear view of tower three or Asher.

"No time. I'll lose him," he responded, his breathing labored as he spoke, already in pursuit.

"One, do you copy?" she asked. "This could be a trap. He likes to distract and deflect."

"Copy, T—" Luke's words were cut off when a loud boom roared, and the van shook like an earthquake had erupted beneath her feet.

She checked the cameras. The crowd started to scatter just as the alarms sounded. But there was no sign of anything on screen.

"This is One. The alarms are going off. Sounds like an explosion. What happened?"

"Shit. I don't know." She grabbed her pistol and tore out of the van, finding the mass of people flooding through the arena's exit.

Her gaze fell upon a burning car down the street. It was outside of the security search perimeter, but close enough to set off alarms.

She pressed her hand to her ear. "Bravo Three, do you copy?"

Nothing.

"This is Bravo Four. From my vantage point, it appears the target set off a car bomb to get the crowd to run. A backup

229

plan for an escape," Liam said over the line. "Bravo Three was still in pursuit of the target last I saw. Copy, TOC?"

"Copy." Relief settled in her chest. "You have eyes on Bravo Three? He's not coming in over comms." She stowed her firearm before anyone could spot it.

"I lost visual on Bravo Three," Liam said, and her lungs burned.

"Bravo Three, come in," she tried again. "Do you copy?" She caught sight of Luke, Owen, and Knox exiting the arena on fast approach.

They split three different ways with Luke heading for her.

"You okay?" he asked, weapon now stowed.

"No. We can't lose him," she whispered, her mouth going bone-dry.

"Asher can handle himself. Don't worry," he said.

"But will he bring us Egon back alive?"

CHAPTER TWENTY-SEVEN

"How are you holding up?" Owen circled the desk where Jessica sat.

She stared at her computer, the images of the shooter becoming blurry before her unblinking gaze.

There was nothing left of Egon's face. Asher had basically blown his head off.

And yet, she couldn't look away.

This man had killed her friend. Tortured her.

Her stomach didn't roil at the sight. Nausea didn't bubble in the back of her throat.

No, she felt . . . nothing.

Numb.

"I'm good," she whispered when she realized she hadn't spoken yet.

"You sure?" Owen asked.

"Um, yeah, I'm fine." She swiveled in her desk chair to face the room, finding Asher removing his vest, blood splattered on his clothes. Thankfully, it wasn't his blood. "You really didn't have a choice to kill him, huh?"

"He grabbed a hostage, Jessica." Asher glared at her,

disappointment toward her suspicions raging in his eyes. "I had to take the head shot."

She lightly nodded. "Yeah, I'm sorry. If an innocent died because of us . . ." Too many people had died already. "Well, I uploaded the DNA sample into the system to double-check that it was him," she said as Luke exited the en suite bathroom, freshly changed.

"Good," Asher said. "But I promise, it was the son of a bitch."

"Did you jailbreak his phone yet?" Luke strode between Jessica and Asher, as if attempting to cut the tension that had just slammed through the room.

"I've only had five minutes with it."

He smiled. "Exactly. You should be done already."

"And I am." She grabbed the phone off the desk and tossed it to him. "Last GPS location—a home outside Salzburg. Looks pretty secluded, too."

"Did you check satellite cams already?" Luke arched a brow.

"Yeah, since the jailbreak took all of sixty seconds." She stood.

"Salzburg isn't far. As soon as Max takes the body off our hands we'll head out," Luke said.

The body. Bravo had hidden Egon's dead body until their German friend could arrive. "You scanned his palm?" she asked Asher. "In case we need it to get into his home?"

"Of course." He removed his tee, and he stood in only cargo pants and boots. Being shirtless in front of her wasn't a first, even with the team present, but now that they'd slept together again . . . she could feel the heat rise in her neck and into her cheeks at the sight. Even if she shouldn't be thinking about him sexually, her body wasn't getting the memo.

"What's Max's ETA?" She refaced the team, thankful Asher was pulling on a clean shirt.

Luke checked his watch. "An hour."

"So, he'll take the credit for the kill, but what about the hostage? Will he be a problem?" She crossed her arms and studied the team.

Knox, Liam, and Owen were packing up everything from the room, and Asher now stood alongside Luke, a few feet away from her.

"We'll be fine," Asher said, dark brown eyes thinning. This wasn't their first time being exposed in the field like this, and as long as POTUS didn't shut them down, it wouldn't be their last.

"How's your dad?" she asked Knox.

He finished zipping a duffel bag and straightened, hands going to his hips, a slight tilt to his head. "Fine. I told him if he plans on running for president he'd better get used to shit like this."

"Hoping to deter him?" Asher asked.

"You blame me?" Knox asked as Luke's phone began ringing.

"Wyatt's calling," he announced.

"He must have something." Her eyes met Asher's, and everything inside of her tensed.

He could deliver so many thoughts and provoke so many emotions with a simple look, even at a time like this.

Their talk—and kiss—buzzed around in her mind.

Luke placed the call on speaker. "What do you have?"

"They got a new message and hopped into a van twenty minutes ago. I accessed their GPS, and it's a match to the address in the ciphertext Samir sent them. They're heading to New York City," Wyatt said.

"Up until now, Samir only used those messages for

meeting times." Jessica dropped into her chair and flipped open her laptop.

"What are you thinking?" Luke asked. "This is a diversion?"

She stared at her screen, trying to get the wheels of her mind to work again.

Before she could respond, Luke said, "Text me the address. I'll send some guys from the company to check out the building."

"It's a hotel in the Bronx," Wyatt answered. "They reserved two rooms. No aliases used."

The room was quiet for a moment, the team collectively coming to their own opinions on the matter.

"I'm with Jessica," Asher said. "This is a diversion."

They were a good team. The two of them.

She cleared her throat and attempted to think again. To focus.

"They may try and lose the Feds," Asher said. "The GPS address could be bogus."

"Well, we'll stay on them," Wyatt responded.

Jessica's lips pursed in thought as an idea rolled around in her mind. "Maybe Samir's reaching out to these guys in another way. The newspaper messages are for the Feds, but they're getting their signals as to what to do from another source. Or there are more than five guys. Another contact somewhere?"

"We haven't found anything else out of the ordinary aside from what we've provided you," Wyatt responded.

"So look for something that wouldn't raise flags," Asher commented.

She could feel him standing close behind her now. She could *always* feel him whenever he was near—the same tingling sensation would move up her spine like a warm whisper.

"He's right." Jessica nodded and worked at her laptop. "Company emails. Texts with friends and family. Samir could be sending messages under the guise of someone they're in regular contact with, which the Feds wouldn't pay attention to. Could've used a classic substitution cipher."

"Got it. I'll see what I can do on the drive," Wyatt answered.

"Keep me informed," Luke said. "Asher took out Egon; we've got an address for him. Bravo will be heading to Salzburg in an hour."

CHAPTER TWENTY-EIGHT

"Well, the guy was certifiable." Liam handed Jessica a cup of coffee in the hotel suite in Salzburg, Austria.

"What'd you expect from an assassin?" She took a sip of the drink and set it on the nightstand next to her, directing her focus back to the laptop.

"I didn't think he'd rig his place with so many damn explosives." Liam dropped onto the bed next to where she was stretched out, working.

They were alone in the room right now, and she was grateful for a reprieve from Asher. "For a guy who likes to cover his kills with explosions—" She dropped her words and closed her eyes, but at the feel of Liam's hand resting over hers, she drew in a ragged breath and peered over at him.

He scooted a hair closer and squeezed her hand. "Is it too soon for you to be back? Especially on this particular op?"

Her gaze veered to his green eyes, a touch of blue in the outer rim. "I'm—"

"Fine." He squinted one eye. "Heard that before."

"Well, that's because it's true." Her hand slipped free of his, but her throat thickened at the lie.

"He's crazy about ya, you know?"

"What? Who?" The laptop nearly fell off her legs and to the floor.

"You know who I'm talking about. And he'd do anything for you. He'd lay his life down for you."

She didn't do heart-to-hearts. What could she say? The truth?

Her chest expanded as her lungs filled with air. "You all would . . . and, me, too—for you and the team," she blurted.

The flicker of a smile faded fast. "So, then, what's your excuse for not being together? We love you, and you love us. And I don't feel like my life is in danger because of it." He lightly lifted his shoulders. "I feel safer, actually."

"It's different."

"At least you're admitting something. That's a start." He rubbed at his cheek, his eyes shifting to the ceiling. "I have my own reasons for not settling down, but at least I gave it a shot once before."

Her brows drew inward. "When?"

"We'll save that story for another day." He stood.

"You expect me to open up and share my deep, dark secrets, but you won't do the same?" She moved the computer off her lap.

His hands disappeared into his denim pockets, and he narrowed his eyes. "I just don't want to see anyone get hurt."

"Asher would never hurt me." Sharing his name like this for the first time had her pulse climbing. The admission almost freeing.

He swirled a finger in the air. "Other way around."

"You think I'll hurt him?"

"I, uh, should let you get back to work. That code won't crack itself."

"Actually, it will." She fixed on a smile and rose to her feet.

"So, you want me to stay and waffle on?"

"I don't know what to do," she softly admitted after a moment of silence had passed. "And then there's Luke to consider."

Liam cocked his head, studying her. "I think you do know, and Luke will get the fuck over it. And if not, I'll make him get over it," he said, his face almost stoic.

She couldn't help but wonder about his past, a past he'd never shared before. Had Liam been in love once? It was hard to believe, but maybe something had happened to shape him into the person he'd become.

"I—" The click from the key card being inserted in the door had her backing up a step and pressing her palm to her chest to gather her thoughts.

Once the door was open, Liam twisted around to view Asher.

Asher shut the door behind him and inched closer to them. He scratched at the back of his short hair, eyes on her.

"Where's the rest of the team?" Her fingertips bit into her arms now as she tried to swallow the emotions surging to the surface. Her defenses flimsier than ever since Berlin. Maybe even before that—maybe the culprit for her near-crumbling walls stood before her now.

"They're checking in with Echo," Asher answered. "Any luck on your end?"

"Uh, yeah. Tracing the funds from Egon to Samir wasn't that hard, but now my program is running to track down where Samir's storing his money."

"Good." Asher nodded.

"I'll let you two talk," Liam said a beat later and started

for the door—leaving before either of them could protest his departure.

Asher jerked his thumb toward the closed door. "Is he okay? Why does he think we need to talk?" He rubbed his palms down his face. "Did he say something to you, too?" He walked past her, and she turned to find him sitting on the bed, pressing his elbows to his knees, his eyes on the floor.

"He spoke to you about me, didn't he?" She pulled the hair tie off her wrist and whipped her hair into a messy bun atop her head as she waited for him to speak.

"He may have said a few words." His brown eyes journeyed to her face. A tight line darted across his forehead. "We, uh, should probably focus on the op, though."

"That's what I told him, but . . ."

"But what, Jessica?" A slow whistle of breath left his barely parted lips.

He had every right to be angry. She'd made love to him. Given herself to him, knowing he'd wanted her for years. Only to turn her back on him afterwards.

When he stood, his height dominated hers. The close shave of his beard accentuated the strength of his strong chin. His jaw clenched as if he were attempting to grind stone with his back teeth.

He stroked his short beard, and a flurry of emotions crossed his face so fast that if she'd blinked, she'd have missed it.

"I should never have proposed meaningless sex," she admitted. "It was a ridiculous idea." Her eyes traveled to his mouth. To the lips she wished could steal her sins with a kiss and make everything okay again. If only it were that easy. "I'm sorry."

"You should be." He turned and strode to the window, bringing both hands to cradle the back of his head.

"What's going to happen between us?" she softly asked.

He placed a palm to the window. "Nothing, right?"

"I'm pretty sure we'll never be able to go back to the way things once were." The break in her voice had been unplanned, and she was pissed at herself for allowing it to happen because it had Asher facing her now.

"What are you saying? You don't want to work together?" He crossed the room to her in three quick strides.

She reached up and pressed her palm to his face, her eyes on the brink of brimming with tears despite the protest of her brain to keep it together.

His cheeks filled with air before he allowed the breath to leave his lips. "Jessica."

"Thank you." Her eyes fell shut. "Thank you for killing Egon. I thought I didn't want him dead, but I don't know if I could've handled the alternative."

He pulled her against his chest, wrapping his arms around her, and rested his chin atop her head, holding her tight in place.

He knew what she needed. He somehow always knew.

"Asher." His name was a soft sound vibrating against the hard planes of his sculpted chest.

He pulled back to find her face.

Right or wrong—she didn't know anymore. Sex with him and offering more sex was evidence of that.

But the indecision pulling at her was unbearable.

And so, she pressed up on her toes and brought her mouth to his.

He didn't kiss her back. Not at first. It was as if he were afraid she'd burn him again.

But then his hand dipped beneath her shirt to touch her back, and his fingertips scorched a hot path over her skin.

His mouth relaxed against hers, and his tongue parted her

lips. And right now, she'd give him entrance all day. Every night. To hell with the consequences.

She gripped his arms and pressed against him, needing to be even closer.

"What the fuck?"

Her shoulders jerked at the harsh words, and she stumbled away from Asher. Her eyes winged straight to Luke who stood in the doorway.

Asher swiped a hand over his jaw and down his neck before he pivoted to view Luke—only to find the door slamming shut behind him.

"I'll talk to him."

"No, I should." But her legs were weak, and so was her frame of mind.

"I'll be right back." He nodded and strode toward the door.

CHAPTER TWENTY-NINE

"Wait up."

Luke faced him in the hall with both palms in the air—a warning to stay the fuck away.

"We need to talk." Asher stopped in front of him and placed his hands on his hips, not sure what the hell to do with them. Maybe Luke would deck him? And he'd probably let him.

"I was right about you two." Luke stabbed at the air in the direction of Jessica's hotel suite. "How long have you been together?" His lips became a white slash on his tanned skin.

Asher closed his eyes for a second, trying to find the courage to deliver the truth, when in all honesty, he still didn't know what was going on with her. She was warm one minute and cold the next.

Luke closed the short distance between them and locked his arms tight across his chest as if to deter himself from hitting Asher square in the jaw.

"We, uh, had a thing long before I knew you were her brother." The truth settled in the air between them, and his heartbeat ticked up as he waited for Luke to speak.

"The Aleppo op?" His eyes became razor thin, his mind working fast. Anger flaring.

Asher nodded. "I didn't see her again until you guys offered me the job." He wasn't about to place the blame on her shoulders for the lie, so he added, "I thought if you knew you wouldn't want me on the team. I asked her not to tell you."

Luke cursed under his breath. "So, all this time? Are you kidding me?"

"No." Asher shook his head. "We kept it professional." His mind went blank for a moment. "Er, until recently. Working together while you were gone, and then after Berlin, things just—"

"How could you?" His brows knitted, and his eyes darkened to a familiar shade—to the same color as Jessica's whenever anger stirred inside of her. "She's family, man. You crossed the line."

His hands tightened at his sides. "Yeah, well, I can't help who I fall in love with."

"Yes, you . . ." His words seemed to die as he shook his head. "Love?"

Asher scrubbed both hands down his face, almost unaware of the words he'd spoken until Luke repeated them. But everything was on the table now, and so, he said, "Yeah, I love her. I've tried not to. I've tried really fucking hard." His voice gave out, his words nearly falling through the cracks. "But I can't help it." He swallowed. "I'm sorry."

Luke's mouth opened, but his gaze shifted over Asher's shoulder.

Asher turned. His heart plummeted at the sight of Jessica in the hall. Her lips parted, and her eyes locked onto his. "My program's done," she said, her voice barely audible. "I located Samir's bank." And then she retreated into the room.

Asher gripped his temples with his right hand. "I'll, uh, get the team together." He started past Luke toward their other hotel room, his mind racing like a greyhound around a track.

"Asher."

"Yeah?" He glanced back over his shoulder.

"Does she love you, too?" he asked, his voice still tense, but less strained than before.

He looked down at his boots. "Probably not."

"What do we have?" Owen examined Jessica's laptop as he stood behind her at the desk in the hotel room.

Asher pressed his back to the window and bent one knee, pressing the bottom of his boot to the wall.

Luke knew he'd had sex with Jessica. And now Jessica knew he loved her.

Things hadn't gone exactly as planned.

But then again, when in his life had anything gone fucking right?

Jessica glimpsed Asher over her shoulder, a visible tightness to her face. Her cheeks were only now sweeping back to their normal rosy hue after she'd become so pale in the hall.

He'd only been able to give her five minutes alone to absorb his confession to Luke, his words like those of a man taking his last dying breath.

"Jessica? You good?" Owen asked when she still hadn't answered him.

She lightly shook her head. "Sorry." She lifted her laptop and turned to face the team. "Samir had money in offshore accounts divided over seven countries, but then he funneled all the money into a bank in Cairo."

"Is it still there?" Luke asked, crossing the room as if his boots were trudging through the muck to get to her. He slowly looked at Asher, and it had Asher's spine straightening against the window.

"Unfortunately, the money was withdrawn. I'm about to access the bank camera feeds, so I can try and figure out who made the withdrawal because it was done on-site."

"Whatever he's planning is about to go down soon," Knox said. "Should we head to Cairo?"

"Probably a waste of time. Whoever took the money is long gone," Luke said. "Any idea where he got the money from?"

"Not yet. I've gotta change some of the code and see if that helps."

"Owen. Liam. You guys work the CCTV feeds at the bank while Jessica handles the account," Luke instructed.

"Roger that." Owen grabbed his laptop from his bag by the door.

"Something feels off, though." Asher couldn't help but notice the slight tremble in her fingers when she'd spoken.

God, had he thrown her off her game? Talk about timing.

But would there ever be a right time for them?

"Why do you say that?" Luke tucked his hands beneath his armpits and rocked back in his boots as he studied her.

"The encryption is heavy. Military-grade heavy. Wherever this money came from—they sure as hell didn't want to be found." She looked up, her blue eyes touching upon Asher.

His palm went to his chest in an attempt to calm the heavy beats of his heart.

"Military? As in ours?" Knox approached the desk.

245

"I-I don't know." She wet her lips. "I think I might need my lab back in New York to make progress."

"Well, we don't need to be here or Cairo," Luke said. "I'll get us on the first flight back. Besides, with Echo heading to New York—"

"We should be there, too," Knox interrupted. "In case anything goes down."

"Agreed," Asher said.

"Why don't you, uh, help pack up the other room and then check in with Echo to see if they know anything else," Luke issued the command to Asher.

It was a dismissal– they'd just checked in with Echo. But hell, maybe he needed to go, to clear his head.

He quickly surveyed the team, and he knew they could tell something was up, especially Liam.

Asher glanced at Jessica and saw her eyes back on the screen. So he forced his boots to move, to leave his team.

Out in the hall, he tucked his fingertips into his palms and pressed his fists to the wall, trying to get a grip.

I love her. Christ. He'd never thought that before, let alone said it.

Why the hell did those words have to leave his mouth tonight, of all nights?

God, he needed to get inside a cage. To lose himself in a fight.

Killing Egon hadn't made him feel better.

He'd knocked the shit out of Egon for touching Jessica, for murdering Ara. The damage from the battery of hits to Egon's face would never be seen, though, since he'd put a bullet in his forehead right after.

He wasn't sure how he'd tell Jessica, or the team, the truth about what had gone down earlier.

That there'd been no hostage.

He'd taken justice into his own hands and killed a man in cold blood.

Guilt over his actions started to weigh down on him, and he rubbed at the dull ache in his chest, willing it to go away.

What the hell have I done?

CHAPTER THIRTY

"Better?" Owen smirked as he assessed her back in her element at their office in Manhattan.

"I'm useless without my lab. It's good to be back." She tucked her black wig into her bottom drawer and fixed on a smile.

They were alone while the rest of Bravo met up with Echo near the hotel in the Bronx.

Had she really been wrong about Samir's plans? Having the men from Detroit show up in New York felt too easy. Maybe she was so used to messy and complicated she couldn't believe they had unturned every last stone.

"It's been a crazy twenty-four hours." His brows drew inward.

"A crazy few weeks . . ." Between the op and what had happened with Asher, she felt like her head was stuck inside a pinball machine.

Asher's words from the hotel yesterday kept rolling around in her mind, knocking the breath out of her.

Yeah, I love her. I've tried not to. I've tried really fucking hard. Had he said those words in the heat of the moment? To prove a point to Luke? Or . . .?

Owen dropped down behind her desk and opened his laptop as her cell began ringing.

It was Grace. She was probably worried, but Jessica couldn't tell her Egon was dead. Her team had "never been" in Austria.

"Not going to answer that?"

She put the call to voicemail and tried to ignore the twinge of guilt.

Grace didn't even know what had happened with Asher on Valentine's Day. She couldn't open up, not even to her best friend.

"Does Samantha know you're back?" she asked as he input his password into the laptop.

"Yeah, of course. The woman would kill me if I didn't call her the second the bird touched the ground."

Owen had someone. Her brother had someone. And she had Asher. Well, sort of. She was doing a damn good job at pushing him away.

And now her brother knew everything. He'd barely spoken to her, aside from operational details, since he'd caught her and Asher kissing.

He probably had no idea what to say, but she didn't want him angry at Asher.

Asher didn't deserve anger from anyone. He was a good man, a better man than he gave himself credit for. A man worth fighting for—but was she capable of *that* fight? A fight with herself, apparently?

"Let's see if your program can get a name for the guy who emptied Samir's bank account."

"What?" She circled the desk to view his screen. "You didn't tell me you snagged an image."

"You were asleep on the flight, and I didn't want to wake you. Besides, we couldn't do anything until we got to the office, anyway."

"Owen." She smacked the side of his arm with the back of her hand. "You should have woken me. Someone from Bravo—"

"They agreed to let you sleep." He shook his head. "You're no good to us if you're totally spent."

She cursed under her breath. "Fine. Show me what you have."

"I got three great angles of the prick."

When he showcased the images of the man on the screen, her heart catapulted into her throat, and she snatched the laptop from the desk to study it closer. "Shit."

"What? You know him?"

"Yeah, I'd say." She handed him back the laptop and briefly closed her eyes. "He's a CIA field officer."

* * *

"You were given direct orders to back the fuck down." Rutherford massaged his temples as he sat behind Luke's desk as if it were his. "It was you who took out our assassin? You gift wrapped him for the Germans?"

"Did you really expect us to stop?" Luke remained standing in front of the desk.

Jessica took a seat alongside him. "When did you turn Samir into an asset for the CIA?"

Rutherford stood, walked to the bar, and poured himself a Scotch. He raised the tumbler to his lips and faced them. "When Samir's brother, Arif, died eight months ago, Samir was approached with the same offer he got."

Shit. She'd been afraid he'd say that. Her skin crawled,

and her fingertips buried deeper into the leather arms of the chair. "The CIA recruited Samir's brother to be an asset after the op in Aleppo?" She tsked. "The agency was so hell-bent on making sure I wouldn't help Ara and the others, and then . . ."

"What'd you give him in exchange for being an asset?" Luke asked.

"Money. Training. The usual." He polished off the rest of his drink and set the empty glass atop Luke's desk before perching a hip against it.

"Didn't you learn anything from what happened with bin Laden?" Luke snapped.

"Samir lost his brother," Jessica said. "His state of mind would be too volatile for him to honestly consider the same position you gave his brother. How could you not see that it'd be a risky move? If he found out his brother had died because he'd been helping the CIA—"

"Assad killed Arif," Rutherford interjected.

"Yeah, and it was probably because Assad found out he was an informant for you," she responded.

"Samir's brother was an invaluable asset. And he didn't help us for money. He just wanted Assad gone. When ISIS dug their claws into Syria, he also helped provide us with intel that brought down multiple HVTs."

"And so you thought Samir would follow suit?" She pressed her hands to her thighs, fighting the tremble in her legs. "You were clearly wrong."

Rutherford was quiet for a moment, his pupils constricting. "Everything was fine until a few months ago."

"What happened?" But did she want to hear the truth?

"Samir approached us with an idea."

"Let me guess." Luke's voice was so low the hairs on her neck stood. "Take control of his uncle's old group. There was a power vacuum at the time. Since the group's against both Assad and ISIS, why not have a man on the inside?"

Rutherford's chest slowly rose and fell, and a visible redness advanced up his neck.

"You guys taught him how to code so he could communicate intel, and then you armed and funded a loose cannon." She shook her head. "And then he went and disappeared on you. Is that why you protected the girls in Berlin—worried he'd hurt them . . . or were you using them to try and draw out Samir?"

Rutherford loosened his tie and eyed his watch. "It's over, Miss Scott." The use of her last name right now felt almost condescending. "He's not going to win, so there's no point in further discussing this."

"How do you know for certain?" Luke braced his palms against the desk.

"We emptied his accounts and took into custody the arms dealer Samir had been working with."

"How'd you find who he was working with?"

He coughed into a closed fist. "Actually, we owe your team for that, I suppose. The arms dealer was on the list of names you retrieved from that laptop in France last month. We'd been tracking him when we discovered he was working with Samir."

"What were they planning?" she asked.

"A chemical attack in New York. Subway station. Something about wanting to hurt Americans the same way we let Assad hurt Syrians."

"We?" Luke lifted his hand from the desk.

"He blames us for Assad still being in power." Rutherford stroked his graying beard.

"I don't think he would've gone through with that," she said, needing to believe her words.

"The point is—it's over," Rutherford began. "You didn't need to involve yourselves in this situation. We would've gotten the assassin, too."

"Samir is still out there, though. And the men from Detroit, the ones he's been working with, are in our city right now." Jessica gripped the back of her neck.

"Officers are about to pick those men up for questioning. I'm sure your buddies, who are also tailing them, will be calling you soon," Rutherford announced. "And as for Samir, he should be getting off a plane at JFK as we speak. Homeland is waiting at the gates."

"That's why you were already in New York when we called." She tensed. "I don't believe it, though." Her arms went limp at her sides, and she observed her brother as he looked back to find her eyes. The same concern in his gaze.

"Well, it's true. Samir took a flight out of Egypt under one of the aliases his arms dealer provided him. We have him on camera boarding the plane."

"But you emptied his accounts, and he probably figured out you took his guy into custody, which means he wouldn't be stupid enough to fly with that passport." She glanced heavenward in thought.

"He's twenty. Not Einstein," Rutherford sputtered.

"Smart enough to pull the wool over your eyes and mastermind all of this." She took a breath. "What about his mom?" She looked back at him. "Samir wouldn't leave his mom behind. And since she's not in Syria, which you know because you had a DEVGRU team go—"

"If she has anything to do with this, we'll find her." Rutherford moved to stand directly in front of Luke and Jessica. "I like you two, but orders are orders. And you were instructed to back off this case."

"Yeah, because you had to protect your ass." Luke shook

his head. "Your mistake almost got my sister blown up. And now an innocent woman is dead. How about a fucking apology?"

She grabbed hold of his bicep, urging him to back down. "Luke." She didn't want him throwing away his life's work because of her.

"*You* trusted Ara," Rutherford said to her. "That was your mistake."

When the director backed up a step, Luke relaxed his shoulders, and she released her grip on his arm.

"Let's hope it's Samir who gets off that plane," Luke began, "because if it's not, any deaths will be on your hands."

Rutherford's phone began ringing a split second later. "This should be Homeland now."

She crossed her arms and waited as he answered, but when he turned his back and lowered his head, her stomach dropped.

"Check again. The flight manifest says he was on that plane." He paused to take a raspy breath. "Find him!" He ended the call and slowly faced them.

Jessica glimpsed Luke out of the corner of her eye before directing her focus back on Rutherford. "Are you ready to admit you need us now?"

CHAPTER THIRTY-ONE

"Why the hell is he so stubborn?" Jessica looked at her brother as he sat on the edge of her desk with folded arms.

"You know Rutherford hates admitting when he's wrong. Plus, the Feds have more resources than us, especially on American soil."

"And their resources led them on a goose chase." She blew out a flustered breath and focused on her computer screen again.

"Samir's brother may not have been his trigger point. He's been in Syria witnessing atrocities for a while. But the CIA inadvertently gave him the nudge he needed for revenge."

"You thinking Samir didn't, uh, kill Ara because he wanted to gain control of the group?" She grabbed her black-rimmed glasses off her desk, realizing her eyes were beyond tired.

"He did it to ensure support from Yasser's old allies. Like the enforcer. The men in Detroit."

She leaned back in her leather desk chair. "He needed to

build a team to enact his plans for revenge." *Revenge* . . . a strong enough lure to pull Samir to the dark side.

Luke pinched the bridge of his nose. "And those five men offered themselves as sacrifices to distract the FBI from whatever Samir has been planning."

"Which means there has to be another player out there helping Samir. And I'm guessing one of those men knows who it is. But they'll never tell. They've been waiting years for a moment like this to come along."

The anger and hatred for America, bubbling beneath the surface. Ready to explode.

"Samir improvised when he lost his money and realized he'd have to get help from someone other than his team in Detroit."

"Which is when he was smart enough to throw the Feds off by copying his uncle's old form of communication," she noted. "But we're still looking for a rush job, and damn it, those are always the messiest."

She leaned forward and paused the terminal footage from Cairo on her screen when she spotted someone who looked like Samir. She zoomed in closer. "It's him." She'd recognize him anywhere after having seen his face in Berlin. "He even made sure to glance right at the camera as he handed over his ticket."

"He wanted the Feds focused on New York, but no way is he still in Egypt."

"Agreed." She rubbed her eyes beneath her glasses. They'd been going at this nonstop. Her only rest had been on the plane. "It's a big airport. Lots of people coming and going. A needle in a haystack. But I'll try to find him."

"You think his mom was in Cairo and flew with him out of there?"

"Maybe. I'll pull a photo from her passport and try to get

a match in the system since I'm sure she used a different name to travel this time."

He nodded. "My money is on her. Wherever she is, he'll be there, too."

"The problem is, I think they could already be Stateside."

He stood, cracking his neck. "We'll find them. I'll have the team focus on locating this other contact Samir must have Stateside." He started for the door.

"How far are Bravo and Echo from the office?"

"Five minutes." He shifted to face her from the doorway and braced a hand against the interior doorframe. "Jessica, um . . ." His brows knitted. "Are you doing okay?"

Oh, God. This wasn't the conversation she wanted to have right now. There was a possible attack about to go down, and the last thing she needed was Luke worrying about her instead of the mission—a mission they still weren't tasked to be part of, but to hell with that stopping them.

"I just want to find Samir and stop him."

"Yeah, okay. Me, too." He scratched at the back of his head. "After this is all over, we can talk."

"Mm-hm." She stared back at her screen.

"And, Jessica?"

"Yeah?" She forced her eyes to his.

"You know I love you. Right?"

"I, uh . . ." She swallowed, pressed her lips together, and slowly nodded.

CHAPTER THIRTY-TWO

"Right under our nose," Asher said with a shake of the head. "Jessica was right."

"She's always right." Owen and Liam crossed the office to look at Asher's laptop.

"This guy," Asher said, pointing to his screen, "has a friend living in Arlington. He communicates regularly with her, and so it wouldn't have triggered any alarms when Echo was watching them in Detroit."

"Did he use the same code as Samir's uncle?" Owen asked.

Asher nodded. "Yeah. He asked for a list of supplies. No time, date, or location, though."

"Whatever Samir's planning is in Virginia or D.C., I'm guessing." Owen started for the door. "I'll round up the rest of the team."

Asher looked to his left at Liam. "Samir's going to use an IED. Kill himself, probably. But where?"

"This was a last-minute change since his plans fell through," Liam said. "I doubt he's targeting any specific events now."

"Gotta be a government target, given the location." Asher pulled up a file on the woman in Virginia, and a few seconds later, Luke and the rest of Bravo and Echo entered the office, crowding the place. They stood before his desk, all eyes on him.

Not Jessica, though. Laptop in hand, she dropped down at the table off to the side of the men and started working right away.

"What do we have?" Luke asked.

Asher explained what he discovered and waited for a response from Luke. When Luke didn't speak, he said, "If the Feds pick her up, we'll lose our lead on Samir. So, what do you suggest?"

"If we withhold this intel from the FBI, they'll probably arrest us." Luke's hands landed on his hips.

"I need to call Samantha. If it's a D.C. hit . . ." Owen cupped the back of his neck and turned toward the door.

"Emily," Liam added, drawing the team's attention. "She lives there, too, right?" He coughed into a closed fist.

"The hit will be personal," Jessica said softly, as if in thought—her mind calculating.

Asher considered her words. "Instead of combing through security footage at the airport in Cairo, maybe we check all incoming flights from Egypt into the Virginia area?"

"On it," she said without glancing his way.

"How fast can we get to Virginia?" Liam asked.

"The drive will take too long. A commercial flight just as bad." Luke rubbed at his beard. "Eva's brother Harrison is in town. I can see if we can borrow his private jet and get a last-minute flight scheduled with the FAA."

"Are we telling Rutherford about this woman or not?" Knox looped his thumbs into his front pockets and observed him.

Luke glanced at Jessica, but she kept her eyes on the screen. She removed a hand from the keyboard only to shift her glasses before returning her fingers to the keys.

"It's possible the exchange was made. Samir may already have the materials needed to make an explosive device," Asher said.

Luke nodded in agreement. "So we turn this woman's name over to the FBI, and we focus on Samir and his mom."

"Works for me," Wyatt said.

"In twenty-four hours, this ends." Luke whistled out a low breath. "And then we're all taking a vacation."

"You just took two months off," Wyatt said with a laugh.

Luke brought his phone to his ear. "Yeah, well, I'm thinking I'm gonna need two more."

After a few minutes, the guys left the office, leaving Asher and Jessica alone.

"You good with the plan?" Asher strode closer to where she worked.

She removed her glasses and rubbed the bridge of her nose before finding his eyes. "Yeah. We go to Virginia. Stop an attack." Her tongue traced a line over her bottom lip.

"But are you okay with coming? With being so close to all of this?"

"I went to Austria, didn't I?" She closed her laptop and rose.

"Yeah, and we needed you then—"

"And you need me now." She crossed her arms, defiance glinting in her eyes.

"But if the ship goes down, I don't want you going with it."

"What does that even mean?"

He lifted his hands and edged a step away from the table.

"We've broken Command's orders twice now. Three strikes, and we might be out."

"You think I'm worried about that?" She circled the table and stood before him.

"I also don't want to see you getting hurt," he admitted, his mind racing back to Berlin. To the s-vest.

"I just want this to be over." She lifted her eyes to the ceiling, and he observed the movement of her throat. When her eyes raced back to his a second later, her pupils dilated ever so slightly.

He gently gripped her bicep, and her arms relaxed at her sides. His eyes remained steady on hers, but he couldn't bring himself to speak. Years of banter, and now the words were stuck in his throat.

"I'm not ready to talk about . . ." She let her words fade into the air.

He released his hold of her arm and blinked a few times, worry about his own decisions cutting through him. He cleared his throat and shook his head. "That's okay. I don't think I'm ready to talk either."

* * *

A CHILL BLEW DOWN ASHER'S BACK AS HE STARED AT THE woman. It'd been six-plus years since he'd seen her, and he wasn't sure if she remembered him.

But the narrowing of her brown eyes as she studied him suggested a glimmer of recognition.

"Why are you doing this?" Fatima's English had improved over the years, but had she changed, like her son? Did she now support terrorism?

Jessica and Asher remained alone with her in the room at the safe house, just two klicks east of downtown Arlington.

Luke was hoping she'd feel more comfortable around familiar faces.

"Do you know your son killed Ara?" Jessica's arms were locked tight across her chest as she stood in a wide stance alongside Asher.

She swept her fingers through her long, dark hair. It was normally covered, but Samir must've asked her to lose her hijab to better blend in with the crowd when they'd arrived in Dulles yesterday. Either that, or she'd made the decision herself when they'd separated at the airport.

After identifying Fatima's taxi, Jessica had convinced the driver to pinpoint where he'd dropped her off. Thank God, she'd still been at the motel in Virginia.

She was probably waiting for Samir's contact to pick her up.

Jessica reached inside the computer bag by her boots and retrieved a set of photos. "He had her shot right in front of me —before her body was blown up."

It couldn't be easy for Jessica to voice those words, or for her to hand the images over to Fatima, but she did it. Somehow, she did it.

So. Damn. Tough.

"That's all that was left of your niece." Jessica's voice was composed, and he knew she was doing her best to keep it that way. "He hired an assassin to kill her, and it's your fault."

"No." She shoved the photos off her lap, and they fluttered to the floor.

"You pushed Ara to give you her location," Jessica began, "and when she wouldn't give it to you, you faked being sick to draw her out. What happened to you? To your son? What changed?"

The woman was quiet for a moment, her eyes dropping to the images on the floor. "I lost my husband. My brother.

Friends. Cousins. And eight months ago, I lost my eldest son." Her voice wavered, and when she looked up, her eyes brimmed with tears.

"And you're about to lose your other one," Asher said in a low voice. "He's going to kill himself, and for what? For whom?"

Fatima's lower lip trembled.

Jessica averted her attention to the ceiling in the small interrogation room. "He won't even make it to his twenty-first birthday, because when the police find him—and stop him—they'll put a bullet in his head. They won't hesitate."

Asher glanced over at Jessica. Her eyes were focused back on Fatima.

"Maybe you didn't know everything he was planning, but I believe you don't want your son to die." Jessica's booted feet edged closer to her, and she crouched before the woman. "Help me, and I'll do my best to ensure he doesn't end up in a body bag like his brother."

Fatima closed her eyes. "The war has gone on long enough. There are too many bodies. No one to stop it."

"And you think killing innocent Americans will help save Syrian ones?" Asher bit down on his back teeth, attempting to control the curl of anger wrapping tight in his chest, threatening to unleash.

"Samir was never supposed to die."

"No," Jessica whispered. "He planned a chemical attack, like the kind used on women and children by your own president. Samir wanted us to suffer the way your country has." She stood upright and glimpsed Asher over her shoulder before returning her gaze to Fatima. "But I don't think it's too late to stop him. To save him." Fatima didn't speak, so Jessica continued, "I can't begin to imagine what you and your people have gone through. But killing people—your son taking his own life—won't end the pain and suffering in your country."

"It'll do the opposite," Asher said. "It could make things a lot worse." He surveyed the woman. Her shoulders were breaking into a full-on tremble.

"Someone has to pay." Tears began to slip down her cheeks. "Who will pay?"

Jessica briefly shook her head. "I don't know. But when I met you and Samir, you were good people. I saw it in your eyes, in the warmth of your gestures. You invited me into your home. We broke bread together." She paused for a beat. "Don't do this."

Asher couldn't take his eyes off Jessica as she spoke. His heart was drumming hard in his chest. She was getting through to her; he could feel it. He could see it in Fatima's eyes.

But he could also see something in Jessica—forgiveness, maybe? She was allowing her emotions to guide her through the line of questioning, which hadn't been typical of her in the past. Was she changing? Opening up?

"You're not these people. Tell me where your son is so I can stop him from hurting anyone else." Jessica knelt before her again, and this time, she reached for her hand.

The woman looked up at Asher, took a breath, and then found Jessica's eyes. "You won't be able to stop him, I'm afraid. He won't back down for you. He's still just a boy. It's hard for him to understand his own pain," she cried. "He's hurting."

Jessica stood again and glanced at Asher. He gave her a slight nod—knowing what she was thinking. "But, Fatima, maybe he'll stop for you?"

CHAPTER THIRTY-THREE

"What's your position?" Rutherford asked.

"We're almost to Langley. He may not be there yet, but he's en route," Jessica answered as she looked into the mirror to reposition the short red wig; she didn't need anyone from the CIA recognizing her.

"You should've handed his mother over to us." The line crackled from Rutherford's heavy breathing.

"Everything happened quickly when we got here. We had to move on the intel," Luke said as he drove, sitting alongside Jessica in the front of the Chevy Tahoe. Fatima was with Asher, Owen, Liam, and Knox in the other SUV following behind them. Echo was in the third vehicle.

"She'd never have talked to you," Jessica added. "Not in time, at least."

"Well, if Samir really thinks he's going to waltz into Langley and blow himself up, he's out of his goddamn mind." Rutherford was quiet for a moment. "Our people are in position if he shows," he added. "You can stand down."

"Sir, with all due respect, no." Luke glanced at Jessica. "We promised his mother we'd keep him alive if possible."

"If he approaches the building with a bomb strapped to his chest, what do you think we're going to do?" Rutherford sputtered.

"Let us talk to him," Luke said with a plea to his tone. "We can try and get him to back off."

Samir's mom was right. He was still practically a kid.

Maybe he didn't deserve saving after everything he'd done, but it also wasn't her decision to make, was it?

"You may have gotten his mom to talk, but we're dealing with a loose cannon here," Rutherford hissed. "Your words. Remember?"

Her eyelashes fluttered as memories from her past operation—the reason why they were even in this situation—clouded her mind.

There's no place for emotions in this job. No feelings. I thought you of all people understood that, her boss at the time had said after she'd requested the agency help Ara and the others in Aleppo.

This isn't an emotional request. It's about what's right. We promised to help them in exchange for information. They won't have a chance at survival if they stay here. And anyone who supports or protects Ara will be targeted: her cousins, her friends. She'd pleaded her case.

I'm sorry. Request denied, he'd responded.

After, she'd caught a plane out of Aleppo and never even said *goodbye* to Asher. And when the dust had settled, she'd returned to help the girls—telling herself it had nothing to do with her emotions and everything to do with keeping a promise made.

But she'd lied to herself, hadn't she? She had cared. And helping Ara over the years, teaching the girls . . . it was because she did have a heart. She'd tried to convince herself otherwise over the years, and for what? For whom?

She pressed a hand to her stomach as the realization continued to light a fire inside of her. *I'm not cold.* "I'm not like you," she whispered. "I tried to be. I thought I had to be."

"What?" Rutherford's word snapped through the line.

Her gaze winged to the phone. "I—"

"If anyone dies today other than Samir, you're done," Rutherford cut her off. "All of you. Understood?"

"Roger that." Luke ended the call.

"I'm going to make things right," she said as her brows drew together. "Or I'm going to die trying."

Luke slowed the vehicle at her words, and she glimpsed Asher in the side-view mirror in the SUV behind them. "Samir's not in the right state of mind, Jess. There's a really good chance the only way we'll be able to stop him is with a bullet."

"You have to give me a chance. All of this is my fault."

"No, it's not. You can't blame yourself."

She took a steadying breath. "I won't be able to live with myself if I don't at least try." Her hand trembled atop her thigh, and she rested her other over it to hide the slight shake.

"After Berlin, I can't risk . . ." He pressed his foot back onto the pedal at normal speed. "Under no circumstances am I letting you put yourself in danger."

"This is what we do."

"No, it's what *I* do. What Owen, Asher, and the others do. *Not* you." His jaw tightened. "I never agreed to you being in the line of fire when you convinced me to start this team six years ago. And it's something I'll never support."

She exhaled through her nose. "That's how you do it, huh?"

"Do what?"

Her gaze skated to his face, to his brows drawing inward. "Work with me. You were never worried about me getting hurt because you made sure to keep me behind the scenes."

"What's wrong with that? You're my sister. Not a SEAL. You've never been in combat."

"But I have field training. I've killed people, Luke. I'm not some innocent woman. I'm not just a brain." She leaned the base of her skull against the headrest.

"Bravo. Echo. We'd all fucking die for you. But under no circumstances are you allowed to die for us."

Her body tensed at his words. "My life doesn't matter more than any of yours."

"Jessica," he said nearly under his breath and pulled the Tahoe off the road.

She could hear the screech of the tires from the other two vehicles behind them as they rolled to a hard stop. "What are you doing? We need to go." Her tongue pinned to the roof of her mouth.

He shifted in his seat and draped his arm over the wheel. "I'm not going anywhere with you, not if you think I'm going to let you risk your life. Not today. Not ever." He bowed his head, blocking his eyes. "I'll pull the team back and let the Feds maintain control."

"No." She scrubbed her hands down her face. How had she let this conversation get away from her like this? She knew in her heart she might be the only one able to stop Samir and save him from an early death.

She looked to Luke's side window and found Asher standing there.

Luke looked up, followed her gaze, and rolled down the window. "We're turning around."

Asher glanced at Jessica before focusing on Luke. "Why? We're a minute away."

"Because she thinks she's made of steel," Luke rasped, clutching the wheel.

Asher's eyes closed and his mouth pressed into a tight line. He was thinking, his mind racing. She could see it happening. Feel it.

And then he asked, "If Samir shows, did Rutherford give us the go-ahead to approach?" His eyes opened now, and his shoulders arched back.

"Yeah, with a condition. We don't fuck it up, or we're out of a job." Luke released the wheel and leaned back in his seat.

The corners of Asher's lips depressed, his eyes thinning. He was quiet for a moment, as if fighting some internal battle, before he said, "Jessica's our best bet, then."

She took quick, shallow breaths as she caught his gaze.

"She's part of the team. If she says she can do it, then we have to let her." There was real pain gliding through his tone, but he was making the right call for the sake of the mission.

"Thank you," she mouthed, trying to fight the quiver in her lip.

"No." Luke shook his head and looked at her.

She reached for his forearm and gripped it. "How many times have you used yourself as bait? Hell, you used Knox just the other day." She swallowed. "I even used Eva. Remember?"

His forehead tightened at the mention of his fiancée. "This is different. This is approaching a man who may be a walking IED. And we just got you out of an s-vest; I'm not about to let you go stand in front of another one."

"She's always had our backs in the field," Asher said, a rough texture to his tone. "What makes you think we won't have hers?"

Luke pulled his arm free of her grip and dragged his

palms down his face. "How can you, of all people, suggest putting her in danger?"

Her pulse spiked higher when Asher's eyes touched upon her face. This wasn't easy for him, but the man came through for her. And it was time she accepted that he always would—regardless of emotions. Maybe even because of them, something she hadn't realized until today.

"We're a team," Asher said pointedly. "All of us." He looked back at Luke. "But you should know"—his lips briefly turned down—"I'll never let anything happen to her. And I mean never."

* * *

He should've been there by now. Jessica's gaze swept left and right. No sign of Samir.

Snipers were waiting, but there were no agents in sight, no one to tip Samir off. The last thing they wanted was for him to show up to a place crawling with Feds and take off to a neighborhood or to a store or mall, where he could hurt other people.

"Bravo Three, anything?" she asked Asher over her comm from inside the vehicle in the parking lot.

She prayed to God Fatima hadn't set them all up. It was a possibility, but at this point, they didn't have a choice but to trust her.

"Nothing yet," Asher answered. "Copy?"

"Copy that." She glanced at Fatima alongside her.

"Maybe he discovered you have me," she said. "But no, he'd come for me if he realized his plans fell through."

"And what was his plan for you? To live under a fake ID in the US?"

"I have a cousin who lives in Cleveland. I was going to go

there." She clasped her hands in her lap and stared out the passenger window.

"Is that why you've been working on perfecting your English?" At Fatima's silence, her attention diverted to thoughts of Berlin. "Was it your idea to threaten the refugees in order to get Ara to give me up?" Anger bubbled back to the surface at the reminder this woman played a role in Ara's death. "You knew how much those girls meant to her based on her emails to you. She'd have done anything to protect them."

"I would never suggest such a thing." Her voice wavered as she spoke. Her fingers fanned across her collarbone. "But Samir read the emails. So, I suppose it is my fault."

Jessica looked out the window. "How could you be okay with your son killing himself? How can any mother want that for her child?"

Asher's voice came over the line, ending her conversation with Fatima. "I have visual confirmation of the target. He's heading toward the front entrance. Eight hundred meters north of your location."

"Roger that." Her heart stuttered in her chest. "Samir's here. It's time." She retrieved her pistol and motioned for Fatima to exit.

"You promise not to kill him?" Her eyes filled with liquid.

"That's the plan," she said before exiting the vehicle, and Fatima joined her on the sidewalk.

"I'm moving into position," she alerted the team.

"This is Bravo One. Target is closing in on the front steps. SWAT is getting anxious," Luke warned a few seconds later.

At the sight of Samir in an s-vest, Fatima screamed out his name in panic.

Samir flung around, firearm in one hand, detonator in the

other. His lips parted as he laid eyes on his mother, and Fatima shifted away from Jessica to run to him.

He started shouting at her in Arabic. Orders to leave. To get away.

Fatima held position ten feet away from him, palms in the air in surrender.

"Samir. Please." Jessica kept her arms locked, her weapon drawn in front of her. "You don't want to do this." She tried to keep her voice steady as she moved closer to him. "If you walk into that lobby, the only person you'll kill is yourself."

His eyes darted from his mother to her. Indecision clouded his eyes. Fear.

"You don't have to hurt anyone else." Her breath floated with the cold air as she edged closer, within range of a possible blast. "I forgive you," she said as steadily as possible, willing her words to be true.

If she could truly forgive him and make peace with what had happened to her, to Ara, she could move forward, be stronger.

His arm shook slightly, and his brown eyes shifted to his mom. He threw his hand out in front of him, motioning for both of them to back away.

More pleas in Arabic sailed from Fatima's lips, but Samir returned his focus to Jessica.

"I know you'd never have gone through with the chemical attack," Jessica said slowly, hoping she was right. *He's a kid. Just a kid.*

"I killed my cousin. I tried to kill you." His jaw clenched. "You don't know what I'm capable of."

"You're smart, Samir. Smart enough to realize the only people who will suffer if you push that button are you and your mom." She took a step closer. "What is it that you really want?"

He was quiet as if contemplating her question, and she took the moment to assess his vest.

From the looks of it, homemade explosives were tucked into the pockets, blue and red wires tangled in the front like a ribbon tying everything together. But it was the two tubes of liquid flanking both his sides that had her worried.

Oil and vinegar? Or did he have a chemical weapon ready to spread when the bomb exploded?

If it was TATP, *the mother of Satan*, the chemicals could explode because of friction without the heat of the blast. She had to end this and now.

"I want the war to stop," he finally said, his voice breaking, emotion leaking out.

He was a confused kid who'd grown up surrounded by violence and death. She had to try and remember that.

"This isn't how you end a war." She clicked back on the safety of her gun and slowly stowed her weapon in the holster, praying she was making the right decision.

He cocked his head and studied her.

"Your brother, Arif, was a good man." She stood alongside Fatima now and saw tears dripping down the woman's face like blood seeping from a wound. "He helped take down bad guys."

"And it got him killed!" Samir yelled, liquid gathering in his eyes.

She was getting through to him.

"But he died trying to help his people. What will you die for?" She swallowed the lump in her throat and moved so she was only a foot away from his outstretched arm, from his gun.

His hand shook, and she wasn't sure if he'd accidentally fire the weapon, but she couldn't back down now. She couldn't turn and run.

No, Asher was right about her. She was a fighter.

"Please, Samir. I don't want them to kill you," she said, realizing she meant every word now. Too many people had already died.

She tipped her chin to the windows in the building behind him, letting him know snipers were in position.

"After what I did to you? To my own flesh and blood? Why do you care?" He lifted the gun and rubbed it against his forehead. His other hand still clutched the detonator, and she knew she was seconds away from this situation ending in one of two ways.

"People make mistakes," she said as calmly as possible. "But you can make the right choice now." She glimpsed his mom over her shoulder before directing her focus back to him. "It's not too late."

He looked heavenward, and the world became blanketed in silence.

She wasn't sure how many seconds ticked by, but his bottom lip shook, and then his entire body began to tremble as he sank to his knees in a broken sob.

She eyed the vials of liquid. He was moving too much.

He lifted both hands, flipping them palms up, offering the gun and detonator as he continued to cry.

"Stay back," she said to Fatima. "The chemicals may be unstable."

Samir looked up at her, and he lightly shook his head. "They're not real."

But could she believe him? Was it a trap? A fake surrender?

Her heart climbed in her throat as she weighed the options.

"You need to get out of there," Luke's voice came over

her comm, interrupting her thoughts. "Don't take a chance. The bomb squad is gearing up. Let them handle this."

"I need to remove the vest. Protective gear won't keep those men alive if this vest accidentally blows up," she said as she disarmed Samir of his weapon and the detonator. "I need to make sure these chemicals aren't TATP."

Samir's eyes thinned at her words. At her doubt.

In her line of work, she had to be certain. She wanted to believe him, but how could she trust a kid who went through such lengths for revenge? Emotions had guided his decisions, and she'd once thought hers hadn't been—only to realize today she'd been wrong.

She crouched before him to study the wires.

"This isn't your area of expertise," Luke reminded her. "If you're not going to wait, I'm sending Bravo—"

His words faded into the air when Bravo Three exited the building from behind Samir. Worry and fear ripped through Asher's gaze.

"Let me help." Asher produced a knife from his pocket, the knife she'd given him at Christmas, talk about déjà vu. "Step back. I've got this."

She followed his request because he was the explosives expert, even though it pained her for him to put himself in danger.

Upright, she edged back and stood alongside Fatima a few feet away; the woman wouldn't leave without her son.

"I'm going to get this off of you. Got it? Don't move. Not a goddamn hair." Asher's back was to her, which hid his movements as he worked at the spirals of red and blue. "You telling the truth about the chemicals?"

Samir was on his feet a minute later, the vest now removed and in Asher's hands. "I promise. It's only acetone," he said as his gaze veered to his mom. "I'm sorry." He sidestepped Asher and hurried to his mother's open arms.

Asher slowly knelt to the ground and set the vest down before facing her. "Just in case he's lying—how about we get the hell out of here?"

CHAPTER THIRTY-FOUR

"You sure you don't want to hitch a ride back with the team tonight?" Asher asked.

Jessica wrapped a hand around the nape of her neck, observing the pilot do final checks of the plane inside the hangar.

"I think I'm going to take a few days off. I have a couple of friends I'd like to visit in D.C." She found Asher's eyes.

"Taking time off, huh? You turning a new leaf?" He tucked his thumbs into the front pockets of his worn-out jeans.

"Yeah, well, I need to clear my head, and I'm not ready to go back to New York."

"I was thinking about not going back, too." He was quiet for a moment. "You get a chance to talk to Rutherford before he rushed us away from Langley?"

"Yeah. He didn't exactly say *thank you*, but . . ." She rubbed her neck, an achiness radiating down her spine. "Samir and his mom will be handed over to the Germans for a trial, and the men from Detroit will finally end up behind bars where they belonged a long time ago."

"What happens to our team?"

"Two weeks of mandatory vacation."

"I don't think the boys will complain this time, especially since Luke wanted two months."

She smiled.

"I could sure as hell use the time off."

"Me too." She bit into her lip. "Today could've gone much differently. Thank you for the assist back there. I'm glad you're okay."

"You, too, Peaches."

A tightness stretched inside her chest at his choice of words. "I missed this." She took a sobering breath. "Not the possibly dying part, but . . . you know, you being you. And me being—"

"A hero."

Her eyes drifted to the floor. "I wouldn't call it that."

"Well, I would." He closed the space between them and lifted his hand to her shoulder. "You did something I couldn't have done. Something I probably wouldn't have done."

She swallowed and met his eyes. "What's that?"

"Forgive Samir."

Her brows drew inward, her throat squeezing.

"You pulled off a miracle today and without a single drop of blood shed." He quietly observed her, and she couldn't help but wonder what he was thinking. A slight touch of darkness traveled across his face. Guilt, maybe.

She lowered her arms to her sides, and he dropped his hand from her shoulder at her movement.

She had to get the words out. To tell him how she really felt. After the day they had, he needed to know.

"I miss us."

"Us?" His lids lowered halfway. "You miss the way

things used to be, you mean?" His voice dropped a couple dozen octaves.

"I miss being comfortable working together." She gave a half-hearted shrug. "I miss being Peaches." Her fingertips lightly bit into the outside of her thigh, her nerves trekking into her throat, an attempt to kill her words like usual, but she didn't want to let them this time. "What I'm trying to say is—"

"Jessica, you have a minute?"

Luke . . . He was standing a few feet away with his hands in his pockets.

When she looked back at Asher, his eyes locked with hers. There was so much going on in his head, wasn't there? And part of her worried it was something she wouldn't want to hear.

Concern coated her insides in thick and heavy strokes, so much so her body nearly sagged from the discomfort.

Asher turned and observed Luke before walking past him and toward where the guys were crowded just outside the hangar, open to the runway outside.

"You okay?" Luke stood before her now.

She smoothed a hand over her jaw, trying to dismiss her nerves. "Yeah, I think so."

"You were brave back there." He dragged a palm down his face, and his eyes widened a little. "I shouldn't have second-guessed you. I'm sorry." He blew out a breath. "It's going to be hard letting go, though."

She leaned forward and placed her hand over his forearm. "I don't want you to stop protecting me, but I don't want you doubting my decisions, whether they're in the field or my personal life."

"Well, if you make a shit call in the field, you'd better believe I'll call you on it," he said in all honesty. "Listen." He cleared his throat. "Mom and Dad were never good at affection. They never said the right things to us. And I know I haven't been the best example, but I want to be better. I want to be here for you if you'll let me."

Liquid threatened to fill her eyes at his words, at feelings she'd kept locked tight inside for years. "Mom and Dad weren't the best role models. That's true, but they aren't to blame for me becoming so screwed up."

"You're not screwed up." His broad shoulders fell forward a touch. "You're tough, but—"

She held up her palm. "It's more than that. I thought I had to separate my emotions so I could make the right calls. But when Marcus died, I really buried myself behind some pretty heavy-duty walls." She stole a breath. "I thought it was to protect the team, but the more I think about it, it was to protect myself from getting hurt."

He blinked a few times as if fighting his feelings. God, they were so similar. But he had managed to change for the better in the last year, and so maybe she could, too.

"If Berlin, or today, taught me anything, it's that I don't want to be that person anymore." *I want to be loved. To love.*

Her mind skipped to Asher, to the man she's wanted for years.

"You can be whoever you want to be, Jessica." He braced her shoulders. "I believe in you."

A tear glided down her cheek, and her stomach muscles tightened. "And, Luke?"

"Yeah?"

She focused on his eyes. "I love you, too."

CHAPTER THIRTY-FIVE

ASHER CROSSED HIS ARMS AND LEANED AGAINST THE WALL, eying Jessica as she kicked off her boots and sat on the hotel bed. "You sure you don't want to take Samantha and Owen up on their offer to stay with them while you're in D.C.?"

"No, and surely it's for the same reasons you're at a hotel." A grin touched her lips. "Eva warned me you can hear everything through their walls." She wet her lips. "I have no interest in listening to Owen have sex." She cringed. "He's like a brother, so . . ."

"Yeah, I don't blame ya." He lowered his hands to his sides and pushed away from the wall. "What time are you meeting your friends tomorrow?"

"Ten a.m. brunch. So, we have plenty of time to finish our conversation from earlier."

He angled his head, and she reached for his forearm. The same distress appeared in his eyes. Maybe he was worried she was going to write him off again? He really did love her, didn't he? She only hoped she hadn't messed everything up.

"I fought for Samir today, to save the life of a man who had me strapped with an s-vest. A man who murdered my friend." Her lungs burned with the memory. "And yet, for a long time, I've been scared to fight for the one thing I've wanted more than anything."

"And what's that?" His tone was rough. Hard. And it had her legs growing weak.

She rolled her lips inward, her heart beating wildly. "You." She lifted her shoulders. "I want to fight for you." She forced her eyes on his. "For us," she corrected.

His thumb swept over her bottom lip before he cupped her cheek, but he remained quiet.

"I want you, Asher Hayes. I want you to have every part of me. I always have. Always will." Liquid pooled in her eyes, the admission freeing. "If you still want me, that is."

"Jessica," he whispered and lowered his face near hers.

His lips hovered, tauntingly close, and despite the crazy turn of events of the day, all she wanted was for this man to wrap his arms around her.

"Be with me," she whisper-said. "And not just for tonight."

"There's, uh, something I have to tell you first." Emotion squeezed his words. "It could change things."

She shook her head and focused on his dark eyes. "Nothing could change how I feel." She was desperate for his touch. "Please."

His lips parted as his hand went to the small of her back. There was a fight, or conflict of some sort, in his eyes.

"Whatever it is, I promise it doesn't matter. We've waited so long and . . ." She let go of her words when he hooked her leg up to his hip with his free hand, holding her tight. His length hardened against her, and a sharp ache of need settled between her thighs.

He sucked at her bottom lip and grunted as he rotated his hips, pressing her pelvis into him.

D.C. or New York. Hell, anywhere—it didn't matter. With Asher, she felt like she was home, a feeling she hadn't known she'd wanted until today. Until him.

"I need you," she whispered when he tore his mouth from hers, both of them gasping for air. "So much."

He lightly tugged at the braid resting over her shoulder and tipped her head back. He lost hold of her leg with his other hand, and his rough palm skirted up her neckline to her chin. "Tell me what you want." His eyes possessed hers, and a shudder of excitement rocked her body.

"You. Inside of me," she said when he eased his hold on her braid and sucked at her neck. Her eyes rolled skyward. "However you want me."

He lifted his mouth from her neck and found her eyes, his other hand tracing a line down the side of her body before he grasped her hip. "No. Tell me how *you* want me."

"On top," she nearly breathed out. "Hard and fast." Heat flooded her stomach and traveled south. "No protection. I want to feel all of you."

"Fuck." The word died inside her mouth as he ravished her lips again before kissing her neck. Cheek. Throat. His teeth at her earlobe.

"On the bed," he commanded a minute later. "Naked." His eyes narrowed as he removed his clothes, and she hastily stripped.

He sat on the bed, and she straddled him, looping her arms around his neck as she shimmied on his lap, anxious for him to fill her.

A hard pulse of desire tore between her legs, and she was sure he could feel it.

"I've never wanted anything more." His velvety words had her breasts puckering, and she kissed him, harder and full of more intensity than ever before.

283

When he flipped her to her back a few minutes later, her fingertips skirted over the hard lines of his chest, and she whispered, "Make love to me."

"Yes, ma'am." He lowered the weight of his body onto her. Their eyes remained connected as he pressed his tip to her center.

She nodded. "I'm on the pill," she told him before he filled her.

His beard scratched a path up her neck before his lips found hers again. He continued to kiss her as they made love, as their bodies moved together.

No regrets. Not anymore.

Life was too short to go without the person she needed the most in this world. And maybe it'd taken her a while to get to this place, but she was grateful she had finally gotten there.

Her stomach muscles tightened, and her body tensed. The need to release and let go had her hanging on the edge.

"Asher," she sputtered his name as she fought to hang on to control. "Oh, God." There was no way she'd last any longer. "Yes. Yes. Yes!" Everything inside of her built up higher and higher, and then . . . "Asher," she cried as she came, her body rocking with his as she released, unraveling in his arms.

He spilled inside of her, warming her from head to toe, and then slowly lowered his sweaty body closer to hers but without crushing her.

Bracing above her with one hand, he moved her braid off her chest, and his fingers skimmed up the slope of her shoulder to her cheek. "This day didn't turn out as I expected."

"I—" Her phone shrieked from the end table, but he didn't take his gaze off her.

"Ignore it," he said. "We have two weeks off, remember?"

"Right." She kissed him, but the moment the call ended, her phone began ringing again. "Let me turn it off. One sec."

He grabbed it for her, but then cocked his head to the side as he eyed the screen. "It's my mom. I, uh, gave her your number for emergencies." He shifted off of her and to his feet. "Mom?" he answered.

Italian floated from the other end of the line. Jessica's Italian was decent from having lived on a base in Naples as a kid for a few years, but she couldn't make out enough to translate what Asher's mom was saying.

She didn't have to, though. Based on the clench of his jaw and the blanching of his skin, something was wrong.

"I'm on my way." He ended the call. "I must've left my phone at the hangar," he said in a daze. "She's been calling me."

She gripped his forearm as he blinked a few times. "What's wrong? What happened?"

His forehead creased, and he stared down at her phone, still tight in his hand. "There was a shooting." His eyes flicked back to hers. "Sarah was shot."

"What?"

"She's . . . okay." His arms hung heavy at his sides, the phone slipping free from his hold. "But Angelo's dead."

CHAPTER THIRTY-SIX

"I THOUGHT YOU SAID SHE WAS OKAY." ASHER STARED AT HIS sister in the bed, hooked up to monitors. Her eyes were blank, focused on the ceiling.

His mom grabbed hold of his arm. His body stiffened as he looked over his shoulder at her. Every fiber in his being was ready to shred the bastards who had done this.

Tears poured down his mom's face, and she pulled him toward her for a hug. "The doctor gave her something to relax." Her voice was muffled against his chest as she cried. "Sarah was trying to get off the bed. Screaming. Crying."

His throat burned, anger torching a sharp line down the center of his body. His hands gathered into fists at his sides as he pivoted out of her grasp to observe Sarah in the bed. "What the hell happened?" His temper flared so hard, his words were a hard echo striking the very air in the room.

"There was a shooting at that club Angelo owns." She dropped down into the chair by the bed.

He knew that part, but he'd hoped his mom would know more. He'd read the news about the shooting on the flight back to the city, but the details had been sparse: it was still an active investigation.

He moved closer to the bed, where his sister remained lifeless. The bullet had torn through her bicep, but thankfully, the rest of her had been untouched.

"Did you know your sister was hanging out with Angelo?" He could hear the blame pinging off the walls.

He nodded without facing her. "What happened to Angelo? How exactly did he die?"

"Someone . . . shot . . . him," she said between sniffles. "One of the bullets hit your sister."

A targeted kill. And his sister had gotten hurt in the crossfires.

"No idea who is responsible?" Nausea swelled in his stomach; he pressed his closed hand against his abdomen.

"The police say it was a gang-related hit, but Angelo's mom told me he wasn't involved anymore."

He whirled to face her; he'd had no idea she still spoke with Angelo's mom. After their fathers had gone to prison, he had assumed they'd lost touch.

"The detectives tried to question Sarah, but when she learned Angelo didn't make it . . ." She closed her eyes. "I had no idea she was seeing him. His mom didn't know, either."

"Asher."

His stomach dropped at the sound of his sister's voice, and he turned to her, reaching for her hand. "Sarah."

She blinked a few times and rolled her head to the side to see him.

He gave her hand a gentle squeeze. "I'm so sorry." He bent down to kiss her head. "I'm sorry I wasn't there for you."

"He's gone," she said, liquid gathering in her eyes. "Why?"

He gulped. "I'll make this right. I promise." He kept his hold on her hand, but he looked back over his shoulder to see Luke and Jessica outside in the hall.

He'd felt her presence somehow.

He'd told both Luke and Jessica not to come because this wasn't their fight. But more than that, he was worried they'd try and stop him from what he had to do next.

* * *

JESSICA STOOD BEFORE HIM, HER EYES WIDE. "THIS ISN'T war. You can't take vengeance into your own hands. Not here. Not like this."

He eyed the ink on his arm, the brush of failure darting down his spine, leaving pain in its wake. "What difference does it make where I kill? Murder is murder." His shoulders shook at his words. "And that's what I already am: a killer."

He'd been grappling with what he'd done in Austria, and now . . .

How easily had he succumbed to wanting to kill again in the name of justice?

She grabbed hold of his bicep and lifted her chin to peer into his eyes. "No, you're not."

"I am," he seethed and leaned in closer to her. "I killed Egon." The truth dropped hard between them.

She didn't respond.

He added, "There was no hostage."

Her eyes thinned.

"And maybe I would've killed Samir if it weren't for you." He had no idea anymore what he was capable of.

Jessica had almost died.

Now his sister.

Two women in his life had their lives on the line, and he'd do anything—even sacrifice his soul—to make things right.

"No." A line crossed through her forehead. "If you killed Egon it was because you had no choice. I know you. You don't—"

"Maybe you don't know me at all." He needed her to see the ugly truth, to know he wasn't such a good guy after all.

He could never be like her. Forgive a murderer.

No, hell fucking no.

"The guy was on his back with his hands in the air, begging me to live, and I put a bullet in his forehead," he said through gritted teeth, allowing the anger at what Egon did to Jessica to thrive inside of him again, so he could feed off it like fuel.

Her gaze cut to the floor as if she couldn't look at him, as if she finally realized he truly was a monster. And it was what he wanted. What he needed so she wouldn't try and stop him from going after Angelo's killer.

He shifted out of her reach, stormed to the window in his office, and pressed his palms to it. But damn her, she came up behind him and touched the center of his back. "Whatever happened to Egon . . . it doesn't matter." A quietness filled the space between them, but only for a few moments.

"You can't just forgive me for that. It doesn't work—"

"I can, and I will."

He spun to face her, almost hating her for taking it so easy on him. He didn't deserve it.

"If you go after him, you're not just off the team—they'll put you in prison." She shook her head and her eyes closed. "Do you want to end up alongside your dad?"

His breathing slowed a touch. The team was everything to him. She was everything.

Could he throw everything away for the sake of retribution?

Her lids lifted, and the liquid in her eyes made them shimmer. "I just got you, Asher. Please. I can't lose you."

"I need to fix this," he said, his voice calmer now.

She was winning the fight—breaking him down, even though he didn't want her to.

She pressed her index finger to his chest. "How? How will you fix this? You'll either end up dead yourself or behind bars, and—"

"That was the choice I was faced with once before, and I—"

"Joined the Navy and made the right call." Her palm went to his chest, his heart beating erratically beneath her palm.

He heaved out a deep breath and looked heavenward. "I can't let these animals roam the streets."

His hands tightened into fists at his sides as he thought about Angelo, about the bastard who'd killed him and nearly murdered his sister.

He peered out the window, doing everything he could to avoid looking at her. But he squinted in the harsh light of day as the gleaming sun reflected off the building across the street and hit him, placing his sins on view. Everything exposed.

"Angelo was trying to be a better person, right?" She brought her hands to his face, forcing his eyes to behold hers. "The last thing he'd want is for his death to have you going backward when he'd been trying to go forward." Her eyes glinted with unshed tears. "Sarah needs you. Your mom does, too. The team. Me. We can't lose you."

He reached for her right wrist, her pulse climbing beneath his thumb, matching his own. "I'm a fighter. A killer. What if it's the same damn thing?"

"No, Asher. Every life you took in the past was—"

He removed her hands from his face and looked away. "Was what, Jessica? A bad guy?"

"Yes!" She reached for him again, refusing to give up on him.

His gaze lowered to her face, to the tears gliding down her smooth skin. She'd been keeping so much of herself hidden for years, but now, the evidence of her emotions was in plain sight. She was baring everything, but what if he didn't deserve it?

He wanted to wrap his fist around his heart and squeeze so it turned to dust. The struggle for breath grabbed hold of him, and a tremor rocked through his body.

"Let me help you find the men responsible for Angelo's death, and we'll put them behind bars where they belong." She tilted her head. "We're a team, remember? You go." Tears flowed down her cheeks now. "I go."

CHAPTER THIRTY-SEVEN

Knox, Liam, and Luke walked into the conference room where Asher and Jessica had set up, drawing his eyes from the screen.

"You called the guys?" Asher glanced at Jessica from across the table.

"Of course." She shifted her dark-rimmed glasses to the bridge of her nose and looked back at her laptop.

"We've got your back, man." Knox sat next to Jessica. "Owen's stuck in D.C., but Echo's en route."

"I, uh—" He didn't know what to say. He'd kept this part of his life from his team for a reason, and now here they were, being roped into his past.

"There aren't many cameras outside Angelo's club," Jessica began. "I have to spread the search area a bit wider during the time of death."

"You could've told us about Angelo. About your past," Liam said in a low voice as he positioned himself next to Knox.

Asher placed his hands in prayer position beneath his

chin, struggling to find the words to say. It was never easy to lay the truth out. "It's complicated" was all he managed.

Liam slowly nodded. "No witnesses came forward?"

"None," she said with a shake of the head.

"Most people at the fight club weren't exactly eager to talk about being there," Asher noted in a glib tone.

"If the NYPD did snag any statements, they're not uploading them into their systems for me to find," she added. "They'd want to protect a witness from retaliation, especially if this is gang-related."

"But he got out of all of that." Asher looked at the images of all the known gang members from Angelo's part of town in the file Jessica had miraculously pulled together in the last twelve hours.

Jessica grabbed her tablet and pointed at the screen. "This is Zander Jameson." She handed the tablet to her brother. "He runs a small Irish crew in Hell's Kitchen. He's known for throwing some illegal fights as well."

"What makes you think he's a suspect?" Luke asked, speaking for the first time, and Asher wondered what the hell he was thinking.

Had Jessica told him about Egon? Or how yesterday he'd been hell-bent on finding the killer to put him six feet under himself?

"Sarah and Angelo were at the club we were all at on Valentine's Day," she explained. "And I saw Zander arguing with Angelo that night. I pulled his image from the CCTV footage and ran it through my program to get a name."

Valentine's Day. The day his dad had been arrested, and now this. His stomach lurched at the memory of his father's arrest. His mother's homemade pasta all over the floor. The trail of marinara sauce spreading throughout his home as officers tossed the place.

"Zander was arrested for murdering two teenagers last year," Luke said while scrolling through the details on the tablet. "He really got off on a techni-fucking-cality?"

Asher's cheeks filled with air as he thought about the possibility Zander had murdered Angelo. He didn't know the guy, or why he'd want Angelo dead, but one thing was for certain—he sure as hell wouldn't get away with it.

"I think there's someone who might know who did this," he said as the realization hit him.

"Who?" Jessica asked as Luke handed her back the tablet.

Asher dragged a palm down his face and blew out a hard breath. "My father."

* * *

ASHER HAD MEMORIZED HIS DAD'S EIGHT-DIGIT PRISON ID a long time ago, even though he'd never used it. His father had sent him letter after letter, and each envelope had the same number attached to it on the return address.

He'd never opened the mail, but he used to stare at the envelopes before heading to the fight club. It had helped provoke and fuel his rage before entering the ring.

He wasn't sure if the letters had stopped coming to his mom's place during his time in the Navy; his mom had known better than to bring his dad up during his deployments.

He'd been seventeen when his dad had gone to prison. Had twenty years really gone by without a word passing between them?

Hell, he'd been out of his life for longer than he'd ever been in it.

"You're already on the approved visitor list," the guard said when he entered the building.

He'd nearly expected to be turned away, assuming he'd need preapproval to come, but apparently, his father had hoped he'd show some day.

A flicker of pain grew in his chest, and he rubbed at his pec muscles while he filled out the paperwork before turning it in with his ID.

After fifteen minutes of waiting, he was escorted with nineteen other people through two security checks, before entering an expansive room filled with rows of chairs. Vending machines took up one of the walls.

It wasn't what he'd expected, but then again, the movies weren't always the best at depicting reality with respect to his own line of work.

"Over there." A guard pointed to a blue chair, the uncomfortable kind he remembered from grade school. "He'll be out soon."

He anxiously rubbed his hands up and down his denim-clad thighs as he scanned the faces of the other visitors waiting in the room.

When two guards opened a door near the security desk, his heart damn near exploded, as if he'd been hit with a bullet. Twenty men, all dressed in khaki from head to toe, entered the room.

He slowly stood at the sight of his father at the back of the group. His black hair had turned silver. His once tan skin was now weathered with age.

As he moved closer, his deep-set eyes thinned.

"Son," he mouthed on approach, and Asher sat back down, not able to hug him or even shake his hand.

His dad slowly occupied the seat across from him, but Asher couldn't bring himself to look into his eyes.

Twenty fucking years—gone.

And he wasn't sure who to blame.

"What are you doing here?"

He leaned forward and pressed his elbows to his thighs, his fingertips rubbing at his forehead.

"Is Sarah okay? Your mom?"

"No." His spine went erect as he found his father's eyes. "But I'm betting you know what happened. No way does Angelo Moretti die and you not hear about it." The muscles in his arms tensed, along with his jaw.

His father's aged hands went to his thighs, and he gripped his khaki-covered legs. "Yeah, and I know the son of a bitch almost killed your sister. Hell, she may have been the original target."

His heartbeat escalated, and he edged to the end of the chair, on the verge of standing. "What do you mean? Who did this?"

"It's being taken care of; you don't need to get yourself involved." His dad crossed his ankle over his knee and observed Asher.

Asher looked around the room as it became more crowded, buzzing with conversation. No one was close enough to them for now, though. "What are you talking about?"

"Angelo gave up the life."

"Yeah, I know," he quickly replied, anxious to hear the things he didn't know.

"Not everyone was happy about that. When Angelo went legit, he began to draw the attention of more people. His fight club became more popular. Hell, word was the UFC was taking notice." He stroked his graying beard. "An Irish thug took a hit on his business because of it, and he blamed Angelo for stealing his crowd."

"Zander Jameson?"

His dad's eyes widened. How was it possible his father

knew so much while being locked up? Then again, he interacted with criminals on a daily basis through the revolving door of the prison. "So, you've heard of him."

"He was arguing with Angelo at a club on . . ." He couldn't get himself to utter the word without taking a damn pause. "Valentine's Day."

His father's brows drew inward, and he sat farther back in the blue chair, shifting uncomfortably. "Angelo told his father Zander had threatened to hurt Sarah."

Fuck. "Why didn't he stop seeing her, then? Why the hell didn't he protect her?" His veins burned, anger reigniting inside him.

"You know the Morettis. They don't back down from a fight." He shook his head. "The Jamesons are done. You can count on that."

"Angelo's dad ordered a hit?" This was what he'd wanted, wasn't it? To have the man responsible pay? But . . .

"Let's talk about you." He cocked his head. "My boy's a Navy SEAL. Did your mother tell you how proud of you I am?"

He bit down on his back teeth. "Let's maybe not talk about that in a room full of criminals," he seethed, catching his eyes.

"Even criminals are thankful for the military."

"Sure," he grumbled and roped a hand around the back of his neck, an edginess buzzing up his spine.

"I guess it's a good thing your mom met Bill, or maybe you'd be right where Angelo is now." He paused. "Of course, what you do is probably not all that safe, but if you're going to go out of this world, I couldn't think of a better way."

"What?" *Who the hell are you?* He wanted to stand, to pace—but he figured the guards wouldn't be in favor of that, so he kept his boots grounded to the floor.

Asher closed his eyes, unable to view his dad. Worried he'd see a reflection of himself in those brown eyes.

"I'm sorry, Son. I'm sorry I screwed up so bad."

"I shouldn't be here." But . . . he remained sitting.

"I'm glad you are, though."

He gulped and took a breath to calm his nerves. "I wanted to kill whoever hurt Sarah, who killed Angelo." He forced his eyes onto his dad, needing to know if he was, in fact, the same man as him. It was the other reason why he'd come, but he hadn't known that until this moment. "I've lost count of how many people I've killed over the years." His stomach knotted at his words. "So, I think I would've done it, but—"

"Nobody fucks with family," his dad interrupted. "But you're not me. You're not Angelo's dad. So, no, Son, you wouldn't have done it."

Asher shifted so his back touched the seat now, and he crossed his arms. "I am capable of . . ." He didn't know if he could voice the truth aloud, though. "I did something else." He swallowed. "I killed someone without orders." The surrounding chatter absorbed his words.

"I'm guessing that person hurt someone you care about? Someone you love, maybe?"

What'd his father know about love? "Maybe I should go."

"Please," he said while holding a palm in the air, "don't."

Asher rubbed at his beard, trying to make sense of the fact he was truly sitting across from a man he'd written off twenty years ago.

Jessica. His mind blew to images of her, to the woman who'd been like a reset button in his life, bringing new meaning to everything.

She'd forgiven Samir. Forgiven him for Egon. Could he forgive his father?

"Call off the hit." His words—his request—took him by surprise.

"What?" His dad's head jerked back.

"I'll make sure Zander ends up behind bars. You can count on that."

"That won't be enough for Moretti. You know that. Zander could end up back on the streets like he did last time he was arrested."

Asher rolled his shoulders back. "Or he could end up in here. With you. With Mr. Moretti."

"So, you *are* okay with him dying?" He lifted a brow.

"It's not up to me. It's up to the courts," he said, knowing deep in his gut he'd made a mistake back in Austria by taking Egon's life. And it was a mistake he wasn't entirely sure he could come back from, even with Jessica's forgiveness.

"I guess . . . we'll see if justice prevails then," his dad slowly said.

CHAPTER THIRTY-EIGHT

ASHER BLOCKED AN UPPERCUT AND DUCKED OUT OF THE WAY of a follow-up punch. He shifted on the balls of his feet, but when his eyes landed on Luke heading his way, he took a kick to the jaw at the loss of focus.

"Talk about timing." Luke draped his arms over the rope of the fighting ring. "Sorry about that."

Asher shook it off and looked at the fighter in the ring. "Give me five." He grabbed a water bottle and sucked it down before approaching Luke. "How'd you find me? My phone is off."

"This is the closest fighting gym to your hotel."

"I switched hotels," he grumbled back.

"Yeah, you could've given us the heads-up before we banged on the door this morning and scared the hell out of an old man." Luke climbed over the rope to step inside.

"Why are you here?"

"The funeral is tomorrow, and you've been off the grid ever since Zander was arrested five days ago." Luke eyed him steadily.

"For a reason." He shook out his arms, trying to loosen the tension inside of him.

Zander and his crew were behind bars, thanks to the evidence Jessica and his team had anonymously offered the police. Ironclad case. No technicalities this time. But he didn't feel better. And he wasn't ready to have round two of a conversation with Jessica yet.

"The team's worried about you," Luke said. "Your mom. Sister."

His words had Asher dropping his gaze to the padded floor.

"How is getting beaten up going to solve your problems?" he asked. "Because, based on your face, you've been letting someone hit you." He stripped off his jacket and tossed it to the side. "If you want someone to fight, you can fight me instead."

Asher nearly laughed. "I'm not fighting you."

"Why not? You think I can't handle you?"

"You can hold your own," he said with a sigh. "But—"

"But what?" Luke positioned himself in front of him with raised fists. "We throw down all the time. And we'll keep doing it if it helps."

"Not gonna happen." His shoulder blades pinched together, and he turned his back on him. "Go home."

"Not leaving here without you."

He motioned for the fighter waiting in the wings. "I need time."

"You need to grieve, but maybe you shouldn't do it like this." Luke wouldn't back down, damn it.

The fighter outside the ring did, unfortunately. He turned and walked away.

This wasn't what he needed right now. No, all he wanted was to hit something. To be hit. "I don't know if I can be on the team anymore. Maybe I should never have been on it to begin with. You should've let my superiors can my ass three and a half years ago." A bitter anger barked up his spine.

"No." Luke shook his head. "You're Bravo. One of us."

Asher swallowed. "I broke orders in Austria," he unleashed the truth. "I took the kill shot. There was no hostage."

He waited for Luke to process the news, but there was no change in his eyes, or in the way he stood. He didn't look the least bit surprised, actually.

"How'd you know? Jessica told you?" He locked his arms across his damp chest.

Luke pinched the bridge of his nose. "No, she didn't tell me."

"Then, how?" His mind raced as he digested the fact Luke had known the truth and had never said anything to him about it.

"Because when I did a sweep of the area where you killed him, I found a camera we hadn't accounted for. I scrubbed the footage to hide the evidence," he said in a low voice when he met his eyes.

A tightness stretched across his chest. "Why didn't you say anything?"

"What was there to say?" he asked. "I probably would've done the same thing. The man was an assassin who tortured my sister." He paused for a moment. "Egon had thirty-seven confirmed kills before you took him out. And you want to know how many kids died when he covered a kill with one of his explosions in Hong Kong last year?"

Asher held up his hand, not able to hear more.

"Egon belongs in a place worse than hell," Luke rasped.

Asher hung his head. "Doesn't change the fact you once said we don't take justice into our own hands."

And he'd been on the verge of doing it again with Angelo's killer had Jessica not talked him off the cliff.

"Shit changes when it comes to one of our own."

Asher's shoulders flared backward at his words.

"You used to stay so far on the right side of the line you could barely even see it. And now, you're saying it's okay I did what I did?"

"I told you when you joined the team that every once in a while I need someone to remind me what's right isn't always protocol. Austria's one of those times."

"I don't believe you would've killed Egon." The muscles in his body grew more rigid. "You're a better man than me."

"Yeah? If that were true, why would I be okay with you being with my sister?"

His words practically nailed him to the floor, and he rubbed a hand over his jaw.

"I want her to be happy, and apparently, *you* make her happy." Luke gripped the back of his neck and closed his eyes for a brief second. "After the funeral, take some time to clear your head. Get away for a while."

"What makes you think I'll come back?"

"Because you love her, remember? And I know you'd never hurt her."

CHAPTER THIRTY-NINE

BRAVO AND ECHO WERE THERE. THEY HADN'T EVEN KNOWN Angelo, but they'd come. They'd shown up at the funeral, and now they were at the reception.

Jessica hadn't said a word to him since she'd appeared in her black dress and heels. Her eyes would meet his for a fleeting moment over the past few hours and then drift away.

That was on him, though.

He'd been avoiding her all week.

But right now, he could feel her eyes on his back as he sucked down a drink, nodding at something a buddy was saying to him, even though he was in a total daze.

He'd considered going to some of the old haunts this past week, but he couldn't bring himself to walk down memory fucking lane to remember the days before he'd left for the Navy.

"You've been fighting again?" Sarah's arm was still in a sling, and it had his jaw clenching at the sight.

His friend parted ways with him now, and Asher lowered his tumbler from his lips and cocked his head, giving his sister his full attention. "What gave you that idea?"

She reached for his cheek with her good arm, and her fingers lightly feathered over his bruises. "The fight club's been closed down; so, where have you been going?"

Once she dropped her hand to her side, he finished his drink. He couldn't bring himself to say anything. His thoughts were still cloudy.

"Angelo changed, Asher. I know you didn't believe him." Her lashes swept down as she gathered a breath.

"I know."

She peered back at him. "Dad said you visited. That meant a lot to him."

He'd learned his mom still visited his old man, but was his sister really in contact with him as well?

"Yeah, we, uh, talk." She finished her wine and rolled her lips inward before finally speaking. "After college, we reconnected. I decided to visit him on a whim, and then it turned into a regular monthly thing."

"Monthly?" His hand snaked up to the back of his neck, and he squeezed as tension shot through him. "Why?"

"Bill's great and all, but Dad's Dad. You know?"

"No, I don't know. He's a murd—" He cut himself off, realizing the hypocrisy of his choice of words. Wasn't he technically a killer, too? *Shit.* "And Mom visits, too, huh?"

She glanced toward their mother; she was talking to Angelo's sister, who'd come down from Boston for the funeral. "She visits once or twice a year. Always has."

He looked down at the floor, his mind racing. "Does Bill know?"

"Of course." She reached for his arm, and he looked into his sister's big brown eyes. "Dad may have killed someone, but he promises it was an accident, and I'm choosing to believe him."

Her words had him stepping back and out of her reach.

More forgiveness. It was going around, apparently.

"But let's not think about that right now. Today is about Angelo." Her eyes began to well. "And you were right about one thing in regard to him. You warned me. You said he'd hurt me." Her voice cracked. "Falling in love is painful, and so, I guess if you never do it, you can't get hurt."

"That's not what I meant, but—"

"I'm done, you know? Everyone I ever care about leaves. Dad. You. Greg." A tear rolled down her cheek. "Now, Angelo."

"Don't talk like that." He set his glass down on the bar top table near him.

What was he supposed to say right now? Something insightful? Hopeful? He was too messed up to think straight himself, let alone offer words of wisdom.

"I'm so sorry," he managed and pulled her in for a hug. He held her tight against him as she cried, but his eyes landed on Jessica's as she now stood with his mom, ten feet away.

The beats of his heart seemed to slow as he observed her, everything inside of him tensing as he eyed the woman he loved.

His sister was right. Falling in love was hard. And it did hurt.

But he also didn't know if he could handle the alternative —a life without it.

A few minutes later, he pulled away from his sister and found Sarah's eyes. "I'm going to be a better brother. I promise."

She forced a smile to her lips, but before she could respond, a friend placed a hand on her shoulder and pulled her in for a hug.

Asher strode across the room to Jessica.

"Can we talk?" he asked her.

"Um." She blinked. "Yeah." She looked at his mom. "Excuse me."

He grabbed her coat by the door and offered it to her before they stepped out onto the street.

"Are you okay?" She tightened the belt of her coat and observed him.

"I will be." He brushed his hands down his face. "But I need to get away, to take some time to process everything that's happened."

Her breath floated into the cool air. "Okay." But there was hesitation in her eyes.

Without thinking, he closed the small gap between them and took hold of her face between his palms the way she had back at the office last week when she talked him off the ledge.

She stared at him with parted lips.

And then he brought his mouth to hers.

He kissed her hard, his lips burning from the touch.

When their mouths broke, she whispered, "Go." She lightly nodded. "But come back to me, okay?"

CHAPTER FORTY

"Were you Skyping with the girls?" Luke leaned into the doorframe to her office.

She closed her laptop. "Yeah, they're back in Berlin." Memories of Ara flitted to mind. "I thought it'd be better for them if I stayed out of their lives, but—"

"You smartened up?" A smile crossed his lips, and he strode farther into her room and stood on the other side of her desk. "How are they holding up?"

She squeezed her eyes shut. "They miss Ara. And me. They're confused about everything that happened, and I didn't have the heart to tell them the entire story."

"Probably best not to."

"I went to see the girls in the Bronx yesterday, too. It's been too long. I've sort of been distracted by—well, everything. I need to make more time for them. For everyone in my life."

"You want to step back?" He cocked his head and looped his thumbs into the front pockets of his jeans. "Need a break?"

"No, but I did have an idea." She motioned for him to sit. "I want to bring someone else onto the team."

"Who?"

"Harper Brooks."

"The same Harper from the CIA who nearly died in France?"

"Yeah, from the op that had you nearly tripping all over yourself as you fell in love." She smiled as she thought about Eva. About her baby niece. She'd barely had any time to spend getting to know her niece. It'd been one thing after another.

"Harper's smart. Her tech and cyber skills are comparable to mine."

He scoffed. "I doubt that."

"It's true, but anything she doesn't know, I can teach her."

He stroked his trimmed beard and dragged his focus down to the floor. "You think she'd want this, though, especially given what happened to her?"

Harper was also a fighter, like Jessica; so, she'd be up for the challenge. "She has family in New York. I think she'd like to come back home."

Home. New York had been Jessica's home for years, but did she really know her own city?

"Let's run it by the team and call POTUS to see if we can bring her in." He paused for a beat. "Speaking of the president, Rutherford called before I came in here."

She rolled her eyes at the mention of his name. She was still pissed at how he handled everything. "Yeah, and what'd he want?"

"Guess POTUS ripped him a new one, because he called to apologize."

"Yeah, well, the president didn't exactly help our situation all that much, either."

He nodded in agreement. "Rutherford won't be calling you, though. I told him he owes you an in-person visit." He mumbled something incoherent under his breath, clearly still clinging to his anger like her.

"I'm not in the mood for a social call from him. Tell him to send me an *I'm sorry* memo," she said with a smirk.

"Will do." Luke briefly dropped his head, stealing his eyes from view. "I owe you an apology as well."

"For deleting Asher's text?"

He looked back at her. "It was an asshole move. I wasn't thinking. I'm so sorry."

Her thoughts veered to Asher's two-week absence now. "Well, apology accepted." She looked out the window, the sun filtering through the partially open blinds. "How do you think Asher's doing?"

"We all deal with death in our own ways." His voice had been low, as if remembering when he'd lost Marcus, or another SEAL during his time on the Teams. "Asher told me about Egon."

Her forehead lifted in surprise. "He told you what happened?"

"I already knew, but yeah, he mentioned it."

Her stomach sank, and she brought her thumb between her teeth.

"I think he's worried he can't come back from what he did." His nostrils flared as their eyes reconnected.

"And what'd you tell him?" She rubbed her arms as goose bumps scattered over her skin.

"That I would've done the same," he quickly answered, and her gut told her he was telling the truth, but she doubted Asher would've believed Luke's words.

The team revered Luke—he was Bravo One—but he was still a man. He bled. And she knew when it came to family, to his fiancée and daughter, he'd chase a demon to hell and back if it meant keeping his loved ones safe.

"I got his knife back from the Feds—the one you gave him for Christmas," he said. "I put it in his office this morning." He tipped his head toward the door. She'd nearly forgotten Asher had been asked to turn it over to the Feds since he'd used it on Samir's s-vest outside Langley. He hadn't been thrilled about that. "Do you want to give it back to him?"

"If"—she cleared her throat—"*when* he comes to the office, I'll let him know it's there."

She thought about their goodbye. The way his mouth had slanted over hers just before he'd taken off. The hard sting of regret poured through her for ever letting him leave, though. Maybe being alone was the exact opposite of what he needed. *He* had been what she'd needed during her toughest times.

"Maybe you should stop waiting for him to come back and just go get him." He lifted his shoulders. "He needs you."

Her eyes widened. "I don't know where he is." Her fingertips smoothed over her mouth at the memory of his kiss.

"And you're going to let something like that stop you?"

* * *

"Asher? The door was unlocked. Are you in here?" She set her carry-on down and closed the door behind her. "Hello?"

She scanned the visible living area of the two-story cabin before her gaze swept up the stairs to where she heard faint sounds.

She gripped the railing, needing the support as she climbed the stairs.

Muffled cries came from above—*Oh, God.* Maybe someone was in trouble.

She raced up the last few steps and followed the sounds to the last door on the right. But she hung her head as she stood frozen outside the door.

No one was in trouble.

She'd tracked him all the way to Colorado, and now . . .?

Her hand pressed to her abdomen, and she rested her head against the door, fighting back tears.

"Oh, yes. Yes. Yes!" A woman was full-on grunting like an animal in the wild.

Jessica shoved away from the door.

"Bloody hell, you're a wild one."

Her palms landed back on the door, her body tensing at the sound of . . . *Wyatt?* Not thinking, she grabbed hold of the knob and pushed the door open.

"Wyatt! What the hell are you doing here?"

"Jessica?" Wyatt peeked around the naked woman still riding him, and his gaze narrowed on Jessica. "What are *you* doing here?" He shifted the woman off his lap and plopped her down next to him before standing.

Jessica shielded her eyes with her hand and then turned her back. "Could you do something about your nakedness?" Heat crawled up her neck, but the guilt at ever believing, even for a second, that Asher could've been in the room with another woman absorbed her thoughts.

"I don't know who she is, but she's hot," the woman said. "You want to join us, sugar?"

"Fuck no," Wyatt rasped. "She's my boss. And like a sister."

"Are you decent now?" She slowly faced the room and lowered her hand to find Wyatt in jeans.

He strode before her and reached for her forearm. "What are ya doing here?"

"I was looking for Asher. I don't understand why you're here, though." She stepped back.

He brought his hand to the nape of his neck and squeezed. "This is my place." He blinked a few times and looked over his shoulder at the woman. "You think maybe you could cover those things up? You know, seeing that my boss is here and all."

The woman blushed and pulled the sheet up over her breasts.

"Sorry about interrupting, but I thought you were—"

"Asher?" He chuckled. "The bloke thinks he's a mountain man or something. He's probably out chopping wood."

She dragged a hand down her face, trying to process everything. "Maybe you can shed some light on all of this. You know, like, what the hell is going on?" Her tongue pinned to the roof of her mouth.

His arms crossed. "Asher needed a place to lie low for a bit, and so I offered my cabin. No one knows I have a place in Boulder, and so . . ."

"Yeah, speaking of that, I do need to know about every place you own."

He smiled. "Oh, do ya, now?"

"Yeah." She nodded and forced her thoughts back to what Wyatt had said. Was Asher outside? Had he seen her drive up? "So, why are you here, then?"

"He's had his phone off, and he's been up here for a few weeks. I got worried, so I flew in two days ago to check on him."

"You could've told me this back in New York."

"I couldn't narc on him. Sorry." He scratched at his

trimmed beard. "But it's probably a good thing you came. I think he needs you. He's a bit out of sorts."

"Sixteen days without a word." She gathered a hard breath and released it. "And you came and did what, exactly?" She peeked over at the blonde in bed.

"Asher didn't come into town with me. I got in trouble all on my own. No worries."

She flinched at the sound of the door closing down below.

"It looks like the man of the hour is back."

"Do you think he's going to be pissed to see me?" She turned toward the door and caught a flash of bluish-black fabric from over the railing.

"He'll be something—doubt it'll be angry." Wyatt nodded. "Go ahead. I'll be down in a second."

She took slow steps out of the room and strode to the top of the stairs to find Asher's back to her, his gaze on her bag by the door.

"Jessica." Her name from his lips had her spine straightening, and he turned in her direction and looked up. "Wyatt ratted me out?" His right brow arched.

She forced her feet to move, but she couldn't take her eyes off him as she came down the steps, her pulse climbing. "No. I got impatient, so I looked for you."

"This place isn't on the map."

"Yeah, I'm wondering what else Wyatt's keeping from us." She stopped at the bottom step and clutched the railing, worried she'd lose her footing. "Are you okay?"

He was in jeans, boots, and a blue and black button-down flannel. Wyatt was right. Asher, of all people, looked like a man who belonged in nature—not a guy raised on the streets of New York City.

"Luke got your knife back from the Feds," she said when he didn't say anything.

His eyes were steady on hers, but for some reason, she couldn't get a read on him. "You came all the way here to bring me it?" He cocked his head.

"Uh, no." Her lips parted into a near smile. "The airline frowns upon knives in carry-ons."

"So, why are you here?"

She rolled her tongue over her front teeth, buying her a second of time. "Do you want me to go?"

Instead of answering, Asher looked up over her shoulder, and she assumed Wyatt was on approach. She should've been able to hear him, but her heartbeat competed with nearly every sound in the cabin.

"I didn't tell her. I swear." Wyatt walked past her, followed by his partner, who glanced at Jessica from over her shoulder once they reached the door.

Asher stepped out of their way, sidestepping Jessica's bag.

"I think you two might need to talk, and there's a pint with my name on it in town." Wyatt patted Asher on the shoulder and then opened the door and left with the woman without another word.

Silence spilled into the room once they were alone. "I guess I made a mistake in coming," she announced when Asher remained casually standing, rubbing at his beard, which had gotten thicker during their time apart.

"I needed time to think, Jessica."

The way he said her name was like a gut-punch. She did her best to stay upright, her fingers nearly whitening as she continued to clutch the railing. "Do you need more time?"

He turned his back and walked through the living room and to the kitchen. There a bottle of Scotch on the counter, and he filled a glass halfway before facing her with the drink in hand. "You want one?"

"Sure." She came into the kitchen and took the glass from him.

He braced one palm on the counter at his side and stared at her instead of pouring another drink. "I'm sorry I haven't been in touch."

"I understand. Kind of went through the same thing after Ara died," she admitted, remembering when she'd banned the team from visiting while she grieved. She was pretty sure Luke was right, though, and Asher's disappearance was about more than Angelo's death. "I got worried. Sorry."

He was quiet for a moment, and she waited for him to talk, needing to hear what he had to say. "I told the president about what I did. I needed him to know the truth."

She nearly dropped the glass as she moved toward him, worry flowing down her spine. She set the glass on the counter.

"Do you know what he told me?" He shook his head. "If he'd been me, he would've sacrificed his job and killed Egon for hurting someone he loved." His eyes fell shut, and his cheeks filled with air before he released the breath.

"Asher?" Her hands went to his chest as she peered up at him. "Remember when you told me to find the fight inside of me—is that what you were doing here?" God, she hoped so.

"I guess so." His brows lowered. "Angelo died. I nearly killed his murderer. And I *did* kill Egon."

"That's a lot to process."

He lightly gripped her biceps, and she kept her hands positioned on his pecs.

"I don't want to lose you," she softly admitted.

His deep brown eyes thinned, and then he leaned forward and pressed his forehead to hers. "I want to come home," he said after a minute.

"New York?" She pulled back to view his eyes.

He nodded. "I'm ready to settle down in one place."

"But you hate—"

"I was scared I'd become who I once was if I lived there."

Emotion thickened in her throat. "And now?"

"I realized I never stopped being that guy."

She thought about his words, trying to make sense of what he was saying.

"Maybe it's time I stop running from who I was." The back of her hand raced over his cheek. "Maybe I never needed to run."

She took a breath. "Well, I want all of you. Whoever you are. Whoever you want to be. And you know why?"

The muscle in his jaw tightened, but he waited for her to continue.

"Because I love you." Tears rolled down her cheeks, and her bottom lip trembled.

His brows knitted, and his chest rose and fell with slow breaths, but he remained quiet, observing her.

"I have some issues I still have to work through, and so I'm not perfect by any means, but—"

His mouth captured hers, and she groaned against his lips as he stole her breath.

"I love you so fucking much," he rasped between hungry kisses.

"Mm. You and your love for the word *fuck*."

He laughed, and his beard tickled her lips into a smile. "I see you're back to busting my balls already." In one fast and hot movement, he pinned her to the cabinets with his body and cocked his head, his mouth close to hers. "And I fucking love it, Peaches."

CHAPTER FORTY-ONE

"My brother's cool with us being together, but if he walks in on us having sex on my desk, he still might kill you."

Asher bunched her skirt up to her hips and tugged her panties down to her ankles. "I'd say it's worth the risk." He kissed the inside of her thighs and pressed two fingers inside of her, noticing her legs slightly trembling as she stood in her black heels, her lower back to the desk. "Do you know how many times I've thought about you and me in your office?"

"You promised never to think about me naked —remember?"

"I lied." He rose to his feet and cupped her ass cheeks before placing her atop her desk. He dipped into his pocket and produced a condom from his jeans. "I hate these things, but since we're in your office, and we'll be in a hurry—"

"Yes. Please, hurry."

He grinned. "Well, now . . . I feel like slowing down." He set the foil pack on the desk. His fists bore down on each side of her, and he arched a brow and brought his mouth near hers.

"Mm, if you don't get inside of me right now, I'm going to fire you."

"Under one condition."

"What?" she growled out.

"Tell me, the cherries—do you really love them that much, or were you fucking with me for months?"

"Like you're any better," she said with a laugh. "Every time you sunk your teeth into a peach over the last three years with your eyes pinned to mine—where do you think I got the idea of such torture?"

"Good point." He slipped a hand over her black silk blouse and popped the top buttons. He unsnapped her bra, freeing her tits, and his cock grew even heavier and thicker in his jeans.

He glanced at the locked door before focusing back on the woman he loved, ready to devour every inch of her.

"We really do have to hurry. Harper's going to be here soon to meet the team. I prefer to keep you and all your sexiness to myself, and so—" He kissed away her words and snatched the condom.

She reached between their bodies and worked at his jeans to free his shaft. "I want you to give it to me hard. Okay?"

"Got a pillow to muffle your screams?" The memory of their first time at the barracks blew to his mind as he sheathed himself.

"Your thumb will do," she said, and he followed orders.

He buried himself deep inside of her a moment later, and her back arched—her hands bearing down on the desk on each side of her.

She squeezed her tight pussy around him, offering even more resistance, and she bit down on his thumb as he moved in and out of her, watching her nipples harden, and her tits shake as he thrust harder and faster.

She shifted, rotating her hips as they moved together.

Moaning so loud she nearly let go of his thumb in her mouth, she tipped her head back, her eyes on the ceiling as she came.

"Jessica," he said under his breath as the blood rushed south, and his balls tightened almost painfully before he exploded inside of her.

"Yes," she murmured. "You were right. The risk was worth it." She stared at him, her eyes hazy. "We might need to do this again after lunch."

He smiled as he helped her to her feet and then removed the condom.

"Hey, you guys decent?" Liam asked from the other side of the door.

He rolled his eyes. "Naked. One second."

She slapped his chest, and he grinned as he reached out and palmed her breast. "I don't feel like working right now."

"We've been back for three weeks and haven't gone on a single op. Don't jinx us." Her teeth sank into her lip as he pinched her nipple. "Are we still on for dinner with your family tonight at your sister's restaurant?"

"Yeah, if you think you can handle it."

She smiled. "Of course I can." She casually rested her arms over his shoulders and wet her lips. "You've been a great brother since you've been home," she noted, her tone a touch more serious. "You know that, right?"

He tilted his head to the side. "Well, I have a lot of time to make up for."

"Hey, you guys done in there?" It was Knox this time.

Asher shook his head and zipped up his pants.

"Does everyone know what we were just doing?" She pulled her skirt down and started to work at her blouse buttons. "I thought I was pretty quiet."

"They can probably smell the sex," he said with a laugh.

"The guys are going to enjoy screwing with us for a while." She smirked.

He wrapped a hand around her hip and tugged her back against him, greedy for more of her. He wanted to be close to her every chance he could get. *They* also had lost time to make up for. "Probably." He raised a fist beneath her chin. "But according to Liam, we've been driving them nuts for years with all of our, uh, tension . . ."

"So we owe them a few jabs?"

"Something like that."

"Harper here yet?" Jessica called out.

"Not yet," Knox said.

"Then why are you banging on the door?" She lightly chuckled.

"Because Luke called," Knox answered.

"I thought Luke was in his office." Asher went to the door, peeked at Jessica from over his shoulder to make sure she was dressed, and then unlocked and opened it.

Knox crossed his arms. "He left an hour ago."

Jessica moved to stand next to Asher. "Something wrong?"

"We're needed on an op. We roll out in two hours."

Jessica pivoted to face Asher and slapped him on the arm. "See, you jinxed us."

Asher surrendered his palms apologetically and tossed in a smile for good measure before he shifted his gaze back to Knox. "I guess Harper will start working straight away. Where're we headed?"

Knox fingered the collar of his shirt and glanced between the two of them. "Vegas." He cleared his throat. "And he said we'll need tuxes." Knox smiled. "You'll need a dress. Something that won't draw the attention of every guy with a pulse." He rubbed his palms together. "Vegas and all."

"What aren't you telling us?" Jessica asked, but Knox turned away. "Knox? Knox!"

"Are you thinking what I'm thinking?" Asher gathered her into his arms once he was out of sight.

"What?"

"We have two more hours."

"Harper will still be here soon."

He smiled. "Yeah, well, I'm sure one of these guys will rudely interrupt once she gets here. So, in the meantime . . ." He gently kissed her, and when her mouth slanted and her lips parted, he lost control and pulled her back into the office.

"Back at the desk," he said, his voice rough, once the door was shut and locked.

"Is that an order?" She fought a smile. "I thought I was the boss."

He grinned. "A team, remember?"

EPILOGUE

ASHER KEPT HIS EYES LOCKED ON JESSICA, UNABLE TO LOOK anywhere else even though Luke and Eva, and Owen and Samantha, were tying the knot right now.

Jessica looked gorgeous in a long, strapless pale pink dress that touched the ground, hiding her heels. But it was her blue eyes—pinned to his—that captivated him.

Their op: a double wedding. Not too incognito with the entire Hollywood Reed family present, but it was pulled together pretty damn fast since both couples had decided wedding planning was overrated. They'd rather duck away to Vegas with a few friends and family members and then jet off to honeymoon in Hawaii after.

He didn't blame Luke and Owen, but he'd been surprised the idea had come from the brides.

But now that Asher was standing alongside his brothers-in-arms at the altar, all he could think about was how much he wanted to marry Jessica, to make her his, officially and forever.

She'd shown up to Boulder less than a month ago, and yet, he didn't need any more time to know what he wanted:

her. Of course, he wouldn't drop to his knee tonight. After Owen's epic proposal, he'd have to up his game, but he knew for certain a wedding between them would happen.

The woman loved him for him. She didn't want to change him, but she damn sure made him a better man, whether she realized it or not.

He coughed into a closed fist as emotion gathered in his throat, and he finally swept his gaze to Luke and Eva as they shared their first kiss as husband and wife. Next, Owen and Samantha.

Two of his best friends had fallen in love, but Asher was pretty sure he'd fallen long before they had. It hadn't been the right time for him and Jessica then, but it was their time now.

He found Jessica's blue eyes again, his chest tightening. "I love you," he mouthed from across the way, where they stood at the Venezia pool gardens beneath the dark sky, the moon glowing above.

"I love you," she mouthed back, and then they clasped hands to follow the brides and grooms down the aisle after the ceremony ended.

He caught sight of baby Lara atop Eva's dad's lap in the audience as he walked, and he'd swear Lara smiled at him. Being a father was an idea that had never crossed his mind. Not until now, at least.

"Are you okay?" Jessica whispered as they walked.

He held on to her hand even tighter and looked over at her, her long blonde hair swept up, showing her long, slender neck. "Never better," he said when his attention drifted from the pearl earrings he'd given her to her beautiful blue eyes.

"Me, too," she said as they entered the hotel.

After the introductions, food, and a few hilarious speeches—especially when Wyatt and Liam took control of the mic—Asher pulled Jessica onto the dance floor.

"Did you know your brother was as romantic as Owen?" He slung her arms around his neck and then held on to her hips as they started to dance.

"I had no idea." Her white teeth flashed. "But I think this night suits them. They're not exactly ostentatious kind of guys. An impromptu trip disguised as an op to Vegas is much more their speed."

He twirled her around, which elicited a gasp of surprise, and then she pressed a quick kiss to his lips. "Keep that up, and we'll be bailing on this night early."

A few seconds later, she turned her back to him and rotated her hips, her ass cheeks grinding into his cock. "Payback later," he said into her ear before spinning her back to face him.

She slung her arms around his neck again. "Promise?"

He kissed her bottom lip, sucking it between his teeth before whispering, "Ti amo tanto. Voglio essere sempre con te."

"Mm. Love it when you talk Italian to me." She briefly lifted her eyes to the ceiling as if in thought before capturing his focus again. "Senza di te non posso più vivere," she said. "How'd I do?"

"Molto bene." He winked and stared deep into her eyes, losing himself. "What kind of wedding do you want?" The question had drifted from his lips before he'd realized what he'd asked.

"I never thought about it before," she softly replied. "But if the right man were to ask me, I'd say on a beach somewhere. Alone."

"No family?"

She lifted one shoulder. "Fine. Family only."

"Everyone here is family, though." All the Teamguys—they were the same as blood, so . . .

"Okay, we can make more room on that beach." She chuckled.

He flashed a grin. "Are you saying I'm that lucky guy, then? The 'right man'?"

"Oh, no. That guy is upstairs, waiting in my room. You're just too damn hot in this tux to pass up at the moment."

He leaned in and brought his mouth near hers. "I'm pretty sure you'll forget about him once you've been with me." He could tell she was fighting either a laugh or an eye roll.

"You feel like making a bet?"

He raised a hand to his head. "I'm growing my hair back out."

"Mm. I miss it, actually." Her fingers raced over his hair. "A different wager."

"What do you have in mind?" He nuzzled his face into her neck, smelling her delicious scent, and then he brought his mouth to her ear. "Please tell me it involves you naked."

"It does, in fact. Also involves the belt to my robe."

"Oh, does it?" He pulled back and smiled.

"If I can make you come within sixty seconds—you move in with me."

"And if you don't?"

"I won't lose." She bit into her lip.

His eyes narrowed. "How about we buy a place together instead?"

"A fresh start?"

He lost his hold on her and rubbed at his chest, his heart close to exploding, which seemed to happen whenever he was around her. "I like that idea."

She gave a slight nod, and then her gaze drifted over his shoulder. He tracked her eyes to Harper—the latest recruit. "She's alone," Jessica murmured. "We should go over there."

"And leave my balls blue?" He reached between them to adjust his pants.

"Well, you're the one who wouldn't let me finish going down on you in the bathroom between songs twenty minutes ago."

"Because your cock-block brother knocked on the door."

Her lips stretched into a smile, a reminder of how she'd deep-throated him earlier while cupping his balls. And there went his cock again. Hard. Hard. Hard.

"Rain check?"

"Mm. It's gonna be one hell of a check." He cursed under his breath as they walked toward Harper, chuckling as a few of the Teamguys twirled their jackets over their heads near her. Tequila had to be the culprit.

"Not what you expected for your first op, huh?" Jessica asked Harper once they were within earshot of her.

Harper's dimpled cheeks lifted as she smiled. "No, but can all ops be like this?"

Asher loosened his bow tie. "I'm not a huge fan of this getup, so that'd be a *no* from me."

"You look so hot, though." A smile teased Jessica's lips before she rolled her tongue over her teeth, seducing him— challenging him to take her right there.

But shit, her dad was about twenty feet away, so he'd be on his best behavior. He'd try, at least. But if she shook her ass against his crotch again while on the dance floor, no adjustment of his slacks would ever ease his erection.

"Surprised to see you guys in tuxedos and not your dress blues," Harper said.

"Yeah, well, Luke's not a fan of standing out as SEALs. Owen's the same," Asher pointed out.

"Right. You guys are more secretive than I had to be in

my previous gig," Harper said before Emily came up alongside them.

"They're going to throw their garter belts, I think." Emily tipped her chin to the center of the dance floor, now clearing out.

Eva sat on a chair next to Samantha. She braced her hands against Luke's shoulders and laughed when he ducked his head under her dress to search for her garter belt.

And, of course, Owen used his teeth for his turn.

"Come on. Ninety percent of you guys are single," Luke hollered to the crowd of SEALs. "Get your asses over here."

Owen tossed the white strap of lace first—and Wyatt nearly dropped it when he caught it.

"That's why you should take an interest in football—the American kind," Knox teased. "You could learn to catch."

Wyatt tipped his chin. "Funny," he grumbled and twirled the lace around his index finger.

"You're not going to go out there?" Jessica asked as Asher remained standing on the outskirts of his semi-inebriated brothers.

"No, I don't need one of those to know I'm getting married." He stole a quick kiss from her and threaded their fingers together.

"Confident, huh?"

"Damn right." He winked before catching sight of Luke chucking the garter into the crowd.

Liam caught it and tossed it right away. "Hell, no," he said with a laugh.

"Our turn," Harper announced.

"I'm good. The flowers are all yours." Jessica leaned against Asher, and he wrapped his arm around her, pulling her tight into his side. "Who do you think Harper will end up with?"

"Why? You think she'll have one of our guys falling at her feet?" he asked as the few single women stood before Eva and Samantha to catch the flowers.

"Oh, come on. Look what happened with us working together." She whistled and clapped when Harper scored the first bouquet. "See?"

"Hm." He looked at his buddies in the crowd, wondering if Jessica was right. But he also knew they were as stubborn as he was, so it'd take a lot for them to change tunes.

"Emily caught the other one," Jessica said a moment later as the DJ walked onto the dance floor.

"Gentlemen, how about a dance with the ladies who caught the bouquets?" the DJ suggested.

"Oh, um." Harper shook her head as the DJ approached her. "We don't need to—"

"Come on," the DJ insisted and motioned for her to head toward Wyatt.

"She reminds me of someone," Grace, Jessica's best friend, said as she came up alongside them.

"Who? Harper?" Jessica looked at her.

"Yeah"—Grace snapped her fingers—"Meghan Markle. The one who married Prince Harry."

"Wyatt's British," Asher said with a laugh. "A match made in heaven."

"Yeah, well, I think we should protect Harper from Wyatt." Jessica's cheeks reddened. "Did I mention that I walked in on him naked in—"

"Say what?" Asher whirled to face her.

She chuckled. "Yeah, I thought it was you."

"You thought I . . ." He couldn't voice his thoughts. Instead, he pinched his eyes tight to try and let go of the memory of Wyatt naked in front of Jessica. He rubbed his face, trying to physically scrub the image away. "Yeah, well, you're right. Wyatt's—"

"A bad boy?" Grace smiled.

"You don't know the half of it," Asher said under his breath. "Yeah, let's keep them away from each other."

"What about Emily?" Grace asked, and Asher followed her eyes to watch Emily and Liam dancing.

Even from where he stood, he could tell the guy was working his charm on her.

"Who knows—if a tough guy like you can fall in love, maybe there's hope for them, too." Jessica turned into his arms, and he rubbed her bare biceps, anxious to get her out of that dress and pinned naked beneath him.

"Out of the two of us, Peaches, you were the tough one to crack." He leaned in closer so his lips hovered near hers.

"Yeah, he's probably right," Grace said.

He'd nearly forgotten he wasn't alone with Jessica. Whenever they were together, the world seemed to disappear.

"Thank God you found a way, though," she whispered against his lips before he lifted her off the ground and kissed her.

* * *

"You're much naughtier than I realized."

Asher parted her thighs with his knee and braced himself over her. "And you loved every minute of it." He nipped her bottom lip. "And you want more, don't you?" He raised his brows a few times and smiled.

She arched her back off the bed; her hands were tied to the headboard with the silk belt from her red robe. "And I get whatever I want now since I won the bet."

"I may have purposefully conceded," he said with a smile.

"Sure. Sure. Sure."

He stared at her full lips before settling on her blue eyes. "You're so beautiful."

"Mm. You are, too."

He shook his head, his forehead lifting. "No."

"Okay. Ruggedly sexy. Hotter than your body double Aquaman, which I didn't think was possible, but—"

"My what?" Laughter erupted from deep within his chest. "I didn't take you for a comic fan."

"Oh," she said with a lazy grin, "that's not why I—"

"Well, does he have a queen?" He lowered himself closer, so their bodies touched.

"He's a king, so . . ." Her words converted to a throaty gasp when he buried two fingers into her wet center. He removed his hand a moment later, and she tugged her wrists, pulling at the silk knot attached to the headboard. "Not fair. What are you doing?"

He inched his way down her body, his mouth trailing a line of kisses in the process. "Bowing down to my queen."

"Hey!" a voice hollered through the door. "You awake?"

Asher groaned and pressed his forehead to her abdomen. "Your brother and his damn timing."

She chuckled. "Tell me about it."

"Why isn't he doing the same thing with his wife?" He shifted to his knees and untied her.

"Yeah?" she called out.

"Can I come in?" Luke asked.

"One minute," she answered, and Asher slapped her ass when she stood.

He handed her the belt once she slipped on her robe, and then, for himself, grabbed the white cotton robe that was courtesy of the hotel.

Jessica opened the door, and Luke rushed in. "Sorry, I—"

His eyes landed on the bed, the comforter crumpled at the bottom. "Shit."

"What'd you think we were doing in here?" Asher scratched at the back of his head when Luke forced himself to face him a beat later.

"Yeah, uh . . . POTUS called. We're needed in Argentina."

"What?" Her mouth rounded. "You just got married. You leave for Hawaii tomorrow."

"Yeah, well, you know bad guys don't give a fuck about my vows." He crossed his arms.

"How many men do we need?" she asked, tightening the belt of her robe.

"Five. Maybe seven."

Jessica placed her hands on her hips. "Asher and I can handle this. We'll take Echo. You and Owen stay on vacation. Plus, this gives Harper a chance to get her feet wet."

"You sure?" Luke's arms tensed, the muscles flexing as his fingertips bit into his biceps while he considered her suggestion. He'd had a hard enough time giving up control during his paternity leave—but he sure as hell better do it for his honeymoon as well.

"What do you say?" She turned to Asher. "Want to save the world with me?"

Asher smiled. "Well damn, woman, when you put it like that, how can I say *no*?"

"See?" She faced her brother. "You go on your honeymoon, and we'll handle Argentina."

"I don't know." His arms dropped to his sides. "Maybe ask Liam or Knox to come with you guys, too."

"I've got Jessica's back," he said while finding her eyes. "And she's got all of ours."

Luke expelled a hard breath, a slow roll of tension

dropping into the room. "Shit, okay. Eva would kill me, so . . ."

"Good. Now, how much time until I have to round up the boys?" she asked.

"A couple of hours. But you might need to schedule in some time to find Liam. Knox is passed out, but I haven't seen Liam since the reception last night."

"Maybe he got hitched," she joked.

"Funny," Luke grumbled.

She pulled him in for a hug. "Now, go get laid. Your wife is waiting for you."

Luke mumbled something before pulling away then found Asher's eyes.

He gave him a reassuring nod, letting him know he'd keep Jessica safe. "Have fun in Hawaii. Make another baby." He patted Luke on the shoulder and said goodbye before closing and locking the door.

"So." He cocked his head to the side and strode toward her. Then he reached for the knot of her belt and tugged at it.

"What are you doing?" Her eyes lit with a smile.

"You heard the man. We have time." He peeled off her robe, so she was standing naked in front of him. "Now," he said and lifted her into his arms, "let's get you back onto that bed so I can see how naughty *you* are this time."

"I don't know. I'm pretty tough to crack."

"Yeah, and I wouldn't expect anything less." Chuckling, he set her down and dropped his robe to the floor. "But thankfully, I have the rest of my life to figure it out."

Her eyes thinned, the color a hypnotic shade of blue that sucked him in. "You're a patient man, aren't you?"

"After six-plus years of waiting for you . . ." He wet his lips and smiled broadly. "Yeah, I really, really am."

* * *

STEALTH OPS BONUS SCENE #3: ASHER & JESSICA'S STORY continues in an all-new bonus scene. Available on my website: https://brittneysahin.com/finding-the-fight/

IF YOU MISSED THE FIRST TWO BONUS SCENES FOR THE Stealth Ops Series - they are available on my website to download.

Made in the USA
Coppell, TX
12 April 2020

19773319R00196